new beginnings in
Rosemary Beach

YOUNG AT HEART ~ BOOK ONE

CECELIA SCOTT

Cecelia Scott

Young at Heart Book 1

New Beginnings in Rosemary Beach

Copyright © 2024 Cecelia Scott

This novel is a work of fiction. Any references to historical events, real people, or real locales are used fictitiously. Other names, characters, places, and incidents are the product of the author's imagination, and any resemblance to actual events or locales or persons, living or dead, is coincidental. All rights to reproduction of this work are reserved. No part of this publication may be reproduced, stored in or introduced into a retrieval system, or transmitted, in any form, or by any means (electronic, mechanical, photocopying, recording, or otherwise) without prior written permission from the copyright owner. Thank you for respecting the copyright. For permission or information on foreign, audio, or other rights, contact the author, ceceliascottauthor@gmail.com.

The Young at Heart Series

In a heartwarming saga of family, friendship, and forgiveness, Vanessa Young and her long-lost daughter, Emily, reunite after thirty years. Together, they embark on a fresh start against the backdrop of white sand beaches and the colorful, small-town charm of Rosemary Beach, Florida. As they navigate a sea of new challenges and old wounds, the women find themselves surrounded by the loving embrace of close family and dear friends. The extensive cast of characters faces all of life's ups and downs with laughter, joy, and unwavering love.

Chapter One

Vanessa

Don't die. Don't die. Don't die.

"Do not die." The words came out of Vanessa Young's mouth in a whisper, barely audible.

But her passenger must have heard, because Emily leaned over and peeked at the dashboard.

"Are we going to run out of gas?" she asked, concerned. "Because we just passed a station and there's another one at the next intersection."

Vanessa closed her eyes on a sigh. "I got a text while we were at the last rest stop. From my sister."

"Gloria? What did she say? Is your dad—"

"He slipped into a coma last night." Vanessa felt her throat tighten as she gripped the steering wheel of the car she'd rented for this spontaneous trip.

"Oh, Vanessa. We're so close. The GPS says we're almost at Gloria's Diner." Emily reached over and squeezed her arm, a gesture that was surprisingly tender and empathetic, considering the two women had met each other yesterday.

Their entire connection had been formed on the eight-hour drive across the state of Florida into the Panhandle. And they hadn't even talked that much, since they'd decided to drive overnight and Emily had slept most of the way.

Poor girl had been through so much. Despite Vanessa's burning desire to share life stories, she'd let Emily sleep, knowing the holes in their many lost years would be filled in eventually.

"We are close," Vanessa acknowledged, too distracted by the ticking clock and her dying father to truly take in the picturesque scenery of her hometown. She hadn't been here since she was sixteen, when she ran away and never came back.

Back then, this waterfront neighborhood had been a classic old Florida collection of mismatched stores and houses known as Inlet Beach, but a developer with a vision blew in right around the time Vanessa had blown out thirty years ago. It hadn't taken long for her weathered hometown to be swallowed up by the far more tourist-friendly, ultra-quaint "planned" community that was dubbed Rosemary Beach.

Anyone with property adjacent to or within the new and improved town of Rosemary Beach saw the value skyrocket. So, the change had been good for Vanessa's father, who owned a sporting goods store. Her sister, Glo, recognized that Rosemary Beach would explode and had managed to buy the building next to Dad's and open her diner decades ago.

Vanessa had missed all that transformation, since she'd left and rarely—okay, never—looked back. And her father—the man in a coma at the moment—had never forgiven her for that, or made her feel welcome at home.

"I don't even know which hospital he's in," Vanessa said on an exhale as she drove toward the quaint town square. "Glo has no idea that I'm coming."

"Just call her," Emily urged. "She's your sister."

"I didn't want her to tell Dad that I'm coming." She had to have the element of surprise on her side, she thought as she leaned forward to peer through the blinding sun bouncing off the windshield.

"He's in a coma," Emily reminded her.

She shrugged. "He might hear."

Kind enough not to argue with that, Emily looked around, her eyes wide as she took in the storybook architecture, window boxes full of flowers, and charming storefronts. The change in the area reminded Vanessa of an old woman who'd had a great facelift—the bones were the same, but the skin was young and fresh.

"This place is so stinkin' cute," Emily said on a sigh. "Why would anyone ever leave?"

Oh, Vanessa had her reasons for leaving—and staying away to have a life in California all these years. But then Dad had a stroke and...

Don't die. Don't die. Don't die.

"Is this it? The diner?" Emily tapped on the window. "Gloria's?"

"Yes." Of course, there wasn't a parking space in sight. So Vanessa whipped into a handicapped spot, knowing she'd be quick. Emily's dog, who had been sleeping soundly in the back seat, sat straight up, whimpered, and barked.

"Shh." Emily turned around to soothe the scraggly mutt. "It's okay, Ruthie."

Vanessa took a steadying breath and smoothed her hair. "I really hope Glo's here, or someone can tell me where to find her."

She glanced at the corner property, where the sign that had read "Bill's Sporting Goods" had been removed from the prime location. The storefront was dark now, and sad looking. Surely it wouldn't stay that way for long, not with the value of property in this beachfront town.

Vanessa's focus shifted to the diner next door, where she hoped and prayed she'd find Gloria or a clue as to where she might be.

"You go in alone," Emily said. "It'll be easier that way. This"—Emily gestured between herself and Vanessa—"is a lot to explain right now. If Gloria's not there, find out where the hospital is and we'll go straight there."

Vanessa nodded, grateful that this young woman was so sensitive. It was one of the very few things she knew about her, but one she already liked and appreciated.

Oh, she'd made a mess of her life, hadn't she? Never got to say goodbye to her mother. Barely spoke to her father. Had to give up the career she'd worked tirelessly for...and now Emily.

One problem at a time, Ness.

"Off I go." Vanessa turned and reached for her bag, coming nose to nose with Ruthie. "You be good, Dogface. I'll be back."

She shot out of the car, rounded the front, and rushed toward the glass doors of the brick diner. She peered inside, then pushed the door open, coming face to face with a twenty-something hostess wiping down menus at the front stand.

"Table for—"

"Is Gloria here?" Vanessa blurted out, breathless.

The young woman searched her face, an unreadable expression in her eyes. "No, um, she's not."

"Where is she? I have to find her, right away." Vanessa stepped closer, not entirely comfortable with being this desperate. It was not her personality at all, but these were extenuating circumstances.

Don't die. Don't die. Don't die. I need to give and get forgiveness. I need closure.

"She's out...for personal reasons," the woman said, a frown forming. "I can leave her a message—"

"What hospital? Please say it's close. I need to see them. I need to see him."

The woman's features softened as she came around the hostess stand, her expression softening. "Do you know—"

"I'm Gloria's sister, Vanessa Young. He's my father." Her voice sounded strained to her own ears. "I need to see him."

The hostess's eyes filled as she put her fingers to her lips, as if she couldn't bear what she was about to say.

Oh, please don't—

"Gloria didn't call you?"

Vanessa shook her head, her throat thick. "I know he went into a coma."

She winced, and, really, it was all Vanessa had to see.

"I'm so sorry, I...I..." The woman reached a hand out, which was good, because Vanessa swayed a little. "Bill, uh, your father, passed away about an hour ago."

No!

She stifled a moan, closing her eyes, as if her head—and heart—would actually explode.

An hour ago?

The woman gave her a deeply compassionate gaze. "I think Gloria has left the hospital, but you can—"

Reeling, Vanessa held up her hand. "It's okay. It's okay." But it wasn't okay. Nothing was okay. He was gone and he'd never forgiven her. Never. And now she had to carry that around for the rest of her life...

"I'm so sorry," the hostess said. "Truly, for you and Glo."

Somehow, she managed to thank her and turn around, forgetting to even ask again which hospital. Forgetting everything as she stepped onto a street that was once familiar, but seemed foreign now.

"Nessie?"

The old nickname echoed, tugging her back to reality. She turned, blinking into the sun as a woman walked toward her with a look of total confusion on her face.

"Is that you? Nessie?" The woman brushed back light brown curls as she hustled closer, her face suddenly so familiar, it took Vanessa's breath away.

"Gloria." On a soft gasp, Vanessa crumpled into her sister's arms, the two of them folded into an embrace that didn't need any words or explanations or apologies. Not with Glo.

Ten years could go by and the minute they were together, they were just two sisters who loved each other and had been through a lot. They'd gone on to lead wildly different lives on opposite coasts, and sometimes weeks or even months would pass between phone calls.

But none of that mattered. Just that these two women —now orphans at forty-five and fifty—held each other.

Finally, they parted, both of their faces wet with tears.

"I can't believe I missed him," Vanessa managed to say on a sniffle.

"He was gone long before he died," Gloria said. "Long before that coma. He'd been declining for months and months, which is why he finally closed the store and let the employees go. We cleaned it out, sold everything at cost, and then..." She sighed. "He had that stroke last month and he just couldn't pull out of it. He was so disoriented these past few weeks, I'm not sure he'd have known you were there, and then he wasn't conscious. He definitely wouldn't have known."

Maybe she was trying to ease Vanessa's pain—that would be so like Glo, a peacemaker from the day she was born—or maybe it was true. It didn't matter. Bill Young was gone and Vanessa never had her goodbye. He'd never forgiven her for...

She threw a look at the car, the sun making it impossible to see through the windshield, although Ruthie's tan-and-black head was sticking out the back, staring at her. Of course, Gloria didn't even notice the dog, her attention fully on Vanessa.

"Why didn't you tell me you were coming?" she asked.

"Would he have hung on another hour?"

Glo shook her head, her blue-gray eyes still misty, but warm with affection and all the forgiveness Vanessa should ever need.

"But you're here now, for all the...aftermath. We'll have a small service, read the will, go through his belongings." A smile tugged. "How's that for a good time, huh?"

Vanessa laughed softly, because no matter what the situation, Gloria Bennett could make a person chuckle. "Yeah."

"When do you have to go back to L.A.?" Glo asked.

"Not, uh, for a while, actually."

Gloria's brows lifted. "Really? You'll stay? How long?"

"A month, maybe longer."

Her sister drew back, surprise on her face. "Seriously, Ness?"

"I closed my business, Glo," Vanessa admitted softly. "And I have no idea where to go or what to do next. I came here for a reset. Then I'll consider..." She glanced around at the colorful town, the tourists and flowers and a place that was once home. "All my options."

Gloria visibly melted a bit, her narrow shoulders dropping as her eyes filled with tears.

"Oh, Nessie. A whole month together! This is the perfect place for a reset, and you'll have plenty of time and love and support to figure things out." She grimaced.

"But I'm scared to believe it's true. I'm afraid I'll wake up and you'll be gone."

Might be time to drop the next bomb on poor Glo.

Tick, tick, boom.

"I'm not alone," Vanessa whispered. "I brought someone with me."

"Oh!" Glo's brows lifted. "A special someone? Well, let me meet him. Wait a second—you're not back with Aaron, are you?"

Vanessa groaned, cringing at the thought of her short-lived marriage that ended three years ago. "No. And it's not a man. It's a..." She swallowed and jutted her chin toward the SUV parked in front of them.

"A dog!" Glo exclaimed, already striding toward the vehicle. "Well, would you look at that little angel. You brought—"

Vanessa snagged her sister's arm before she could get any closer to the car. "Wait."

Glo threw her a look. "Is he dangerous? Because he sure doesn't look it. Oh, who's that in the car?"

"That's, um..." She took Gloria by the shoulder, turning her away from the car to look into her eyes. "Do you remember when I got pregnant at sixteen?"

Glo snorted softly. "Yes, Ness. I do seem to recall that little earthquake you caused in this town and our family. And you running away and giving up your baby for adoption. Why?"

"Well, on my way to Florida to see Dad, I made an impulsive decision, and..." She glanced at the car. "Found that baby. Actually, technically, she found me, and—"

"You what?" Gloria barely breathed the word as visible chills rose on her arms. "You...found..." She tried to turn to the car, but Vanessa kept her grip.

"Her name is Emily. She's twenty-nine years old and in the process of getting out of an abusive marriage. She needs to start over. Badly. We both do."

With a soft cry, Gloria broke loose and turned to the car, rushing toward it before Vanessa could stop her. As she reached the passenger door, it opened and Emily slowly stepped onto the sidewalk.

Gloria froze, her hands to her mouth as they stared at each other.

"Hi," Emily said softly, brushing back shoulder-length black hair.

"You're a carbon copy of Vanessa!" Gloria exclaimed. "Well, minus the hair color. But holy cow."

"It's dyed." Emily toyed with the split ends. "Badly, I might add. We do look alike. Are you...Gloria? I guess it's Aunt Gloria."

"Yes!" Glo shrieked and threw her arms around skinny, frail Emily, squeezing the life out of her and making Ruthie bark noisily out of the backseat window. "Yes, I am! This is Nessie's magic, you know?"

"Nessie's...magic?" Emily asked, clearly not sure what to make of the explosion of Gloria-ness.

Glo pulled away reaching out her other arm to bring Vanessa into a group hug. "She makes bad things good. That's what she does. That's why I've longed for her to come home and...and..." She looked from one to the other. "Oh, hallelujah! You're here! You're *both* here!"

Once again, Vanessa let herself be folded into Gloria's loving arms, only this time, she also had Emily in that hug.

Vanessa Young had made a lot of messes in her life. There was a reason that Dad—may he rest in peace—called her Messy Nessie. But right now, with her sister and her long-lost daughter and sunshine and a dog and a new life ahead?

Right now, she didn't feel messy at all.

She felt like this could truly be a new beginning. All she had to do...was take it.

Chapter Two

Gloria

Gloria Bennett's mind whirled with a million questions, all under a cloud of grief she hadn't quite processed. Her father's death was an odd sort of sadness, though, since it was a relief in some ways, and expected.

But nothing about Vanessa's arrival was expected, and it left Gloria reeling.

Part of her was broken and bruised by Dad being gone, because, despite everything, he was her father, and she'd been caring for him for quite some time. Decades, really.

Another part of her? Well, Gloria couldn't hide her emotions one bit, and she was pretty darn happy that the prodigal daughter had finally returned, even if that return was temporary. It was still more time than she'd had with Nessie in many, many years, and for that she was grateful.

And...her daughter! Nessie brought the baby she'd given up for adoption twenty-nine years ago.

That was the twist that spun her around the most.

She somehow managed to have the wherewithal to invite them both to her condo, where she hoped to get all her questions answered and soak up their company. With the beach in view and unable to do anything more for her father, Glo hoped they could share coffee, grief, sisterhood, and somehow cram years of catching up into the afternoon.

She had the beachfront condo to herself these days, as the second bedroom where her twenty-four-year-old daughter, Daisy, had lived for a few years after college was now empty. Not that Daisy had gone far—she still lived and worked in Rosemary Beach, and for that Gloria was grateful. But she'd moved in with her fiancé and that...was a whole other story she'd no doubt share with Vanessa eventually.

"Come on in, you two." She walked them up to the second floor of the two-story building, ushering them to her unit on the end. Getting to the door ahead of them, she turned and watched mother and daughter—how could that even be real?—walk side by side down the wide outdoor corridor above the parking lot.

Even their gait was the same, Gloria mused as she held open her door. Both women had the same slender build, with long legs and narrow shoulders, and shockingly similar facial features, from a slightly sloped nose to prominent cheekbones and matching wide, deep blue gazes.

Emily looked a little more frail, with hollow cheeks and some shadows under her eyes, as if she'd been under a lot of stress.

Though the last few hours and their initial conversation was a bit of a blur, she recalled Vanessa saying something about Emily getting out of an abusive marriage. Oh, and Vanessa had closed her business as one of the top stylists in Hollywood with an impressive client list? Why?

Gloria only knew one thing for sure: She'd better make a big pot of coffee.

"Is it okay if Ruthie comes in?" Emily asked softly, holding up a leash that was attached to the ten-pound creature with a wagging tail and the widest smile of anyone that day. "She doesn't chew or anything."

"Oh, honey, please. You don't even have to ask."

Emily gave a grateful smile and guided the little dog inside, slipping off her leash and letting her trot around and sniff the new territory.

"Glo, this place is lovely." Vanessa stepped inside, her whole face brightening as she took in Gloria's twenty-two hundred square feet of beachfront bliss. The open concept condo with a stunning water view through sliding glass doors was decorated with an eclectic mix of antiques, off finds, and plenty of "coastal" chic. "It's so...you."

"Thanks, Nessie." Gloria smiled, taking that as a compliment. "You remember I bought this place, oh, ten years ago now. After the divorce. It's been a wonderful place to live."

Vanessa's hand raised up to her lips as a shadow of guilt cast across her blue eyes. "It's been a long time since I've been here. I'm the worst sister ever."

"You most certainly are not." Gloria took Vanessa and Emily's hands and guided them into the kitchen, bathed in light and accented with teal and tangerine. After a day at the diner, there was no kitchen that gave her more joy.

"I've been so distant," Vanessa said on a sigh.

Gloria eyed her sister as she pulled out three mugs and set them next to the coffee maker and set to brewing a pot.

Yes, Nessie had been distant. Yes, there were times throughout the years that Glo felt like she was the only one putting effort in. But now was not the time to affirm Vanessa's self-doubts. Forgiveness was what she needed most.

"You've been having a life in L.A. A fun and amazing one."

"Fun and amazing, until it wasn't," Vanessa said dryly.

Gloria gave her a curious look. "You said you closed your stylist business? Why?"

Vanessa puffed out a breath and dropped her head back. "Where do I begin? Probably around the time a little beast called TikTok got popular and the swarms on social media decided 'she should fire her stylist' was a perfectly okay thing to say."

Gloria frowned. "Did something happen?"

"Nothing in particular, but you know my business lives and dies by word-of-mouth among celebrities and influencers and the rich women who listen to them." She sighed and absently turned the mugs Gloria had placed on the counter. "In the past year or so, I just stopped getting work. Everyone is going to younger stylists with more trendy looks that go viral on TikTok. And I admittedly had more misses than hits at some high-profile events."

"Oh, Nessie. You can rebound from that. You have exquisite taste and could wrap a Barbie doll in toilet paper and make me believe it was a wedding gown."

She gave an easy laugh at the memory. "It's a younger woman's business, to be honest. I'm done in Hollywood, and, honestly, a stylist at my level only works there. Sure, there are small segments of wealthy enclaves where rich women hire a stylist for an event, but I can't make a real living like that. I needed the constant work in and around L.A., and I just can't get it anymore. I'll have to find something else to do."

"Maybe you could find it...here," Gloria said softly, trying to keep the ache of high hopes out of her voice.

"I don't know," Vanessa said. "We're taking it one day at a time. Right, Emily?"

From the other side of the room where Emily was following the dog and probably giving them a little privacy, the young woman said, "We sure are."

As they made small talk and got comfortable, Gloria poured out three big, steaming cups of coffee and put them on a tray with cream and sugar, grabbed some biscotti from a tin, and lifted it. "Back deck, girls. My favorite part of home."

Vanessa opened the slider and they all walked out to the wide and private deck to look at the crystalline Gulf of Mexico, white sand beach, and endless blue sky that made this part of Florida's famous panhandle a mecca for tourists.

"Where are you two planning on staying?" she asked as she set the tray on the coffee table and gestured for them to get comfy on the sofa and chairs. There was a small outdoor dining table where she frequently had morning coffee or a light dinner, but this seemed cozier. "You're more than welcome here, of course, if you don't mind bunking in my one and only spare bedroom."

"You're so sweet, Glo, but I found us a rental. Short term, just for a month, with the option to extend. It's a little beach house about five minutes up the road."

"Oh, that's perfect," Gloria cooed, although she wouldn't have minded the company. As she picked up a mug and invited them to do the same, she looked from one woman to the other, a smile pulling. "Where in the world do we begin?"

Emily and Vanessa glanced at each other from across the coffee table, a little deer-in-the-headlights in their matching cobalt-colored eyes.

"How did you two reconnect?" Gloria asked. "How long have you been in contact?"

Emily laughed softly, lifting Ruthie onto her lap, where she settled in. "Since, um, yesterday."

Gloria gasped. "Yesterday? Excuse me?"

"It's a weird story," Emily said, scratching the dog's little golf-ball head.

"I'm all ears." Gloria leaned back and took a deep drink of coffee.

Emily's gaze shifted back over to Vanessa, who

gestured for her to do the honors, each passing second merely ratcheting up Gloria's curiosity about the long-lost mother and daughter finding each other. Everything about the story—even though she knew next to nothing—gave off a ray of hope.

They belonged together, these matching ladies with only sixteen years between them. Gloria knew that deep in her gut.

"So..." Emily shifted in her seat, careful not to disturb Ruthie, who was happily smooshed between Emily's thigh and the armrest. "I guess I'll start at the very beginning. Vanessa gave me up for adoption when I was six months old, as I'm sure you know."

"Yes, I do." Gloria couldn't help but wonder if the fact that Vanessa had tried—and failed—to be her mother bothered Emily, but she kept that particular line of questioning to herself.

"I was adopted by a single woman who couldn't have kids of her own, named Joanna. She actually renamed me Amelia."

"Was she a good mother?" Gloria asked, so hoping the answer would be yes.

"I wouldn't know." Emily pressed her lips together and wrapped her hands around the warm mug. "She died suddenly when I was three."

"Oh." Gloria dropped back with a grunt, her gaze flicking over to study Vanessa. Her sister's gaze was cast into her coffee mug, as if she might be fighting regret. Of course she was, poor thing. "I'm so sorry, Emily. Or...Amelia?"

"Thank you, and...I actually went back to Emily a while ago, which is a different long story." She brushed some of that dark hair behind her ear and smiled. "Anyway, I was raised by Joanna's mother, who also qualified as an angel and is and will always be my favorite human ever, my Grandma Gigi."

"Oh, thank goodness." Glo pressed a hand to her chest.

Vanessa nodded. "It sounds like Gigi was wonderful to you, Emily. I'm so grateful."

"She was the best."

Gloria winced. "Was?"

"She passed." Emily closed her eyes, her grief palpable. "About a year ago."

Gloria shook her head. "I'm so sorry."

"Thank you. She helped me so much. I was married to someone...someone very, very evil. He was violent and abusive and it only got worse as the marriage went on. By the time Grandma Gigi died, it was getting pretty hard to hide the bruises."

"No!" Gloria muttered on a gasp.

Emily just tipped her head. "Yes, I'm afraid. He'd effectively cut me off from everyone in my life. He made me quit my job, stop talking to all my friends...the textbook control stuff. By the time I realized how severe it truly was, I was in way too deep to get out. I had no money, no family, nothing."

Gloria whimpered, emotion tugging at her heart for this sweet young woman who was her own blood relative.

"My goodness, child, how much adversity does one girl have to go through?"

"Too much." Vanessa shook her head.

"Thank you, Gloria." Emily swallowed. "It's made me strong. When Gigi died, she left me a box of cash and this little baby doll right here." She patted Ruthie's head, getting a loving lick in response. "She also left me detailed instructions on how to run away from my husband."

Gloria leaned forward. "And you did?"

She nodded. "It took several months to get my ducks in a row, but I managed to scare up a fake ID first. I needed a new name, so I picked Emily, since that's what..." She smiled at Vanessa. "You first named me."

"Still one of my favorite names," Vanessa said.

"I was on the run for about two months," Emily continued. "I very carefully made my way from Denver to Florida, and ended up in a little beach town called Cocoa Beach, working at an inn."

"I know Cocoa Beach." Gloria nodded. "Near the Space Center, right?"

"Yes, and it was lovely there. But I was living in crippling fear. Doug, my husband, is—I guess was—an FBI agent. He'd never even filed a missing person report when I left, and I know it was because he was dead set on finding me himself in order to protect his reputation. It also meant I didn't feel safe going to the police. That's why I kept running."

"And no one else filed a report? A friend or neighbor? No one else noticed you were gone?"

Emily's face flushed, clearly embarrassed by her plight. "Without Grandma Gigi, I didn't have anyone else. Literally no one. It had gotten that bad."

"Oh, my word." Gloria put her cup down and sighed. "I'm so sorry for you."

"But Grandma Gigi left me one more thing," she added. "In the letter she wrote on her deathbed, she gave me the name and location of my birth mother."

Gloria blinked back, looking at the two of them and realizing that the saga that brought this mother and daughter together was even more shocking than she could have imagined.

"So...Emily, you reached out first, then? Not Nessie?"

Vanessa lifted her hands up. "I had no way of finding her. The adoption was private, and I'd always kept myself from thinking about it too much. I suppose if I had done enough digging, I could have found her, but..." She glanced at Emily, sadness darkening her expression. "I figured she'd want nothing to do with me."

"You figured wrong," Emily said with a gentle smile that warmed Gloria's heart to see. "In a moment of intense loneliness in a crummy old motel, I called her. And once I knew I had the right number, I basically... dumped. Told my entire story without taking a breath."

Gloria shook her head as she sipped her hot coffee, studying her sister as she processed the story. "Nessie, you must have been beside yourself. I mean, this is the girl you gave up for adoption when she was six months old! Calling you out of the blue. What did you do?"

"I hung up." Vanessa closed her eyes, her eyelids fluttered shut with shame. "I was overwhelmed. I had just been fired by a big client, and I freaked out and froze. By the time I gathered myself to call Emily back, the phone line had been disconnected."

"Burner phones," Emily explained. "I had lots of them so that my location couldn't be traced."

"So..." Vanessa raised her brows. "I did what any sane person would do. I sold all my belongings, got on a plane, showed up at the inn where she'd said she was working, and asked her to come with me to start a new life."

Emily leaned forward. "And it just so happened that the night before she showed up...Doug had found me."

Gloria gasped. "No!"

"Yes, and it was terrifying. He showed up at the wedding I was working at the inn, and when I ran back to my motel room to escape him...he was there."

Gloria's heart ached, imagining the fear that Emily must have faced in that horrible moment. "What happened?"

"He threatened me, but thanks to the amazing family I worked for, the police showed up and took him away in handcuffs, under arrest for assault and God knows what else." Emily took in a deep breath, closing her eyes as the breeze blew her hair around her face. "He's gone, and I'm free. Not fully divorced yet, but..." She gave a stressed smile. "Working on that."

"You're free as a bird," Vanessa added. "A bird who spontaneously flew here with a woman she hardly knows."

"But who is still my mother," Emily said.

Gloria chuckled, looking between the mother and daughter, leaning back as she took it all in. "Oh, my darling Vanessa. Your life is many things, but boring is never one of them."

"A big hot mess is what my life is," Vanessa said on a sigh, pushing back a strand of hair and pressing her lips together. "But it's a hopeful mess now. I'm glad to have some time here while I figure things out."

"Hopeful, indeed." Gloria fixed her gaze on Emily. "Goodness, you must have so many questions. Were you able to learn a lot about your newfound mother on the drive up here?"

"I wish I'd learned more," Emily admitted. "We drove overnight and I was so wiped out from all the drama with Doug that I slept the majority of the ride. I did find out that Vanessa was a super successful Hollywood stylist, which is beyond cool."

Vanessa waved a dismissive hand.

"And," Emily continued, "that she was married to Aaron Aldridge for five years but got divorced. And I learned that your mother passed in a car accident when Vanessa was just a baby. So, Glo, you would have been..."

"Five," Gloria supplied. "Young enough to barely remember the woman, but always miss her."

"I'm so sorry," Emily said gently, knitting her brows together in a look of sympathy.

Vanessa took a deep breath and raised her coffee mug to her lips. "I was a baby, so I have zero memories of her. It definitely impacted Glo more."

"Only because we were raised by our father." She

gave a soft groan as the grief hit. "Rest his soul. His..." She looked up. "His not always loving, kind, or sweet soul."

Emily swallowed. "I'm getting the impression he was, uh, challenging."

"It was tough at times," Gloria admitted. "Mostly for Nessie, to be fair. He didn't take Mom's death well and he never really seemed to let go of her. He had a short fuse and high emotional walls. And with Nessie..." Her voice trailed off.

Vanessa flicked her brows. "With Nessie, that fuse was shorter and those walls were...impenetrable," she said on a dry laugh. "Throw in a pregnancy at sixteen and you have a recipe for...an explosion."

Gloria snorted, remembering the fireworks all those years ago. "The smoke that came out of that man's ears would have blinded you."

"It's true," Vanessa said. "He blew a gasket. Said he'd never forgive me, and meant it. So I ran off to L.A., where our dad had a cousin, Kate. She agreed to take me in while I figured things out." She lifted her gaze and locked eyes with Emily, biting her lip.

Gloria knew this was a tragically tough topic for Nessie, and maybe too soon to get into the whole "I'm sorry I decided not to be your mother after six months" conversation, so she took her chance to divert things.

"What else do you want to know, Emily?"

"Right now, I'm sort of just taking it all in." She toyed with the frayed ends of her hair, which Gloria couldn't help but notice looked like a rat had chewed on.

Not the time for beauty advice, Glo.

"I guess..." Emily shifted uncomfortably, her fingers digging into Ruthie's short fur. "I guess I'm kind of curious about my biological father. I...I've never had a dad. I know you were only a teenager and everything, but I can't help wondering who he was."

Gloria held her breath, turning her attention to Vanessa, waiting for the familiar expression that came over her sister's face at the mention of Noah Ellison. There. There it was. A mix of regret and disappointment and, yeah, young love.

Decades later, it was the same face.

"He was my best friend," Vanessa said softly, her voice wavering. "His name is Noah, and we grew up together. We were inseparable childhood friends, and in high school we became boyfriend and girlfriend. He was a good guy, but he's long gone from these parts and we don't have any contact."

"Oh." Emily nodded slowly, rubbing her palms along the tops of her ripped jeans as she processed this. "Well, I'm glad to hear he's...good."

"His mother was like a second mom to us, too," Gloria added. "They lived down the street when my dad moved us here after our mom passed, and she's always been dear."

"That's nice to hear." Emily smiled and sipped her coffee. "So, no hard feelings, it sounds like?"

Vanessa shrugged off the question and glanced away.

"Now, Miss Emily, I have a question for you." Gloria arched a brow, sensing it was time to change the subject and seizing the first thing that came to mind. "What exactly is going on with your hair? I'm sorry but I can't keep it to myself anymore."

All three women cracked up at the much-needed lightening of the mood.

"I cut and dyed it myself."

"Ya think?" Glo teased. "A blind man could see that."

"It was when I was on the run. I'm naturally blond. Same color as Vanessa, actually. But I didn't want to be identified."

"Oh, you poor soul." Gloria pressed a hand to her heart. "You're safe now. Bad hair and all."

The women shared more conversation and a few more cups of coffee as the sun began to set on the Gulf. The waves of confusing and conflicting grief seemed to become less intense as Gloria leaned into these precious relationships.

Plus, she had to acknowledge that however tough it was to lose Dad, it was tougher for Vanessa, who had come here on a quest for forgiveness and closure, and missed it by an hour.

Although, truth be told, Gloria wasn't entirely sure old Dad would have given Vanessa that final peace offering she was hoping for. He was a mean, nasty man, and his old age and sickness had only intensified that.

Maybe it was better that Vanessa hadn't talked to him. It didn't matter, because Gloria had enough forgiveness to go around.

Yes, she'd been badly hurt when she got the phone call at twenty-one in college that Vanessa had run away, and she hadn't even said goodbye. She was brokenhearted about it. But holding a grudge would have only made things worse.

Gloria couldn't help but think about how devastated she'd be when Nessie and Emily left town in just a few short weeks, and loneliness came back hard. The sadness had been intense enough now that her own daughter kept her at arm's length, but for now? The sisters were together again, and a couple of decades of distance faded away into a pot of coffee and a sunset.

Chapter Three

Emily

Emily woke up early, blinking into the gentle morning light streaming in through the windows of her bedroom.

Dare she call it *her* bedroom? She'd only been in the furnished beach house Vanessa had rented for a little over twelve hours, but it was definitely the nicest and most comfortable place she'd slept in since running away from Doug two months ago.

Emily rolled onto her back, the relaxation of her first solid night's sleep in months sinking deep into her bones.

You're safe, she reminded herself. *He's locked up. He can't hurt you anymore.*

The reality of that brought another wave of surreal relief over her as Emily sank onto the plush pillows and breathed out a slow sigh.

Ruthie stirred at the bottom of the bed, wagging her tail when they made eye contact and she saw that Emily was awake.

She reached over onto the nightstand and picked up her phone—her latest pay-per-minute flip phone—which Gloria had insisted they trade in for an iPhone, stat. But the twenty-dollar Walmart cell was enough to receive calls and voicemails, and Emily saw that she had one from Vanessa.

Emily clicked Play and listened to the message.

"Hey, just wanted to let you know that Gloria and I are spending a few hours doing funeral arrangements. I figured I'd spare you that fun and happy errand, but I'll catch you this afternoon. Make yourself comfy! Bye!"

Emily closed the phone, thinking about this new mother of hers. Sure, they'd lived completely separate lives and had only spoken for the first time forty-eight hours ago, but their connection was undeniable.

From their weirdly similar looks down to their mannerisms, which she'd thought were learned and not inherited, looking at Vanessa was like gazing in the mirror sixteen years into the future.

Well, a very put together, clean cut, beautiful mirror...not things Emily had felt too much lately.

She rolled out of bed and looked at the real mirror on the wall above the dresser, groaning at her mess of badly dyed hair and eyebrows in desperate need of a pluck. She missed being pretty. She ached to feel good about herself again.

"Hey, Ruthie," Emily called to her pooch. "We've got a whole morning to kill in a brand new and, frankly, adorable town that demands to be explored. You in?"

The ten-pound ball of joy and energy leapt off the bed, panting and wagging her tail as Emily threw on some jeans and a gray tank top, shoving her feet into her only pair of sneakers.

Some shopping might be in order, too, but that would require money, which would require a job.

"One problem at a time," she whispered to the dog as she clipped on a leash and they headed out the front door, locking it behind her.

Rosemary Beach was like a movie set—perfectly walkable streets and sidewalks all lined with precious shops and restaurants that somehow combined a beachy, coastal vibe with a brick, historic one. Which was ironic, considering Gloria had explained to her yesterday that the town had been "born" right around the time Emily was, and essentially created from scratch.

Its history was no older than Emily's, which kind of made her love it even more. They had the same lifespan in common.

Vanessa had chosen a rental in a prime location—clearly, money wasn't an issue for her—along a row of adorable waterfront homes, all painted in soft tones of pink, blue, and peach. Theirs was sunny yellow clapboard with cheerful turquoise shutters, and looked like it could be on the cover of *Coastal Living* magazine.

It was beyond perfect for a mother and daughter looking for new lives.

She had no idea what would come next for her, but they had decided to just take it one step at a time, starting with a month in Rosemary Beach. Emily had never thought this chance would come. She figured she'd be on the run for ages, living in fear and paranoia for the foreseeable future.

But here she was safe, free, and currently strolling

down a sun-washed street with Ruthie, leaving her worries and fears farther behind her with every step.

She followed her intuition to get her from the beach house to downtown Rosemary Beach, which wasn't far, reaching the heart of town in under ten minutes. Despite being a town that had been dreamed up by a developer, the place felt very local and authentic to her. Few chain restaurants, lots of mom-and-pop stores, and extremely clean.

With three-story, balcony-lined buildings, it was a little New Orleans, a little European, and a lot adorable.

As she turned a corner, Emily slowed her step at the sight of a gorgeous, massive building that looked like it took up a whole block.

"Whoa," Emily whispered, her head tilting up as she drank in the stunning three-story hotel decorated with lacey, inviting balconies, pointed turrets, and a corner clock tower. "That's a beauty."

It was like staring up at a German fairytale castle, and Emily knew it had to be a Rosemary Beach landmark.

The sign out front read "The Pearl Hotel," and it seemingly marked the downtown of beautiful Rosemary Beach like a beacon of breathtaking design.

Suddenly, the sound of laughter and voices floated through the air, and Emily turned her head to catch a glimpse of the wide, grass-covered courtyard behind the hotel. Emerging into the light was a fully gowned bride, all in white, like the literal princess in a storybook setting.

Something shifted in Emily's heart as she took in the moment, transfixed.

The woman, who looked to be about Emily's age, was beaming like the sun as she posed for photographs with her bridesmaids outside the hotel, clutching her bouquet, her joy wafting across the courtyard like their voices and squeals of laughter.

Girl, I hope your marriage goes better than mine.

As Emily gave Ruthie's leash a gentle tug and they headed toward the main street of town, she couldn't help but think back on her own wedding day.

It was no fairy tale like the one she'd just witnessed, that was for sure.

Emily and Doug Rosetti's wedding was tiny, practically an elopement. Doug had insisted on keeping the guest list minimal, as he was a "small circle" kind of guy. That meant Emily had to tell most of her friends and dear sorority sisters from college that they were choosing to keep it private and intimate.

Not her choice, not by a long shot. Grandma Gigi had been willing to pay for a big wedding, but like everything else with Doug, Emily didn't get what she'd wanted. The thoughts of her disappointing dumpster fire of a marriage left a bitter taste in her mouth, but Emily shook it off.

That was the past. This, she thought to herself as she looked around the vibrant and lively town square, *this* was her future.

She stopped at the walk-up window to a coffee shop called 3rd Cup, and treated herself to a latte and a chocolate croissant and a pup cup for Ruthie.

Finding a seat in the sun, she took a bite of the delicious treat, letting out a moan of pure delight. She'd been on such a tight budget since running away, guilty pleasures and superfluous snacks had been a thing of the past.

But now, she could breathe. She could eat again, and Emily was excited to get back to a healthy weight and start working out again. She could run on the beach without fear of turning around and seeing Doug standing there, waiting for her.

After finishing every last morsel of her pastry, Emily strolled down Main Street with Ruthie trotting by her side. A pink sign with a black silhouette of a woman with a swinging ponytail caught her eye.

"Cricket's Beauty Salon," she whispered, smiling at the script below it that read, "Because beauty never goes out of style."

A hair salon! Talk about a treat. Emily had loathed the mess she made of her once beautiful locks in an effort to go undercover. Truthfully, it hadn't been a priority or even a concern, but now that Doug was locked up and her life was starting anew...she could stand to get her hair fixed.

"Hello..." Emily poked her head in, holding Ruthie outside on her leash, checking out the cozy salon with a retro vibe that felt like she'd stepped into the 1950s.

A woman who looked like she could be sixty or seventy stepped out from behind a desk, her long, flowing skirt billowing around a slender frame. She had thick gray hair that bounced around her shoulders, and bright pink, cat-eye-shaped glasses sitting on the bridge of her nose.

"Hello, dear. Can I help you?"

"Sorry, I..." Emily glanced back outside at Ruthie. "Do you take walk-ins?"

"Not usually." The woman arched a brow. "But from the looks of it, we have an emergency situation on our hands, so come on in."

Emily laughed. "I have my dog with me. Maybe I ought to just run her home and come back..."

"Nonsense, bring her in." The woman waved Emily through the front door. "I've got three cats roaming around the salon at all times, so she'll have friends."

"Great. Thank you." She tugged Ruthie's leash and stepped inside, looking from the black-and-white checkered linoleum floor to two hair styling stations complete with bright pink leather chairs. Along the back she saw two more sinks and heat lamps, one with a woman under it reading a magazine while her hair color processed.

"Sit on down, my dear." The woman walked over to the first chair and flipped a cape open, draping it over Emily when she sat. "I'm Cricket, by the way."

"I'm Emily." She glanced at herself in the mirror. "It's great to meet you, Cricket. I really appreciate you taking me in spontaneously like this. And letting me keep Ruthie here."

The dog was already curled up on the floor next to Emily.

"Well, I know a sight of pure desperation when I see one. And this?" Cricket picked up some of Emily's black dyed hair and toyed with the unevenly chopped ends. "This is not good."

"I know." She shook her head. "It's a long story, but...

can you fix it? I'd love to get it back to my natural color. It's blond."

"I can see that from your roots," Cricket said matter of factly, clicking her tongue. "I can certainly fix the cut today, and the color is going to take a couple of sessions, but we'll get you back blond and beautiful, don't you worry."

Emily let out a sigh of relief. "Wonderful. Thank you."

As Cricket began to work on the mess that was Emily's hair, the two women started to chat.

"So, Emily, are you visiting? I know every single person in Rosemary Beach—and everything about them. I don't know you, so I'm guessing tourist?"

Emily was not surprised that Cricket the Hair Guru knew everyone in town, and all the secrets and gossip. "I just got into town yesterday, but I'm staying for a month or so, just taking an extended vacation, I guess. I need a reset and some healing."

"Wow, a newcomer! What brought you to our little beach town for this healing stay?"

"It's a weird, long, and kind of sad story, actually," Emily said, getting a look that told her those were the kind of stories Cricket loved. "But I came with my mom and I'm here now. It's absolutely beautiful."

"Well..." Cricket began mixing up some dyes and color releasers in a dish. "You came to the right place. Rosemary Beach is the most beautiful place on Earth, if you ask me."

She began applying the mixture gently and methodically onto Emily's hair, wrapping strands in foil with such experienced professionalism, Emily knew she was in good hands.

"Have you lived here your whole life?" Emily asked, grateful to be able to connect with other people and start to rebuild a community she'd been so desperately missing since Doug had cut her off from the world.

"Absolutely. Born and raised long before the developers came in and built this 'historic'"—she held up air quotes—"city from the ground up. Don't get me wrong, I couldn't love it more. When this little beach community got new life, I felt like I did, too."

"That's wonderful," Emily said. "Are you married, Cricket?"

"Widowed five years now."

"Oh, I'm sorry."

"It's fine. Gene's waiting for me up there. And I've got a son in his forties, but he moved away when he was young and never wanted to move back. Now he hates this new town, calls it Fakemary Beach, the brat. As if that old dump he grew up in could ever get this many tourists and cash. He lives in Miami, which, if you ask me, is its own kind of hellhole."

She smiled—how could she not—at the colorful older woman. "I'm sure you miss him," Emily said.

"Oh, yes." Cricket's capable hands slowed and her expression changed. "Every second of every day. He's an opinionated man, but I love him to pieces." On a deep inhale, she slathered some more purple goo on Emily's hair. "Believe me, I've tried every trick in the book in an effort to get my boy home, but he won't budge."

"Is he married?"

"He was. Divorced now." She wrinkled her nose. "I'm more than fine with it, though. Never liked that girl. Never. I even tried to break them up myself a couple of times—'cause I can meddle with the best of 'em—but eventually he came to his senses and they split up a few years ago. Thank you, Jesus."

Emily had no doubt Cricket could meddle, and then some. She couldn't put her finger on it, but something about the woman was downright irresistible. Blunt and straightforward, Emily was inexplicably comfortable with Cricket, just like everything else about this town.

"What about you? You married?" Cricket arched a drawn-on brow. "I don't see a ring."

Emily waved a hand. "I was. But I'm...not anymore."

"Another divorcée, huh?" Cricket shook her head as she separated some more layers of Emily's hair. "I swear it's going around like the plague these days. I blame the men, mostly. Except my son. He's one of the good ones."

"Did he have any kids of his own, your son?"

Cricket froze for a second as she was wrapping a hair strand in foil, the question seemingly hitting her like a gut punch.

Emily instantly wondered if it was too personal, or perhaps there was a wound there. "Oh, I'm sorry if I—"

"No, no. It's okay." Cricket shook off the weirdness and straightened her narrow shoulders, focusing back on the hair and quickly pulling herself together. "He, um, he had a child, sort of. Many years ago. It wasn't with his ex-wife."

"Oh." Emily nodded slowly, curious but not wanting to pry.

"He was only a teenager." Cricket pressed her lips together. "And the girl...the girl he got pregnant...she ran off to L.A. and gave the baby up for adoption. It's sad, really, because I always believed they were soulmates. Part of me still does."

Emily felt her whole body freeze from the inside out, and all the blood drain from her head, whooshing down. *Was she...could this...who was...*

Cricket chattered on, but her words sounded like Emily was underwater—and drowning.

"She never came back, poor girl, even though her sister lives right here. And her father, though he passed away yesterday, rest his—"

"Oh..." The word came out as barely a whimper, and Cricket didn't even hear it.

"So, to answer your question, I am tragically not a grandmother, which is a crime against humanity, if you ask me."

"Stop." Emily's hand flew to her mouth as the realization became impossible to deny.

Cricket did, stepping back and looking surprised. "Oh, don't worry, honey. The brassiness will tone out, I promise. I won't have you leaving my salon looking orange—"

"Cricket," Emily breathed the woman's name, locking eyes with her in the mirror.

"What? What's the matter?"

"Was it...Vanessa Young?"

She blinked, cocking her head like a confused puppy. "Excuse me?"

"The girl who got pregnant by your son." Her voice quivered, her throat closing with emotion.

Cricket nodded, narrowing her gaze warily at Emily. "Yes. Do you know her?"

She inhaled, getting a whiff of hair color and...hope. How would Cricket take it? Would it be a happy shock or...not?

Very slowly, Emily swiveled the chair to face her, pressed her hands together and stared at Cricket, as if she needed to pray for help to say this the right way.

"It's me," she breathed the words.

"What?"

"I'm Vanessa's daughter. I'm..." She swallowed against a lump in her throat so big it hurt. "I'm your granddaughter."

Cricket blanched and stared, her whole tiny body looking like it might vibrate as the words hit. "No...it can't be. How did you...how are you...who are...*what*?"

"I am," Emily said on an emotional laugh. "Vanessa and I just found each other a few days ago and...we came here because her father was sick and...yes. It's me. The baby she gave up for adoption."

"My granddaughter." Cricket stepped closer, her hands quivering on her chest as if her heart might actually leap out of it. "No! Yes! I can't believe it!" She let out a soft cry and pressed her hands to Emily's cheeks, laughing tearfully. "My beautiful granddaughter! Of course you are! You're the spitting image of Vanessa. Except for the awful hair."

Emily laughed and placed her hands on top of Cricket's, trying to freeze the moment so she could remember it forever—she had another grandmother! And she was funny and warm and real and...alive.

She could practically feel Grandma Gigi smiling down on this moment.

"So, Vanessa is here, too, then?" Cricket asked.

"She is." Emily nodded. "We're here together."

"For a month, you said?"

"Yes. We came because—"

"Bill passed." Cricket nodded. "Good of her to come for that. Did she see him?"

Emily shook her head. "She was an hour late."

"Oh." Her shoulders sank as if she knew exactly how that had to hurt Vanessa. "How are she and Glo doing? I'm a good friend of the family, you see. Even though things sadly didn't work out between Vanessa and my Noah—that's your dad," she added with a sly smile. "I've stayed quite close with Gloria. And Bill, though he was a pain in the butt."

"They're doing okay, taking it in stride."

"Well, then." Cricket pulled away, gathering herself and patting the salon chair. "We can't let this happy reunion wreck your hair. Sit back down and tell me everything. Every last detail. Your life, Vanessa's life, all of it. You made an old woman very happy today."

"I'm happy, too," Emily said, putting her hand on top

of Cricket's. "I lost my grandma last year and we were very close."

"Well, now you've found me." She gave a heartfelt smile. "And you, my dear, might just be my secret weapon."

Emily frowned as she sat back down and adjusted the cape. "Secret weapon? For what?"

Cricket stared at her in the mirror as if the answer should be obvious. "Why, my never-ending quest to get Noah to come home. If he won't come back for his own daughter, then something's really wrong with him."

Or maybe he wouldn't want to have anything to do with her, Emily thought. That was fine. She already had more family in one day than she'd had in her whole life.

Chapter Four

Cricket

It was so like Nessie Young to show up unannounced with the long-lost baby—now a beautiful young woman—at her side. Nessie was the definition of unpredictable, and that just made her more lovable to Cricket. Predictable people were boring and Nessie was anything but.

And now she was here, in Rosemary Beach, and Cricket Ellison, at seventy years old, was *finally* a grandma. If this wasn't the definition of a miracle, she didn't know what was.

After her long—and much needed—session with Emily, she'd convinced the girl to tell her where she and Nessie were staying. With that information, Cricket promptly took the rest of the day off, canceling some regulars for her far more urgent mission of seeing Nessie.

As Nessie and Glo's honorary second mother, Cricket knew she had to step in and be there for them in any way she could.

Plus, she had to do a little recon to find out what was going on in Nessie's life. She wanted to know if there was hope that she'd stay longer than a month—forever, perhaps. Then she could get Noah home and rekindle the romance that should never have ended.

She marched up the white wooden steps to the cute little beach house that matched the address given to her by Emily. Not that she'd needed an address—Cricket knew Rosemary Beach as well as she knew the hair color wheel. She knew who owned this rental, what it looked like inside, and what it cost to rent.

A lot, which told her Nessie was financially stable after her divorce from that actor. But was she ready for... love? Time to find out.

After a couple of knocks on the freshly painted front door, it swung open.

"Cricket." Vanessa stood on the other side of the door, shock widening her eyes as her jaw went slack.

To no one's surprise, Vanessa had grown into a beautiful forty-five-year-old woman with healthy, glowing skin and a fit figure. Also, she must have found a great hair stylist in L.A., because her blond was toned to perfection with nary a brass hair and a great cut.

"Nessie." Cricket held her arms out and embraced the other woman.

For a brief moment, the history, the years, the distance, and even the past with Noah didn't matter as Cricket hugged this woman she'd loved since she met her as a motherless baby.

Despite their complicated history, and the fact that Vanessa Young had once shattered her son's heart when she never came home, Cricket *still* loved her. That soft spot stayed soft, and their connection was always so real.

She'd been devastated by Vanessa's choices all those years ago—and by her steadfast refusal to come back to Rosemary Beach—but she couldn't completely blame the girl. She understood.

"I've missed you, Nessie." She held both of Vanessa's hands and squeezed them.

"I've missed you, too." Vanessa's eyes were misty. "Come in, please. I just made tea. Will you join me?"

"Sure." Cricket followed her into the kitchen, considering all the things they could talk about, but started with one of the most pressing. "I'm so sorry about Bill."

Vanessa nodded. "Yeah. I missed him by an hour, if you can believe that. I guess you can."

"You and Bill sliding like ships in the night?" Cricket laughed. "I can believe it."

Pouring another mug of hot water and dropping in a bag, Vanessa gestured toward the living room, where they settled onto a comfy rattan couch.

"I was going to come and see you," Vanessa said as she set her mug on a coaster on the glass coffee table. "I only got in yesterday morning."

Cricket purposely kept the meeting with Emily to herself, waiting to see how Vanessa handled the news. This situation called for the right timing, a sense of subtlety, and maybe a little patience.

"Well, it's sad about Bill," Cricket said, getting just enough of a raised brow in response to make her laugh. "It is," she insisted.

"He was never your favorite person," Vanessa said.

"Or yours," Cricket volleyed back.

Truth was, Cricket could hardly stand the crotchety old fart known as Bill Young, who just got meaner with each passing year. She'd begged him to fix his relationship with his youngest daughter, but he'd refused. Stubborn old coot.

"But favorite or not," Cricket said, "he's dead and that's sad. I hope he's up there with Gene playing cornhole. They always liked that game, even though Bill cheated."

Vanessa smiled and took a deep breath and exhaled slowly. "I hate that you lost Gene, Cricket."

She shrugged. "I'll see him again." She blew on her tea, cooling it and considering her next sentence. "I heard you quit your fancy stylist job in L.A."

Vanessa blinked back. "Wow, word travels fast. Who told you? Glo? She couldn't have had time. We just parted ways, like, twenty minutes ago, and—"

"Emily told me." Well, so much for subtlety and patience and timing. None of those things were in Cricket's wheelhouse anyway.

"You...you talked to..." Vanessa's manicured hand flew to her lips. "Oh, boy."

"She wandered into my salon in desperate need of a cut and color." Cricket arched a brow, a smile tugging at her lips. "We got to chatting and, soon enough, discovered that she's my granddaughter."

"Cricket, I should have told you. But you have to understand, I only found her literally two days ago. This was all very sudden and spontaneous and—"

"Nessie, sweetie." Cricket sensed Vanessa's heightening anxiety and placed a hand on her leg to ease it. "She told me the whole story. I'm not mad."

"You're not?"

"Are you kidding? I'm overjoyed! Do you know how long I've waited for a granddaughter? Twenty-nine stinking years, that's how long. And there she was, in my chair, looking like Nessie Young the Second."

The two women laughed together and hugged again as Vanessa breathed a visible sigh of relief.

"We do resemble each other quite a bit," Vanessa acknowledged.

"It's just wonderful, Nessie, really."

She took Cricket's hand and gave it a tight, loving squeeze. "Thank you for always being there. You and Glo...you two have never given up on me, never let me slip away out of your lives, no matter how distant I got." Her eyes filled. "I'm grateful for that. I'm grateful I have a home to come back to, even after being gone for so long."

Vanessa was just one of those people. You could go long stretches without talking to her, but her sparkle was never fully gone. And the instant she was back, the world was a bit brighter.

"You're always welcome here, my darling. And Emily! How fun for you to be just now getting to know your daughter. As adults."

Vanessa nodded. "It's fascinating. We're taking it one step at a time, but I have to say, the connection has been pretty natural so far. Plus, fate was on our side when it set us both up for a complete and total life change at the same moment."

Cricket angled her head. "Fate has a way of doing that."

"Where is she, anyway?" Vanessa asked, checking her watch. "I haven't seen her all day."

"You won't recognize her with her new hair," Cricket said. "She was exploring the town with her dog, sweet little thing. I'm sure she'll be coming back here soon. Of course, as soon as I finished her trim, I headed straight here to see you."

Vanessa smiled, brushing some hair behind her ears and hesitating before she asked the next question, the one they both knew was inevitable. "How's Noah?"

Cricket sipped her tea as her mind flashed with images of little Vanessa and Noah. Always together, inseparable. As children and then teenagers, the depth of their fondness palpable to anyone who was with them.

It had been such an organic friendship. Cricket had met the new neighbors when Bill Young moved down the street forty-five years ago with a five-year-old, a baby, and a very confusing and mysterious past. All he'd say was that his wife died tragically, and he and his two girls needed to start over.

Cricket had eight-month-old Noah, and to help Bill out, she'd take the little ones to the park. The pair were two peas in a pod, and their friendship stayed strong throughout grade school, and became a precious and mutual crush in eighth grade. By early high school, they were "officially" boyfriend and girlfriend, and Cricket was, admittedly, already scoping out wedding venues.

Sure, she'd perhaps gotten ahead of herself, but

anyone with eyes could see that the two were soulmates. They were simply meant to be, and no one could deny their close, once-in-a-lifetime connection.

But it all went sour when one mistake happened at the age of sixteen. Bill lost it on Vanessa when she told him she was pregnant, and she left. Cricket had seen her only a time or two since then...until right now.

Noah was broken when Vanessa ran off, and they'd only stayed in touch long enough for her to tell him she was giving the baby away. She was supposed to come back to Rosemary Beach, but she never did. After that, ties were cut, futures changed, life moved on.

But Cricket had always stayed stuck in those days, stuck in the hope of her son being with the girl—woman, now—that he truly, deeply loved.

"He's divorced," Cricket answered. "Because I know you're curious."

Vanessa's cheeks flushed, and she rolled her eyes slightly at Cricket's bluntness. "Well, so am I."

"That I did know. Glo's kept me up to date on your life."

Vanessa smiled. "I'm glad. I'm sorry I've been so hard to reach. Is he still in Miami, then? Noah?"

"Yes." Cricket curled her lip and groaned with frustration. "For reasons I can't possibly understand."

She chuckled softly. "His job, perhaps?"

"Job, shmob. We have law firms in Rosemary Beach! I keep telling him. He can be a lawyer anywhere, you know. But he lives in a big fancy high rise on Brickell

Avenue and works at a huge corporate firm and..." She flicked her hand. "That's his life. I miss him terribly."

"I'm sure you do."

Cricket studied Vanessa, knowing that she missed him, too. Of course she did. She had to.

And now, for the first time in forever, Nessie was back in Rosemary Beach, and both she and Noah were single.

Could there be hope after all?

"Hello! I'm back." The front door swung open and Emily walked in, her smile brighter than it had been when she showed up at the salon that morning looking rattier than the mutt by her side.

"Come in here, honey," Cricket said, patting the spot on the couch between her and Vanessa. "Show Nessie your new hair."

Vanessa gasped and cooed over the beautifully layered, light brown hair that fell in perfect waves to just kiss the tops of Emily's shoulders. "You look like a totally new woman!"

Emily glanced back and forth between her mother and her grandmother, her eyes glimmering. "I feel like one."

For the next hour, they talked and laughed and gossiped and sank into the indescribable joy of being mother, daughter...and grandmother.

Gah, she loved that word. Grandmother. She'd waited so long, it didn't even feel real.

"Oh, Cricket, there's simply no question. You have to get Noah back here. Whatever it takes." Paula McManus eyed Cricket from above her blue knitting needles, her gray gaze serious.

"God knows I'll try, but..." Cricket looked back down at her own knitting, mindlessly working her way through a lavender cardigan. "There's stubborn, and then there's Noah Ellison. He's a level up from most bullheaded men."

Shelly Jenks, her other knitting pal and the third member of their gossip club, arched her dark eyebrows almost up to her snow-white hair. "Vanessa is back. And those two belong together."

Cricket continued knitting and frowned. "I'm fully aware of that, but I have to be realistic."

Paula snorted. "Why start now? You've been pulling those strings and trying to get him back here for years. Ever since Gene died."

Cricket smiled at the truth of it. And if he didn't come home to his mother after his father died, would he ever? Well, of course, it wasn't like she was lonely.

She had the support and endless fun and laughter of Paula and Shelly, who came over to Cricket's little loft above her salon several nights a week to knit and talk, an activity that they'd rather uncreatively named a "knit-chat."

Shelly lowered her knitting needles. "Well, surely you're going to tell him about Emily."

There was no surely about it. Ever since she'd spent time with Vanessa and Emily, Cricket realized how new and tender their relationship really was. Did she want to be the one to upset things by dragging Noah into it? Obviously, she wanted to, but was that too much?

She simply couldn't bear to do anything to hurt her very own granddaughter.

"I don't know, Shel. They've been through a lot. And so has Noah with that selfish shrew, Rebecca. Maybe I should respect that and stay out of it myself."

The other women looked at her like she had two heads.

"I'm sorry," Paula said, pushing back some silver-threaded brown hair that brushed her shoulders. "I thought we were with Cricket Ellison."

"Really," Shelly added. "Did aliens kidnap our friend and replace her with someone who doesn't stick her nose where it doesn't belong?"

"Exactly," Cricket said. "Well, not the alien part. But if my nose doesn't belong somewhere, maybe there's a reason. Remember a few weeks ago after I did Mary Wilkinson's hair and then I 'accidentally' slipped up and told Ben Warren, the Realtor, that her house was for sale before Mary wanted anyone to know?"

"You were only trying to help," Shelly said with the compassion of a true friend.

"I got them both very mad at me. And I swore I'd stay out of other people's business."Paula lifted a shoulder. "I don't see a reason to stay out of this. Noah is your son, for heaven's sake, not some lady selling a house. He's single and free and enjoying his fancy big-city life and high income as a bachelor. He needs a woman."

She couldn't argue with that. "He *is* a family man to his core," she said. "That's why he settled for that annoying Rebecca in the first place. He wanted a wife, a family, a home. He was just looking for it with the wrong person."

Paula shook her head, looking doubtful. "Personally, I am not sure if Vanessa Young is the right person for him. I mean, just because they were friends as kids and dated in high school? That was three decades ago, darling. Worlds have changed. They're different people. She married a movie star!"

"B-list," Cricket said. "Maybe C."

"Still, they're different."

Cricket turned her attention back down to her yarn, rhythmically stitching as she spoke. "Yes, she's grown up. She's experienced things, she's aged, matured...gone through life. But she's still Nessie and he's still Noah."

"I, for one, want to hear about Emily." Shelly leaned forward, a wide smile pulling her gorgeous, chocolatey skin that Cricket couldn't help but envy.

Black don't crack, Shelly loved to remind them when they frequently remarked that she didn't look a day over fifty.

"Yes, hello!" Paula lifted her needles and laughed. "Your dream of being a grandmother has finally come to life!"

"I know." Cricket grinned, unable to stifle the bubbling joy in her heart. "She's wonderful. Smart, and, wow...resilient and tough. Wait until you hear her story."

The women chatted and knitted the evening away, as

they often did, and Cricket couldn't help the fact that her mind was filled with fantasies of Noah coming home. But should she meddle where she didn't belong?

The last thing she wanted to do was mess it all up.

He was her only child, and Cricket always felt that he only left town for good because Vanessa was gone. He was haunted by the memories, filled with regrets about the pregnancy, and plagued with the guilt that he wasn't able to stop her from running away.

Cricket knew her boy. But Vanessa and Emily were here now. What if they could all finally be a family? The big family she'd always longed for and dreamed of.

Maybe she didn't have to come up with some elaborate scheme to get Noah home. Maybe she could just tell him about Vanessa and Emily and trust his heart to do the right thing.

Oof. That was easier said than done for Cricket Ellison.

Chapter Five

Vanessa

Vanessa could hardly breathe as she stared at her father's closed casket, keeping her eyes glued to the shiny finish on the deep cherrywood. She stood between Gloria and Emily at the gravesite, dressed in black and surrounded by a small group of people who knew Bill Young.

It was a dreary day to match the dreary mood, with rare gray clouds layered in the sky that mimicked the sadness in Vanessa's heart.

The funeral had been long and slow and Vanessa had hardly listened to a word from any of the speeches or the words from the pastor who led the service. Her mind was occupied with only one devastating thought that made her nauseous as she watched that casket lower into the ground.

He'd never forgiven her. Never. Her father refused to give her that moment of peace and closure that she so deeply ached for. He blamed her for the split in their family, for an unwanted pregnancy, for being a disappointment. And all she ever wanted was for him to say he was wrong, he was sorry, and that he forgave her.

That was not to be.

New Beginnings in Rosemary Beach 55

She clenched her jaw as the pastor read some verses and led a prayer, her eyes stinging and her heart pounding.

How could she have failed this badly? How was it possible that he was literally going into his grave without ever making things right with her?

But who was really to blame, she asked herself. She'd stayed away longer than she should have. She should have tried harder. She should have insisted on patching up that relationship before it was too late.

There was plenty of blame to go around, plenty of failure on both their parts. Now Dad was dead and she was a forty-five has-been with no plan, no direction, and no parents.

"You okay?" Gloria whispered, leaning over and taking Vanessa's hand in hers as the funeral came to an end.

"Eh. Who can be okay at a time like this?"

Gloria shut her eyes with grief and sympathy. She'd come alone, since her son, Jeremy, hadn't been able to get away from college in Boston, and Daisy had a shift at the hospital all day that no one could cover. Not even for a funeral?

Her sister had been cagey and weird at the mention of her daughter, who seemed to be wrapped up in work and planning a wedding. But now was not the time to press. Not when they were about to bury Bill Young—alone. Not even next to his late wife, who had been cremated and her ashes strewn...somewhere.

Dad hated the subject, which had been closed many

years ago. Along with his heart, she mused. He never let them talk about her.

"It is with deep sadness and grief that we, the close friends and family of William Patrick Young, say goodbye to a dear member of our community," the pastor droned. "We know that he is now in his heavenly home in the arms of the Lord, and in that truth we find peace, comfort, and hope."

Hope. Vanessa sucked in a breath at the word. Some days, she felt like she had none. No hope for forgiveness or closure with her dad. He was gone, and she had to live the rest of her life knowing that he died hating her.

She did have Emily now, though they were far from deeply connected as mother and daughter. And she had Glo, her steadfast sister.

The pastor invited everyone to a reception at Gloria's Diner to commemorate Bill's life and, finally, blessedly, released them.

"Come on." Gloria looped her arm through Vanessa's elbow, and gestured at Emily for her to follow them. "I'll drive us to the diner so we can get things set up for the party, or whatever you want to call it."

Vanessa managed a halfhearted laugh. "Thanks, Glo. How d'you think that went?"

Gloria huffed out a breath as they walked to the parking area of the cemetery. "Oh, all right, I guess. I still can't believe he's actually gone, but I don't know." She clicked the keys to unlock her SUV as they walked up to it. "I spent so many years taking care of him and looking after him and prioritizing him over everyone else, I guess

I was kind of...ready." Her hand flew to her mouth and she gasped loudly. "Oh, my gosh. That was horrible to say. I don't mean I was ready, you can never be ready, I just—"

"Glo." Vanessa walked over and placed her hands on her sister's shoulders. "I know exactly what you mean, and it's not horrible. You gave up everything for Dad, and your selflessness is...unfathomable."

Unlike Vanessa, who, today, felt selfish to her core.

It was no secret that Dad's mental health had declined long before his physical health did. He'd always lived on the hairy edge between angry and depressed, one wrong incident away from a blowup or a breakdown. That all got worse once Vanessa left, she knew. He was depressed, which sent him to the bottle too frequently, never really able to cope or take care of himself.

As Emily got closer, Vanessa brought her in on the discussion. "It can't be said enough that Glo is a saint and an angel *and* the good daughter all rolled into one, who did the work to keep Dad alive and well, and did it with relatively no complaining."

Gloria gave an appreciative smile as they all climbed into the SUV. "Thanks, Ness," she said, pulling on her seatbelt. "I did give up a lot for Dad. I always put him first."

"You gave up your *marriage* for him," Vanessa gently reminded her. "It's okay to be a little relieved that you can think about yourself again, for once."

"My marriage had problems." Gloria lifted a shoulder, pulling out of the parking lot and heading toward

Main Street. "Christian and I were troubled," she added, glancing in the rearview mirror for traffic and to direct the statement to Emily. "He was a professional athlete and that made it really hard to be a family."

"Really?" Emily leaned forward. "That's cool. What sport? I mean, if you don't mind me asking."

"Ask anything," Gloria said. "You're family and have the right to know the past—which is not all bad, I might add. He played major league baseball, for the Boston Red Sox."

"Wow, impressive," Emily said. "How did you meet him?"

"He was in the Panhandle for a training camp after college, and traveled to Rosemary Beach on a weekend trip. Walked into the diner one day and I might have swooned." She laughed, and so did Emily.

"Do girls still swoon?" she asked on a chuckle.

"They do when they see a guy like Christian Bennett when he was twenty-three and smoking hot." She grinned into the rearview mirror. "Anyway, he ended up playing in the minor leagues for a team only about an hour from here, and after a year or so, we got married... and then I learned why so many professional athletes get divorced."

"The travel?" Emily guessed.

"That's the hardest part. It's doable at first, but then there are kids and it was so hard, because..."

"Because you couldn't leave Dad," Vanessa said, flinching at another gut punch of guilt.

"Well, you know..." She tried to wave off the sacrifice

that Vanessa had never considered making because of how Dad had treated her. But had that been fair to Glo? "Anyway, Christian finally made The Show, as they say, and got a sizable contract with the Boston Red Sox."

"And you wouldn't move there?" Emily leaned closer, clearly invested in the story.

"Well, it's cold up there!" she exclaimed as if that were the reason and not Bill Young and his failing health, deep depression, and many needs. "This is my home," Gloria said. "I had the diner and the kids were in school and, yes, Dad was here. So I really thought we could live apart during the season, but..."

"That didn't work," Vanessa finished for her.

"No, no. We split up." She said the words coolly, underscoring Vanessa's belief that there were more things wrong than just Gloria having to take care of Dad. But her sister always painted things in a glossy light, and Vanessa felt certain she didn't know the whole story, although that might be her guilty conscience talking.

"But my son, Jeremy, is playing Division 1 baseball in college right now, following in his dad's footsteps," Gloria added brightly. "They have a good relationship, especially since they're both in Boston. Daisy, not so much, but there's no hard feelings anywhere, really. It just... didn't work out."

"That's sad," Emily whispered.

Sad was one way of putting it, Vanessa thought. Deeply unfair was another.

The thought made her reach across the console and put her hand on Gloria's arm. "You can let go of all that responsibility now, Glo. You earned your place in heaven and I couldn't be more grateful. Especially because I dug in and didn't help."

Gloria waved a dismissive hand, as if sensing Vanessa's guilt. "Hey, he drove you away, and don't think I've forgotten that. He was responsible for you leaving this town, and I never truly forgave him for that. But, yes, I'm looking forward."

"Do you have plans for his property?" Vanessa asked. "It's got to be worth a pretty penny."

"Oh, it's worth many, many pretty pennies, but I'm not going to sell it."

"You're not?" Vanessa inched back in her seat, surprised.

"I'm going to expand the diner and make it into a full-service restaurant," she said. "I think I'll bring in a chef and remodel the whole thing—I've already had plans drawn up—and turn it all into destination restaurant that should do well in Rosemary Beach."

"Oh, my heavens!" Vanessa exclaimed. "That is an awesome idea."

"Is that your lifelong dream, Gloria?" Emily asked.

"I don't know about lifelong," she said, "but I've been thinking about it for a long, long time. I knew it couldn't or wouldn't happen until we lost Dad, and I certainly didn't want to rush that. But I did hire an interior designer who drew up plans for a very cool place and it seems crazy not to give it a shot with that premier location. Hey, if I crash and burn, then I'll sell it and get all those pretty pennies. But I'm only fifty and I think it's time for me to tackle something new, what with my kids all grown and gone, you know? I need to look to the future."

"I feel ya, sister," Vanessa said, genuinely happy for her sister but deeply longing for a future of her own.

But that's why she was here—to figure it out. And she would. But now, they were pulling up to the diner and it was time to thank way too many people for their sympathy over her loss. Gloria was the one who deserved that sympathy. She deserved everything, Vanessa thought with an affectionate glance at her sweet sister. Everything.

Gloria's staff at the diner had set up a lovely reception for Dad's celebration of life, with tables of appetizers, drinks, a coffee station, and some very nice desserts. It was elegant and tasteful, and got surprisingly crowded pretty quick.

"I guess Dad had more friends than I gave him credit for," Vanessa said to Glo as they reconvened for a moment in the corner.

"Oh, he ran a pretty successful business in a small town; you know how it is. Everyone shows up to show their support."

"I think it's nice," Vanessa said, thinking about her life in L.A., and how drastically different this was. It was almost like being on another planet.

Emily was chatting with Cricket and some other

locals—getting an earful of gossip, no doubt—and the place hummed with a respectful amount of somber conversation and small hints of laughter.

"Hello, my dears." Cricket walked over, arm in arm with Emily, clearly the older woman's new obsession. "Don't mind me, I'm just hanging out with my *granddaughter*." Her eyes shimmered with joy.

Vanessa held her arms out and gave Cricket a warm hug. "Thanks for coming."

"Are you kidding?" She looked back and forth between Vanessa and Gloria. "You girls are like daughters to me, and I am so sorry for your loss."

Vanessa let out a sigh.

"Thank you." Gloria smiled kindly. "For everything."

Cricket winked and gave Gloria a nod, then turned to Vanessa. "I just still can't believe my eyes when I see you in the flesh, Nessie. Have you decided how long you'll be staying in town?"

"As of right now, we're sticking with the one-month plan, but you know. I'm just trying to figure things out."

Cricket pulled Emily close to her, and laughed softly "You cannot take my granddaughter away, I simply will not allow it."

Vanessa smiled. "Emily is figuring her life out, too. We're both in sort of a starting-over limbo."

"I understand." Cricket gave a knowing nod. "You will figure everything out in due time, I'm sure. Now you, Miss Lady." She turned her attention to Glo. "Did you tell them your expansion plans?"

"Yes, I did." Gloria grinned proudly and pointed to

the back wall. "That's coming down and the two buildings will be joined. This whole section will be the front bar and booths, maybe a little more casual, and the back will be tables for a more formal setting. I can really visualize how I want it to turn out."

An ache pulled in Vanessa's chest. Oh, how she wished she had a plan like Glo. A clear vision for what she wanted to do with the rest of her life. Instead, she just had muddy uncertainty and a past filled with regrets.

"Well, you deserve it, Glo. I mean, good heavens." Cricket leaned in close and lowered her voice. "Waiting on Bill's every need for the past however many years! I know we're at his service and everything, but he wasn't exactly a *ray of sunshine,* if you get my drift."

Gloria snorted softly. "No kidding. It's okay, though, really. I did what..." she paused, and Vanessa instantly knew what was about to come out of her mouth.

I did what any daughter would do.

But sweet Gloria caught herself, and said instead, "I did what I felt was right, that's all."

Obviously sensing tension and the guilt that was likely visible on Vanessa's face, Cricket took each of the women's hands. "Well, it's just so wonderful to have you both together again. This town has missed the Young sisters. And I hope you have no intentions of getting this one back"—she used their joint hands to gesture Emily closer—"because she's mine now."

Emily laughed.

"Come on, granddaughter, we have more people to meet. My knitting ladies have just arrived, and they are going to want to eat you with a spoon." Cricket ushered Emily away with a quick wave to Vanessa and Gloria. "Bye, girls."

Alone with each other, Vanessa took a sip of her coffee. "I'm so sorry, Glo. I'm so sorry I've been gone all these years and that you sacrificed so much for him and I was never strong enough to face him or my past and—"

"Nessie, please." Gloria turned to face her, shaking her head. "You were off living your life. I never blamed you. Never. It was my cross to bear."

Vanessa swallowed the lump of emotion that rose in her throat.

Gloria smiled. "If you don't stop beating yourself up, you're going to crumble. New start, remember?"

"A new start of doing what I don't know yet, but I guess I'll figure it out."

"Of course you'll figure it out."

A few moments later, a middle-aged man who Vanessa thought looked vaguely familiar walked up to the sisters and greeted them.

"Vanessa, Gloria, I just wanted to say I'm so very sorry for your loss," he said.

Thankfully, Gloria stepped in and shook the man's hand. "We appreciate that so much, Barry, and thank you for all of your work on sorting out my father's will and affairs, as well."

Oh, Vanessa thought to herself. This was Dad's lawyer.

"Vanessa, have you met Barry Martinez? Rosemary

Beach's finest estate planning attorney. Also a longtime family friend."

"I'm not sure I have." Vanessa extended her hand. "Nice to meet you, Barry."

"Likewise, although I'm sorry it's under these circumstances."

Vanessa gave a solemn nod.

"Um, but do you think I could talk to the both of you for a moment, privately?" Barry glanced around. "Gloria, I consider you a friend as much as a client, and there's something you should know. Both of you should know."

Gloria turned to Vanessa, shrugging as she frowned with confusion. "Sure, we can step outside."

"Great."

The three of them walked out of the front door of the diner and headed a few feet down the sidewalk so they were standing right in front of the corner store, Dad's now-empty shop and Glo's future restaurant.

Barry pressed his lips together as the two women looked at him expectantly. "I've, uh, gone through your father's will."

"Right." Gloria nodded.

"And, well, I wanted to tell you personally, before we do the formal reading in a couple weeks, that it might not be entirely what you're expecting." The man's brown eyes slid over to Vanessa, shadowed with an emotion she couldn't quite identify.

"What do you mean?" Vanessa asked. "It's pretty simple. Everything is going to Gloria. She's been living here and taking care of him for her entire adult life. There shouldn't be any confusion about that."

Barry cleared his throat and took in a slow breath. "Bill left nearly everything to Gloria—his home, his savings, some investments, and his belongings. But..." Barry glanced to his right, jutting his chin at the vacant storefront. "He left this property to Vanessa."

"What?" Vanessa stepped back, her jaw falling open. She couldn't have heard that correctly. She turned to Glo, who was frozen in place, her face blanched in shock.

"No, no, that can't be right," Vanessa said, shaking her head hard. "That has to be a mistake. Gloria has always known she was getting this property. It's not even a question."

"Bill was very clear in his wording," the man said. "I suspected this might come as a shock, so I figured I'd give you both a heads-up and let you...figure things out."

"There's nothing to figure out," Vanessa insisted. "The property is meant for Glo."

"That's not what your father wanted."

"But...but..." Vanessa turned to her sister. "Glo, I—"

"I need a minute," Gloria said through a cracking voice, holding up a hand and hustling down the street toward the beach.

Vanessa did the only thing she could and followed her, crossing a wooden walkover that took them to the sand, which wasn't that crowded on this overcast day.

When Gloria dropped onto a park bench, Vanessa sat close to her sister and faced the gunmetal gray Gulf of Mexico.

"I don't care what Dad wrote or why he wrote it, that property is yours," she said without preamble. "I'm giving it to you. Period, end of discussion. We'll do whatever we have to do to make that legal."

Gloria shook her head, squeezing her eyes shut as a tear escaped. "I just...I don't understand, Nessie." She looked at Vanessa, mascara streaked down her cheeks. "I did everything for him. I gave him my whole life. Ever since Mom died and he spiraled, I was there for him, even as a kid."

"I know you were." Vanessa placed a hand on her sister's leg.

"Why would he take that from me?"

"Because he was cruel and ungrateful, and...I don't know." Vanessa shook her head.

"And I don't mean to say that you don't deserve it, because—"

"Gloria." Vanessa leveled her gaze with her sister's. "I think we both know darn well that I do not deserve Dad's most valuable asset. I don't even want it."

"But he did this for a reason, Nessie." She sniffed, looking out at the horizon. "He *changed* his will or..." She narrowed red-rimmed eyes. "Or he lied when we talked about the property. He told me it was mine, but I never actually saw a will."

"Well, none of that matters," Vanessa replied. "If my name is on it, I can do whatever I want with it, and I'm giving it to you. So it's a moot point."

"But that's not what he wanted."

"I don't care. You have plans. You have a future and a

valuable piece of property and a restaurant to build. He messed up." She gave a dry laugh. "Wouldn't be the first time."

Gloria wiped her eyes, the ocean breeze blowing her hair around her face. "What if this was his way of giving you the forgiveness you wanted so badly? What if he knew that by doing this, he could mend his relationship with you?"

Vanessa held her breath for a second. She hadn't thought of it that way. "If he wanted to fix things with me, he could have picked up the phone. And frankly, I could have, too. There's no fixing what happened between Dad and me. Not now that he's gone."

A shiver slid up her spine.

"I can't do this, Nessie. I can't take from you what's rightfully yours. I mean, he must have had a motive. But why? Why would he do this knowing how much it would hurt me and—"

"Gloria, I promise you." Vanessa took both of her sister's hands. "I'm not taking that property."

"I don't feel right with you just handing it over to me when he left it to you."

"Well, feel differently, because that's exactly what's happening."

Gloria didn't look so convinced.

They sat quietly holding hands, both of them no doubt thinking the same thing.

Why would Dad do this? Did he have some secret issue with Gloria? No, not possible. No one had issues with Gloria. Was it possible that this really was his way of trying to give Vanessa the peace and closure she wanted?

"It was going to be my reward, you know?" Gloria said tearfully. "All the years of sacrifice and selflessness—I was happy to do it—but this was sort of the light at the end of the tunnel. This was my future. Especially now with Daisy pulling away from me, and—"

"Daisy pulling away from you?" Vanessa drew back with surprise. "What do you mean?"

Gloria and Daisy were essentially inseparable and always close, although come to think of it...Vanessa hadn't even seen Daisy since she'd been back in town. What had happened?

"Oh, the fiancé and his stupid rich family and...." She flicked her fingers. "All that garbage. The diner and the expansion plan was just the only thing bringing me joy and hope lately. But now you're here, and that's even better. So I can give up—"

"Gloria Ellen Young Bennett," Vanessa said sternly, leveling her gaze. "You are *not* giving this up."

Gloria chewed her lip. "Can I just ask you one question?"

"Of course."

She inhaled slowly. "If there were some hypothetical situation where you did, in fact, keep the property and turn it into some sort of business for yourself....would it mean you'd stay here?"

Vanessa paused, pondering the question and giving the only answer that would be truly honest. "Not that it matters, but I don't know. Maybe."

Chapter Six

Gloria

"Wait, seriously?" Daisy Bennett, Gloria's twenty-four-year-old daughter, who was growing up entirely too quickly, flipped her blond-streaked hair and sipped her iced latte. "Grandpa gave his shop to Aunt Vanessa? That's a total outrage, Mom! I've only met her, like, twice."

The sun beamed down on the outdoor table in front of the diner where they sat for an afternoon coffee, one day after the funeral and the shocking news. Gloria felt like it had been ages since she'd seen her precious daughter and best friend.

Well, they *used* to be best friends. But lately, ever since Daisy moved in with Kyle, her fiancé, Glo could frequently go long stretches without seeing her. It hurt her heart, but she tried constantly to remind herself that Daisy had to grow up at some point. Still, something about it felt...wrong.

It probably didn't help that her other baby, twenty-one year-old Jeremy, was a thousand miles away, a junior at Boston College. He called when he could, but those chats had grown shorter and less frequent.

"Well, we're still deciding what to do with it," Gloria

said. "I'm sure Dad had his reasons, although I seriously can't think of what they could possibly be."

"Who cares about his reasons?" Daisy frowned. "Grandpa was old and mostly nasty. I can't believe he did this to you. He knew you had plans for the diner!"

"Yes..." Gloria sighed, her heart heavy with grief and confusion and hurt. "He certainly did know that."

"It's next level unfair." Daisy shook her head. "She's giving it to you, right? Aunt Vanessa isn't going to keep the property, is she?"

"She wants to give it to me, yes."

"Thank goodness. At least she's willing to do the right thing."

"I..." Gloria swallowed. "I'm not so sure it is the right thing, Daisy."

Her daughter's dark brown eyes nearly popped out of her head, her face lighting up with a classic Daisy over-the-top expression. "You're kidding, right? Mom, that place is practically yours already. Everyone in town knows it!"

"I know, I know. It just feels wrong to go against what Dad wanted."

Daisy looked skyward without a shred of caring for what her grandfather wanted. "Just let Aunt Vanessa give it to you and call it, Mom. Don't go digging into what that man wanted."

Gloria couldn't argue with that or much of anything Daisy was feeling about the whole situation. She'd struggled all night with many of the same emotions.

"As far as I knew, he disowned Aunt Vanessa long

before I was born and wanted nothing to do with her," Daisy continued. "You've been here, taking care of him and putting up with his crusty old self to the bitter end. Then he goes and *changes his will* and gives his best asset to the daughter he didn't even speak to? It's wrong on every level. How are you not more upset?"

"I'm very upset, honey, believe me. I spent the better part of yesterday crying over...all of it."

Daisy sighed. "I'm so sorry I missed the funeral. I could not for the life of me find someone to cover my shift."

"It's okay. It was just a bunch of people being sad."

Her brows flicked. "Sounds fun."

"Mmm." Gloria sipped her coffee. "A blast."

"It's just so...like her."

Gloria was not terribly fond of the edge in Daisy's voice, or the bitterness on her tongue. What had happened to her sweet daughter who picked every flower she saw and couldn't watch a sunset without turning it into a full photo shoot?

Only one thing could have caused this change in her daughter—Kyle Whittington.

But it wasn't her place to say anything negative about the young man Daisy was going to marry. She'd taken on a whole new life and identity since getting deeply involved with her now-fiancé and the prominent, wealthy family who'd been deeply involved with the building, design, and profit of Rosemary Beach.

She shook off thoughts of Kyle to consider Daisy's last comment. It was so...*like her?*

"What do you mean by that?" Glo asked, stirring her coffee.

"Aunt Vanessa." Daisy sat back in her chair and huffed out a sigh. "It's so like her to just blow into town, drop some crazy news-bomb on everyone that she's now, like, besties with the girl she gave up forever ago, and take the most valuable thing that Grandpa had after having been essentially MIA since before I was born."

Gloria stared at her, and not because it took full concentration to follow a meandering, multi-phrased thought like Daisy frequently spewed.

"Everyone in Rosemary Beach seems to think the sun rises and sets on the mysterious Vanessa Young," she continued. "I think the whole thing is just self-centered."

Irritation rose in Gloria's chest, but she tamped down her anger. Of course, her instinct buzzed with the need to defend her sister, and the frustration that Daisy was speaking on things she knew nothing about.

But arguing would only push her daughter further away than she already was, and Gloria couldn't handle any more distance between them.

"Aunt Vanessa has had a difficult life," she said gently. "Things with my father were very tough for her, and she's been through a lot."

There was still a big part of Gloria's heart that wondered if this was Dad's way of extending an olive branch to Vanessa, but she didn't know for sure.

"We never even see her."

"Nessie lived in California up until this week, and I had no idea she was coming back." Gloria lifted her own coffee and took a sip. "And seriously, she'd love to see you. And you should meet Emily! You two are cousins."

Daisy lifted a hand to shield her eyes from the afternoon sun, angling her head. "Are we, though?"

"Well, biologically, yes."

"Didn't she just meet Aunt Vanessa last week?"

"Yes, but she's her daughter. Vanessa gave her up for adoption and they've finally reconnected. You know this, Daisy."

"I know, I guess." She dropped her hand with a thud and picked up the stir stick. "It's all just kind of...weird."

"You'll get used to it."

"Does Cricket know?" Daisy had always had a special bond with Cricket Ellison. "Because, wow, that would mean this Emily person is Cricket's granddaughter. A real one, not a pseudo-granddaughter like she calls me."

Gloria nodded. "Yes, she knows. They've met." Daisy would know all that if she'd tried just a little harder to get yesterday off and come to her grandfather's funeral.

"Cricket's probably faking an illness to get Noah on a plane as we speak," Daisy cracked. "The woman would move heaven and Earth to get them back together. I've heard her say so myself."

Glo waved a hand. "Hopefully, she's given up that dream by now. Noah's life is far away, and Vanessa's is, well, kind of a mess."

"Can I be honest with you, Mom?"

Gloria resisted the urge to leap across the table and

shout *"Yes! Please! All I want in the world is to be close to you again and I feel like you're slipping away!"*

But she opted for cool, casual. "Of course, hon. What is it?"

"You don't have to be so perfect all the time, you know that, right? Like, no one would blame you if you showed some real emotion about this whole thing. You could flip this table over right now and it would be acceptable. It's super upsetting and unfair."

Gloria paused, thinking about her daughter's words. "I don't need to flip any tables, Daisy, but...yeah. I'm mad. I'm hurt. I'm pretty darn heartbroken."

Although Gloria was trying her best to keep it together and be a role model of selflessness and grace for her daughter, on the inside, she was cracking with pain.

She didn't want to feel resentment and bitterness, not toward Dad or Vanessa or anybody.

Gloria had spent the better part of her life watching what resentment, grudge-holding, and unforgiveness did to a person as it completely deteriorated and destroyed her father. She wanted no part of it. She swore, throughout her entire life since the day Vanessa left, she would never hold a grudge. Not against her sister, or anyone else.

She'd watched Dad become angry and bitter and old...fast. He isolated himself, and by the very end there were few people who cared about him and his health.

Every time she saw her father's regretful, resentful eyes, she'd go home and call Vanessa. And if she didn't answer, she'd leave a voicemail, or, in more recent years, send a text. She refused to let that relationship die.

And now, she so desperately didn't want the anger and outrage of this insane decision from Dad to let tension grow between her and her sister and threaten their fragile relationship. But Daisy was right. It was pretty darn hard not to flip a table right about now.

"Look, Dais. I totally get why you would feel that way, and I know things seems simple, but they're not."

"They look pretty simple to me." Daisy took a sip of iced coffee from her straw. "It was some weird fluke in the will, Aunt Vanessa is giving you the property, so just proceed as planned. And feel free to be mad in the process."

"I am mad." Gloria nodded. "Not at Nessie. At Dad. I could slap him for changing this, knowing what it would do to me, even if she hands it over. He did this knowing it would break me."

"What would she even do with it?" Daisy asked. "I mean, she doesn't want to run a sporting goods store or whatever."

Glo lifted a shoulder. "No idea. As of right now, she's not even planning on staying in town all that much longer."

That truth hurt Gloria almost as much as the will revelation.

Daisy's phone buzzed on the table, and she picked it up and read a text. "I gotta go, Mom. Kyle's family invited me on their yacht tonight. I want to get ready."

Disappointment thudded in Gloria's stomach at the

words. Losing Daisy to Kyle was getting harder every day.

"Speaking of Kyle..." Gloria reached out and grabbed Daisy's hand before she had the chance to stand up. "We haven't had much time to wedding plan lately, with everything going on with Grandpa."

"It's okay." Daisy smiled and slid her hand free. "Kyle's mom has handled a lot of it, which is really cool of her, don't you think? She has connections for literally *everything*, including that amazing dress I picked up in New York. You're coming to the final fitting, right? It's next month."

"I wouldn't miss it for the world," she said. "I've arranged for the diner to be covered and have a hotel. I can't believe the wedding is, what? Four months away? There has to be something I can do for my own daughter's wedding."

"Four months and six days." Daisy grinned. "I'll let you know after I talk to Linda what's left to do. But, please, she *lives* for this stuff and you have to run the diner. It's just easier this way."

She'd get...what was left to do? Gloria didn't know how she could have been pushed so far to the side in the planning of her own daughter's wedding, but again, picking a fight with Daisy would help no one.

She shifted in her seat, an age-old ache in the peacemaking heart of Gloria Bennett. Sometimes, there was a fine line between peacemaker...and pushover.

"Okay, sounds good, Dais." She stood up and gave

her daughter a long, tight hug. "Have fun tonight. Be safe."

"Bye, Mom." Daisy bounced away, her caramel hair flowing in the breeze as she walked down Main Street.

Gloria sat back down at the table, finishing the last few sips of her coffee, and wondering how and when she'd taken a back seat in Daisy's life, and if there was a way to fix it.

That would mean changing Kyle—a slightly entitled, trust fund, prep school kid whose dad was the CEO of a luxury beachfront real estate firm. The Whittingtons had made multiple millions on Rosemary Beach and then even more selling high-end homes all along the Panhandle's beachfront towns.

Kyle had gone to Yale—per his legacy, of course—and returned home to Rosemary Beach to work for his dad's company and begin amassing a fortune of his own.

Daisy had stayed in state, and attended the University of North Florida in Jacksonville, about five hours east of Rosemary Beach. She got her nursing degree, and as soon as she graduated, she knew she wanted to come back to the little beach town she called home.

Gloria had been over the moon with her decision, and they lived together for a couple of years while Daisy worked her first job at Ascension Hospital.

Not too long after Daisy moved back from Jacksonville, she'd crossed paths with Kyle through mutual high school friends, and he took a liking to her. Not that Gloria could blame him for that. Daisy was a captivating, bubbly, enchanting beauty who brought joy to everyone around her.

She'd tried her hardest to see what her daughter saw in the wealthy Ivy League kid, but all Gloria ended up getting was pushed away. Kyle and his family ran in exclusive circles with elite people and spent their time on yachts and planes.

Daisy, understandably, had gotten swept up into the luxury and glamour of it all, and she was deeply smitten with the slick young rich boy.

He'd proposed to her several months ago with a rock that looked almost ridiculous on her tiny finger, but Daisy was beside herself with joy, so Gloria tried to be as excited as possible.

But as time went on, Daisy fell into the Whittington family easily and naturally, and there seemed to be no place in all of that for a divorced diner owner.

As Gloria pondered the reality of that, she wiped one single tear and tossed her cardboard to-go cup into a trash bin as she left.

Was she going to miss out on her daughter's life? Would Daisy always choose the uber-rich Whittingtons now?

All at once, it felt like she was losing her daughter and her dreams. Even if Nessie just handed her the keys to the property, Gloria needed to know *why*. She needed to know what in the world Dad was thinking, and why he'd do this to the one person who was always there for him.

Still stewing over her questions later that evening, Gloria went to her father's house. This time, she wanted to find his copy of his will, and maybe discover a provision or addendum or explanation on why and when he'd changed it.

Unless he'd always planned this post-mortem surprise.

Dad's house—which she supposed was hers now, unless he'd left *this* to Vanessa as well—was a bungalow a few blocks from the beach, in a residential area about ten minutes away from the heart of Rosemary Beach. He'd lived in it for thirty years now, having moved when Glo left for college and Vanessa left for...good.

He had decided he didn't want to be in the home the girls had grown up in anymore, and it was time to downsize, so he'd relocated to this understated three-bedroom just outside of downtown.

For all of his flaws—and there were many—Bill Young kept things minimal and very tidy, so sorting through his things after he passed was not a terribly daunting or frustrating task.

Still, in his seventy-four years of life, the man had acquired a good bit of stuff, which lived in boxes in his attic, neatly organized drawers in his nightstand and desk, and filing cabinets in his office closet.

But as she walked through the halls of the familiar old house, there for the first time since he died, she could only smell the lingering scent of his cigar—which he'd sworn he'd given up—and his beloved Aqua Velva aftershave. It all gave her a certain kind of peace in the solitude.

It had been tough for Gloria all these years, knowing Dad had essentially disowned her sister and that as long as he was in Rosemary Beach...Vanessa wouldn't be. And Gloria had to be. Even when Christian moved to Boston, effectively ending their marriage because of her father.

She had tried to talk to Dad about Vanessa, to encourage him to reach out, but he would have none of it.

Dad was gone, and these walls were no longer haunted with his bitterness and hate. Gloria often wondered where that inner pain in her father came from, and she imagined the majority of it wasn't from Vanessa's pregnancy at all, but rather from Mom's accident.

Gloria could tell from a relatively young age that his mental health was on a rapid decline even before his physical health was, and there was nothing to blame for it but Mom's sudden death.

On a sigh, Gloria flicked the light on in his office, which was a small bedroom at the end of the hallway, and sat at his desk in the middle of the room. The surface was empty except for a few knickknacks, a pen, and his old watch. Mostly it was dust, as he hadn't sat here since he had a stroke over a month ago.

She wasn't sure where a copy of the will would be, but she figured she might as well start looking in his desk file drawer, since that's where he seemed to keep most important things.

After rooting through every folder, all she'd found

was medical files, store paperwork, and old spreadsheets. Moving to the bottom drawer, she saw it wasn't so neatly organized, but a pile of files, binders, and folders.

On a groan, Gloria lifted the huge stack, silently cursing her father for refusing to move any of his records to digital format.

"Because who uses online spreadsheets, right, Dad?" she mumbled to herself, hoping his will might be stored underneath all this stuff, at the bottom of the drawer. "Nope, everything has to be in paper form, just to make it a huge pain in the butt for Gloria one day."

As she plopped the fat stack onto the desk, a manila enveloped that looked stuffed to the gills fell out and dropped to the floor.

Could that be it?

Glo reached down and picked it up, feeling that it was thick and full and...sealed.

Huh. Why would Dad have a sealed, unmarked envelope? It wasn't a likely spot to keep his will, but with him? One could never be too sure.

Except the envelope wasn't unmarked.

As Glo turned the thick envelope around, she noticed Dad's unmistakable all-caps handwriting in tiny print in the corner.

Letters from Violet

"Mom?" Gloria breathed out the word through her tightened throat as she realized what exactly she might be holding.

Letters that her mother had written to her father at some point in their relationship. Maybe it was when they were dating. Maybe it was during the early years of their marriage. Maybe the letters spanned all the way until the very day she died.

She had no clue, but she did know that in her hands was a piece of the mother she'd lost at only five years old.

She clutched the envelope tightly and shut her eyes, unexpected tears springing. For the first time in a week, the reality of Gloria's life hit her like a train at full speed.

She was an *orphan*. At fifty years old, Gloria Bennett had lost both of her parents. They were really, truly gone. And with Daisy keeping her at arm's length and Jeremy up in Boston, Gloria felt deeply alone.

She held the envelope, staring at her mother's name as tears fell onto the old paper.

Family was everything to Gloria. It was her driving force in all of life, to be a mother and a daughter and a sister and, at one time, a wife. Gloria gave her family relationships her absolute all. She always poured her entire heart and soul into her loved ones, and somehow, now, she was left with none of them.

"Except Nessie," she whispered to herself, leaning her back against Dad's wooden desk as she toyed with the mystery envelope in her hand.

Vanessa was here, for the first time in thirty years. Vanessa was her family, her dear, dear sister, and Gloria could not let her go.

Suddenly, sitting on Dad's office floor and clutching this envelope, everything became shockingly clear.

Vanessa *had* to take that property. If it meant she'd

stay in town forever, it was the right decision. It was the only decision.

And the minute she made it, Gloria felt covered in peace.

She shoved the envelope deep into her purse—that would be an emotional journey for another day—and hustled out of there. She jumped into her car and drove as fast as traffic would allow to get to Vanessa's colorful beach house rental, her whole body humming with...well, peace. Maybe something else, too.

Hope. Hope for a family and a future and fun. Years with her sister to make up for the decades stolen from her by their father. Of course that was why he'd left Vanessa the property, of course he knew it would bring her back to Gloria. Even if only to sell it—which maybe he sensed she wouldn't do, anyway.

He did this as a way to give the ultimate gift to Gloria —not a store, not a restaurant, not a place...a *sister*.

She whipped her car into the driveway of the beach house, glancing at the clock. It was after ten, but surely Nessie was still up. Running to the front door, she knocked hard over and over.

Vanessa opened the door wearing pajamas and a confused expression. "Hey, Glo. Is everything all right?"

"Nessie." Gloria fought to catch her breath. "You have to keep the property."

Vanessa shook her head, frowning with confusion. "What? What are you talking about? I already told you, I'm giving it to you. I don't even know what I'd do with it but sell it, and you deserve—"

"My sister," Gloria interrupted. "I deserve my sister. Family means the world to me, Vanessa. You know that. Mom's been gone since we were little, and now Dad is, too. My son is in Massachusetts and my daughter? I hardly recognize her. I want you to take the corner store, open a business, and stay here."

Vanessa stared at her in stunned silence, her jaw gaping. "Come inside, Glo. I'll make some tea."

"I don't want tea. Okay, I do. But I want you, Vanessa Young. You!"

Vanessa smiled and ushered her inside, chuckling as she seated Gloria at a barstool in the dimly lit kitchen and filled a kettle and started heating it.

"Nessie, I'm serious about this."

Vanessa let out a slow sigh. "Honey, I think you've had a long, and extremely emotional few days, and you really need to rest and give this some thought. A lot of hard thought."

"I don't need hard thought. I have feelings. Deep, real, honest, achy feelings."

"You sound like you should be writing country music."

"I mean it, Nessie!"

At the desperation in her voice, Vanessa turned from the stove, staring at her. "Do you, really?"

"Yes. Look, I was seriously hurt by what Dad did by keeping you away all those—"

"I kept myself away."

"But would you have if he'd been nice? Forgiving? Slightly normal?"

Vanessa's face screwed up. "Why was he so...*horrible?*"

Gloria flicked off the question. "We'll figure that out someday. But that's the point, Ness. We'll figure it out together if you are here. Please. Don't you see, this is his way of forgiving you and thanking me."

"By taking away your inheritance, which, by the way..." She dropped tea bags in the cups, lifting up the kettle. "...is worth millions. With an S."

"I don't care," Gloria insisted. "You are worth everything to me."

Vanessa froze mid-pour and looked at Gloria, eyes wide. "Really?"

"Please stay." Gloria locked eyes with her sister, emotion tightening her throat. "Please take the property and make it something you love and stay, Nessie. Mom and Dad are gone, and I need family. I need you. I really think this is the way things are supposed to be."

Vanessa slowly lowered the kettle back onto the stove, shaking her head. "Gloria...you're not seriously considering ditching your restaurant plans for this, are you?"

"Nessie, I love my diner the way it is. Besides, who wants to work nights?" She laughed tearfully, stood up, and walked around the countertop.

"You're serious," Vanessa said slowly, brushing a strand of hair behind her ear. "You really want me to have the store? This is insane, Glo."

"Dad offered you an olive branch from the grave," Gloria

said, sniffing. "Take it. Get your forgiveness and your healing and your closure. And grab those keys to your brand-new life and start thinking of possibilities of what it could look like."

"Gloria." Vanessa pressed her lips together, her eyes misty. "I'm speechless."

"You came here for a fresh start, and now you've got one. You wanted a plan, right?"

Vanessa laughed dryly. "More than anything."

"Now you can make one. Having my sister next door to the diner is so much more important than a restaurant or a dream or...anything. This is our future, Nessie. This is the rest of your life. Our lives."

"Okay. I can't believe this." Vanessa blinked back tears. "I don't even know what to do with it."

"You'll figure it out," Glo said with a laugh.

With a whimper of love, they hugged tightly for a long, long time, both so emotional, they couldn't talk.

"Are those happy tears or sad?"

They pulled apart at the sound of Emily's voice, turning to see her standing in the doorway.

"Happy," they answered in sisterly unison.

"Oh, good. I heard you come in, Gloria, and I thought maybe you two needed some time to grieve and think and talk."

"Tell her," Gloria said, jabbing Vanessa with her elbow. "Tell her what you're doing."

"But I don't know yet."

"Tell me what?" Emily asked, coming into to the kitchen, looking from one to the other.

"It looks like I'm staying in Rosemary Beach for...the foreseeable future."

"Really?" Emily's eyes opened wide. "That's...amazing. Wow."

"And what about you?" Gloria slid her arm around Emily's waist. "Would you stay and add to my family joy?"

"If I had a job," she said, "I'd live here in a heartbeat."

"Can you wait tables? I'm looking for a server."

"Yes and yes, Gloria!" Emily exclaimed without a second's hesitation.

With a squeal, she clapped her hands, then pointed her fingers at Emily. "But that's not what you call me."

"Glo," Emily corrected.

Gloria leaned in and got close to her. "*Aunt Glo*, from now until forever."

They shared one more joyous hug, some tea, and for the first time in as long as Gloria could remember, she wasn't the least bit mad at her father. She loved her inheritance and couldn't stop smiling.

Chapter Seven

Emily

"So that's a French dip, extra au jus, and a side of sweet potato fries." Emily smiled as she jotted down the order on her notepad. "And for you, sir?"

The older gentleman on the other side of the booth gave a kind smile, his eyes glancing across the table at the woman who was clearly his wife, likely of a very long time. "I'll have the Reuben, my dear. And don't go light on that Thousand Island dressing."

"I'll bring you an extra side, sir." Emily slid her notepad back into the front of her apron, grateful she'd dabbled in the service industry while on the run. Also grateful her new "Aunt Glo" ran a diner and had Emily in a uniform and apron faster than you could say the daily special.

It was only Emily's first day on the job, but she could already tell that Gloria's was a Rosemary Beach staple, and a hub for all the locals to gather, eat, and gossip and tourists to get some of the best food in town.

Quite simply, Emily felt so grateful to not be in fear, or checking the front door every twenty seconds, or trying to hide her face when she went out so that she wasn't recognized. She wore her newly trimmed and colored hair up in a short ponytail, and easily made eye contact with every customer she served.

"Emily?" The hostess, a young woman in her late twenties, like Emily, tapped her on the shoulder as she rounded the corner to the kitchen.

"Yes?" Emily turned and was met with a warm smile and bright eyes.

"You're Glo's niece, right? I don't think we've properly met." The other young woman held out her hand. "I'm Liz, I work up at the front."

Emily shook her hand. "It's great to meet you, Liz."

"Likewise," the girl said in an endearing Southern accent. "I wanted to ask...how's your mom, Vanessa? She was so frantic the day she came in here and I had to deliver the awful news."

Emily stepped to the side to continue the conversation out of the main dining area. "She's doing all right. Thank you for asking."

"That's good to hear. Glo has such a heart of gold. I don't know Vanessa, but I'm sure she's the same way."

She seemed to be, but truthfully, Emily still didn't really know the woman who was now her mom, according to perfect strangers like this woman. But Emily just nodded and smiled, not wanting to get into the nitty-gritty of her bizarre backstory.

"Anyway, I wanted to ask..." Liz took Emily's arm and gently pulled her closer, lowering her voice to a whisper. "When is Gloria planning on starting the expansion next door? Not to rush things, of course. I'm just wondering because I'm hoping to get promoted to an assistant manager, and if we're expanding, then Glo's gonna need more staff." She smiled, lifting a shoulder. "Might be my chance."

Emily sucked in a breath, glancing to the side while she figured out how to respond. Liz was clearly a sweetheart, and knew nothing of the muddy past and strained relationships of the Young family. "Actually, um, kind of a surprise but my grandfather decided to give his store to my mom, Vanessa."

"Oh." Liz's face fell a bit. "Oh, of course. I'm so rude. I never should have asked, really. Invading on your family privacy and everything. I just figured since Glo was always around, I'm so sorry—"

Family privacy...Emily had never even had a family before. Maybe she shouldn't have said anything.

"No, no. It's fine, Liz. Really." Emily offered a warm smile. "You seem like you know this diner inside and out. Maybe once things settle down, you could talk to Glo about the promotion, even without the expansion."

Liz pressed her lips together. "All right, I think I will. Thanks, Emily. Now, let's get back to work, shall we?" She nodded in the direction of the corner booth where the older couple sat. "Don't want old Mr. Davenport waiting too long on his Rueben with lotsa Thousand Island dressing."

Emily blinked back. "How did you know?"

"They're regulars. Been orderin' the same lunches for years." She lifted a friendly shoulder. "Don't worry, you'll learn."

The morning flew by, and Emily enjoyed every fast-paced second. She made a point of memorizing orders and asking people their names. She even started saying she was new to town, and every single local she talked to had a different recommendation of something she simply had to do in Rosemary Beach.

These people had a lot of pride in their little city, and Emily could easily understand why. Rosemary Beach was quite possibly the most charming place she'd ever been, and it had an upscale yet welcoming and unassuming feel everywhere she went.

During lulls, Emily would pop over to the hostess stand and talk to Liz, who knew all of the town drama and happenings from working at the diner and talking to Gloria, who knew *everything*, Emily was learning.

Liz filled her in on the townspeople of Rosemary Beach who frequented the diner, sharing whatever juicy gossip she knew about them, and their typical menu orders. The rest of the place was peppered with tourists who, according to Liz, were like extras in a movie.

Emily took it all in—soaking up every moment of peace, freedom, and her new life, which she couldn't imagine in a more perfect place.

"Oh, hang on a sec," Emily said when she noticed a family looking for a server. "I'm gonna go check on table twelve. The..." She racked her brain.

"Christiano family," Liz finished. "Big, happy, Italian family. Lotsa kids. Lotsa chicken fingers, always."

Emily held up a hand. "Christianos. Kids. Chicken fingers. Got it. I'll be back!"

When she finished checking on the family and

bringing their four young children copious amounts of honey mustard dipping sauce, Emily noticed a new guest in her section.

A man in a ballcap, maybe early thirties, seated alone at a two-top in the back corner. He was looking down, so all Emily could see was an Atlanta Hawks logo on his hat. In front of him was a laptop, and the man was typing and staring at the screen intently.

Emily didn't want to interrupt, but she had to take his order.

"Hi, welcome to Gloria's. Can I get you started with something to drink?"

The man slowly lifted his head, warm brown eyes looking at Emily as a slight smile pulled at his clean-shaven face. "Iced tea would be great. Unsweetened."

Emily was suddenly very aware that the man was attractive—really, really handsome, actually, with a strong jawline and whispers of brown hair falling around his forehead under the baseball cap.

Huh. A cute guy. How nice, for someone else. His wife or girlfriend, probably. "Of course. I'll be right back with iced tea."

He looked back down, the ball cap once again hiding his face.

Emily headed into the kitchen and filled up a tall glass with ice and unsweetened tea, then walked back to the man and whatever was on his ever-important laptop.

"Thanks," he said absently, not bothering to look up at her this time.

"Of course." Emily lowered the glass down to the

table, then went to reach for her notepad to take his order. But as she moved her hand, she accidentally bumped the iced tea and in the blink of an eye...she saw it tip and tumble and spill tea *everywhere*.

"Oh, God!" Emily gasped in horror at the scene that seemed to unfold in slow motion, the amber-gold liquid gushing over table and lap and...keyboard!

Swearing under his breath, the man stood up, his white T-shirt sloshed with tea, but all his attention was on the laptop, which was covered.

"Oh, God." He tapped a key furiously. "Oh, no. My *document*. The computer's dead and I didn't save—" His voice rose with frustration.

"I'm so sorry, I'm so sorry." Emily felt her cheeks go burning red. "Let me go grab some paper towels."

"It's all right," he said calmly, finally meeting her gaze. "It's...fine. Accidents happen."

It clearly wasn't fine, but she was relieved that he didn't seem too angry. She jogged to the back room and returned with an entire roll of brown paper towels, soaking up the spilled tea on the table, floor, and laptop.

Emily shook her head. "I'm so embarrassed. I really am sorry."

The man let out a slightly noisy sigh, patting his shirt with the paper towels. "It's okay, really. I just...*man*, I wish I'd clicked Save. Lost some important work that I don't know if I'll be able to recreate."

Emily stood up from the floor where she'd been crouching down to clean up the spill. "Are you sure it's lost?"

"The screen went black when it got wet, and the whole system shut down with an unsaved doc open. Seems like a pretty safe bet to me."

She glanced at him again, feeling yet another wave of relief that he wasn't that angry. She couldn't imagine how Doug would have reacted if she'd made a mistake like that.

"I, um, I actually know a thing or two about computers, and I might be able to recover it."

The man gave her a dubious look, his hat casting a shadow over his mysterious, handsome face. "Really?"

"Well, I mean, I'd like to try." Emily shrugged, balling the tea-soaked paper towels in her hand. "I used to work with computers and there are some ways to access lost files in the case of a crash. No promises, but I want to try. Please, I feel terrible."

The man took in a breath and held Emily's gaze for a few moments. "Okay. I mean, if you think there's a chance of getting the work back, I'll try anything."

She let out a small sigh of relief, knowing full well the chances of her recovering whatever he was working on were pretty slim, but it wouldn't be right if she didn't at least attempt to fix her clumsy mistake. "Great. I'm Emily, by the way." She wiped off her sticky hand and held it out.

The man smiled. It was no joyful grin, but it was a smile nonetheless. "Reed."

"Good to meet you, Reed."

"Excuse me, miss? We're ready to order."

She threw a quick smile at the other customer, then

turned back to Reed. "I can take down your number, and we'll figure out a time for me to take a crack at those lost files." She pulled her notepad and pen out of her apron and set it on the table next to the likely destroyed laptop.

"Sure, that's fine. I appreciate it."

While Reed was scribbling his phone number down, Emily glanced at the black screen of the computer. "What were you working on, anyway? It must have been important."

He clicked the pen closed against the tabletop and ripped off the top page of the notepad, handing it to her. "It was extremely important." He flicked his brows, clearly indicating that's all he was willing to say about that.

So, his computer files were as mysterious as the depth of his brown eyes, Emily noted.

"Well, I'll shoot you a text." She folded the paper and stuck it in the back pocket of her black jeans. "And again, I'm really sorry."

Reed returned to his computer and attempted to give it a reset, waving a hand. "It's okay, um, Emily, right?"

"Yes, Emily." She nodded. "And, I almost forgot, what would you like to order?"

He looked up at her, that same tiny hint of an almost-smile playing at the corner of his mouth. "Surprise me. Just please, no more liquids."

She laughed. "Will do."

As Emily made her way through the restaurant, stopping to take an order, then heading back to the kitchen, a hand grabbed her arm and stopped her in her tracks.

"Um, excuse me!" Liz stared at her with wide eyes and an eager smile. "I need to know everything that just happened, now. What that guy said to you."

She frowned. "What happened is that I made a total fool of myself and spilled a full glass of tea all over him and his computer, which apparently destroyed some insanely important top-secret documents."

"Okay, that's not the only tea you're about to spill." Liz's eyes popped open wide. "What kind of documents?"

"I don't know, he didn't say." Emily shook her head. "I feel so stupid. I offered to take a look at the computer and see if I can recover anything that was lost, but...I'm not hopeful that—"

Liz gasped with surprise. "And he agreed?"

"I mean, I don't think he has a ton of faith in a klutzy waitress, but yeah, I think he was willing to try anything. Anyway, why are you so shocked? Who is he?"

"That's the thing." Liz pulled her in close and lowered her voice to a whisper. "No one knows who he is. He's totally mysterious, and also totally hot, right?"

Emily shrugged, not wanting to admit she thought the same thing. "I guess. How does no one know who he is? Doesn't he live here?"

"No clue. I guess he must, since he comes to the diner to work a lot. Always alone, always with a laptop. I don't even know his name."

"Reed," Emily said. "He introduced himself as Reed."

"Wow." Liz laughed softly. "You made more progress

with him in five minutes than anyone I know in the several months he's been around. And believe me, some of my girlfriends have tried. Go, Emily! Maybe he likes you."

"Hah! After I ruined his precious work and practically destroyed his thousand-dollar MacBook? I doubt it."

Emily felt her cheeks burn at the very thought of him liking her. She didn't want any man to be into her ever again. Romantically, she was off the market forever.

Of course, sweet Liz had no way of knowing that. Of course she assumed Emily was just a normal, single girl in her late twenties who'd get butterflies over any interaction with a cute guy like Reed.

But Emily Young was far from a normal young woman with a normal past. Even the little flicker of anger in Reed's eyes after the tea spill was enough to send her into fight or flight.

Still, she couldn't help but wonder. Who was he? And what in the world was on that laptop?

Chapter Eight

Cricket

Cricket was overjoyed that Gloria Bennett had her usual trim and highlight appointment scheduled for today, because there was no one in Rosemary Beach who she'd rather spend two uninterrupted hours talking to.

"Oh, I needed this." Glo closed her eyes as Cricket tilted her head down in the washing sink and rinsed out all the soft color from her hair, lathering it up with shampoo. "I've hardly done a single thing for myself since my dad had his stroke. My roots are an abomination."

"Oh, Glo, honey." Her roots were, in fact, an abomination, but Cricket didn't need to state her agreement out loud. Plus, it was nothing she couldn't fix right up and make beautiful. "You deserve to relax. I can't imagine the stress you've been under."

Glo sighed and shook her head as Cricket finished up conditioning her freshly highlighted hair and wrapped it up in a towel.

"I know how hard loss can be," Cricket said as they walked back over to the styling chair. "I remember when Gene died, it was so overwhelming. I was grieving, of course, and then on top of losing my husband I had this suddenly monstrous To-Do list. It was far too much for a new widow to deal with."

Gloria pressed her lips together as their gazes met in the mirror in front of them. "I can't imagine. Losing my father is one thing, but I know how hard Gene's death was on you."

"It was tough, but it's been years now. Noah was such a rock for me. He handled everything." Cricket gently ran a comb through Gloria's wet hair. "That's the beauty of sons. They handle things. They stay away, but they handle things."

"I miss my son, too," Glo said wistfully.

"How is dear Jeremy?" Cricket smiled at the thought of Gloria's youngest kid—always a star athlete with a big presence and a charming personality. Handsome and smart, too, and so polite.

"Busy as ever." Gloria huffed out a sigh. "I hardly hear from him these days. He's got baseball practice morning, noon, and night, and when he's not on the field he's doing Lord knows what with his fraternity and their parties." She shuddered. "I don't want to think about it."

"Oh, don't worry yourself. Jeremy is a good boy and you gave him a good sense of right and wrong. He'll have his fun, I'm sure, but he'll always do the right things."

"I hope so. It's hard being so far away."

Cricket began separating sections of Gloria's shoulder-length hair to trim and layer it just the way Glo liked. "Well, that's why you've got your Daisy girl! How's wedding planning going? The date is coming up, right? I must tell you, I'm quite excited to buy a dress. Black tie. So fancy."

"Oh, yeah. Well, that's all the Whittington family, believe me."

Cricket couldn't help but sense the tone of sadness and hint of frustration in her dear friend's voice. "Talk to me, Glo. What's going on here?"

"Oh, the typical stuff." Gloria waved a hand. "You know the family is...rich seems an understatement. Zillionaires, which I suppose gives them the right to plan —and pay for—every detail of the wedding."

"Well, be glad of that. Weddings are expensive."

"I know," she agreed. "But this one is wildly over the top."

Cricket frowned as she gently trimmed the ends of Gloria's hair. "That doesn't sound like Daisy."

"Not the old Daisy, no. The old Daisy would have rolled her eyes and curled her lip at the insane display of wealth that this wedding will be. But I don't know, Cricket. Kyle has changed her. She's very swept up in all of it, and...I'm worried I'm losing her."

"Oh, Glo." Cricket set her scissors down and placed both her hands on Gloria's shoulders, swiveling her to face the mirror straight on. "You and Daisy are two peas in a pod. She'll come back."

Glo bit her lip. "I'm not so sure."

Cricket pointed a finger and arched her brow dramatically. "Gloria Bennett, she will come back."

Glo smiled at this as Cricket got back to styling. "Anyway, enough about me. I'm sure you heard all about how Nessie got the corner property where my father's store was."

"I have heard the buzz, yes." Cricket brought out her blow-dryer, untangling the cord. "I didn't want to bring it up before you did...seems like it could be a touchy subject. I assume she's giving it to you, but that still had to be a massive shock. And so unfair to you. That Bill." She clicked her tongue. "A pain in the butt, even from the Great Beyond."

"Actually, Cricket..." Gloria paused and met Cricket's gaze in the mirror. "Vanessa is going to keep the property."

Cricket froze, styling tools in hand, staring in shock at her dear friend. "She's...*what*? What about your restaurant? Good heavens, is Vanessa that selfish?" Cricket couldn't help but think about the nights she'd spent consoling her heartbroken son over the fact that Vanessa Young never came back.

It was his baby, too. And she'd promised to come back.

Cricket's complicated feelings toward Nessie stirred in her chest as she waited for Gloria's response. It was love-hate, she supposed. She loved the girl and wanted her to be a daughter-in-law, but hated how she'd shattered poor Noah.

"No, not selfish at all," Gloria continued. "She *insisted* on giving it to me, but to be honest, I insisted harder on her keeping it. I won."

"But...why?"

Gloria sighed and fought a smile. "Because she's the

prize, Cricket, not a piece of property. It means my sister will stay in town and we can finally be family, and live close in every sense. That's what I need the most, and she needs a new job and a future and a plan. Bottom line, I need her a lot more than I need a big restaurant."

"Wow." Cricket went back to Gloria's hair as she took this all in, her mind spinning with this news. And the fact that Vanessa was here...*for good*. "That's my Glo." Cricket patted Gloria's cheek. "Selfless to her very core."

"It's just as much for me as for her. I've missed her all these years, and I truly believe my Dad knew that and this was his slightly, uh, unconventional way of bringing us together. It's wonderful, Cricket."

She looked in the mirror and nodded. "I can see that and if it makes you happy, then I'm happy for you. Oh!" Her eyes widened. "Will Emily stay, too? My granddaughter?" She still hadn't gotten used to saying that.

"I think so. She's got a job at the diner and seems to love Rosemary Beach."

Cricket beamed, thrilled to hear that. "You know, I always pictured my first day with my granddaughter would be spent pushing a stroller around a park and cleaning up spit-up, but life has a funny way of surprising you. Emily and I have already made plans to go shopping and to lunch."

"Grown kids are better anyway," Glo teased. "And speaking of...how's Noah doing? After all, he's going to find out eventually that his daughter is in town."

Cricket paused mid-cut and raised her brows in the mirror. "I suppose. Do you think this could be the straw that breaks that stubborn mule's back and brings him home?"

"You haven't told him that they're here yet?"

Cricket sighed. "No, shockingly, I haven't. I feel that the information presents my best chance so far of convincing him to come home, so I want to use it wisely. I don't want to just throw it at him. The drama might make him want to stay away even more."

"But she's his *daughter*." Gloria shook her head. "I know they've never met, but Nessie had never met her up until a little over a week ago, and they already seem to have quite a connection."

"Noah is different." Cricket turned the blow-dryer on low and began waving it over Gloria's freshly cut and colored locks. "He was so hurt when Nessie ran off and gave away the baby, I don't think he has any desire to revisit that part of his life. He's got walls up and I don't know if I should be the one to try and tear them down."

Glo choked on a laugh. "Cricket Ellison, are you suggesting staying *out* of it? This coming from the same woman who actually considered faking an illness to get Noah to come home?"

"First of all, I did not go through with that plan." She pointed the blow-dryer at Glo in the mirror. "And second of all, I simply need a way to get him back onto the streets of Rosemary Beach. Once he's home, he'll stay. I just know it. I know he hates the changes that happened to this beach and how the developers created a town where there wasn't one, but I'm used to it. I love it."

"Well...aren't Nessie and Emily a way to get him back here?"

"I just know my boy, Gloria. I fear they're more a way to keep him in Miami for good. He avoids the topic of Vanessa at all costs. Has for years."

Gloria gently touched her nearly dry hair, admiring the bouncy layers that Cricket had mastered on her thick waves. "Either way, Cricket, I feel like you should tell him. He should know about Emily, and that she's reconnected with Vanessa—not to mention that they are here. He has a right, as the other parent."

"I know, I know. It's just so complicated, and I'm so scared." Cricket rubbed some serum all over Gloria's hair, finishing up her signature style. "He never liked how close I stayed with your family after Nessie left. I guess he expected me to hate her but I just couldn't."

Gloria turned around, a frown pulling at her brows. "Wait, really?"

Cricket pressed her lips together and shook her head. "I guess he thought that Vanessa leaving was a betrayal to him, to us. You know she didn't say goodbye."

"I know," Gloria said with a wince of pain.

"He struggles with forgiveness. I don't know how he's going to react when I tell him that they're here. In town. Together."

Gloria stood up and took Cricket's hand, giving it a squeeze. "You have to tell him the truth. He'll probably want nothing to do with it, but he should know."

"That's the best and worst thing about you, Gloria." Cricket pursed her lips. "You're always right."

After two more clients that afternoon, Cricket went upstairs to her cozy apartment above the salon, pouring a cup of hot tea to sip while she pondered how to word the news to Noah.

She was not typically someone who spent a great deal of time worrying about what she was going to say or how she was going to say it—Cricket told the truth. She said what had to be said, when it needed to be said, and to whoever needed to hear it.

Generally, her blunt nature served her well, and everyone knew that Cricket Ellison was a straight shooter. People needed that, she knew.

But tonight, as she let her tea steep and sat down and ran a hand over her floral sofa, she wasn't exactly sure how to tell Noah that his long-lost soulmate was back in Rosemary Beach...with his biological daughter.

She glanced at the clock, seeing that it was just after six. Noah might be home from the office by now, especially if he'd worked remote today. He did that quite frequently these days.

What a world, Cricket thought to herself, where you could be a corporate lawyer from the comfort of your living room. It meant he could be a corporate lawyer from *anywhere*, including Rosemary Beach, but that was a conversation for another day.

She picked up her phone and clicked the FaceTime button for his number, which always gave her a boost of joy. She loved to see Noah's handsome face when they talked, her dear son all grown up and successful and handsome. It was hard to be anything but proud, sometimes.

"Hey, Mom." Noah answered the call with a smile, his dark brown hair trimmed close around his face, and his blue eyes glimmering. "How are you?"

"My boy." Cricket beamed at the phone screen. "You look wonderful. I'm fine, you know, business is booming as usual and I have to say I feel great these days."

"I'm glad to hear it, Mom," Noah exclaimed. "You still taking walks and knitting?"

"Almost every day." Cricket nodded. "I'm as healthy as a horse, you need not ever worry about me."

"Oh, I don't worry about you," he said on a chuckle. "You've got a busier job and a more active social life than most people I know in their thirties."

Cricket smiled. She *had* built a lovely little life for herself since grieving Gene's passing, and she was quite proud of it. Now that she had a granddaughter, the only thing missing was her son.

Ease into it, Cricket. Don't just drop a bomb.

"How's work been going?" she asked nonchalantly.

"Crazy as ever." He whistled out a sigh. "I'm home for dinner, but I have to head back to the office to work on this brief with my team of associates. I'll probably be there until midnight, and then again at six a.m. Sometimes I think I should just sleep at that place."

Cricket gasped, her eyes widening. His work was getting more demanding, and he could possibly be drained. He needed to slow down, relax, *move home*.

"That sounds horrible, Noah. I do hope you're taking care of yourself, because those are not healthy work hours."

"I'm fine, Mom, I promise." He laughed softly. "I'm all good. It's hectic right now, but that's the nature of the job. It's what I signed up for."

"So...you're happy?"

He raised a brow. "I own my dream apartment, my dream car, live in my favorite city and I'm a partner at a huge law firm."

"That doesn't answer my question." She swallowed. "Are you...lonely?"

Something flashed in his steel-blue eyes, and he glanced away from the camera for a moment. "I'm good, Mom. Really. I'm forty-five years old, you don't have to worry about me. My life is exactly where I want it to be."

"I just know the divorce was tough. Being single again is a big life change for you. I just hope you're adjusting okay. I do wish it had worked out."

"Mom." He leveled his gaze on the phone screen and gave her a "get real" look. "First of all, I've been divorced for almost two years, separated for over three now. Second, you hated Rebecca. Openly. You probably threw a party the night I left her."

Cricket stifled a smile. It had been a small get-together with a few close friends. There had been some champagne. One could hardly call it a *party*.

"I'm just checking in, Noah. These things can come in waves."

"I know," he said, his tone softening. "And I appreciate that. But I'm married to my job these days. And my pretty, new BMW. I'm living the dream."

Was that his dream, though? Because when he was thirteen, he had a school assignment that instructed the students to write an essay about their dreams. Noah's, as Cricket recalled, was to "put bad guys in jail, live on the beach, and marry Vanessa Young."

As a partner at a giant law firm working on mergers and acquisitions and...what was it? Antichrist? No, anti*trust*—which sounded nearly as bad—he probably wasn't putting too many bad people in jail.

She took a deep breath, shifting on the sofa, staring at the little screen in her hand. "I, um, have to tell you something, Noah. And I think it's best to just come right out and say it."

His gaze went serious, probably at the out-of-character hesitation in her voice. "What is it? Is everything all right?"

"Yes, yes. Everything is fine. But, um..." She cleared her throat, taking a sip of tea and leaning back on her sofa cushions. "Just brace yourself, okay?"

"I'm braced."

"Bill Young died a week and a half ago," Cricket said, knowing that wasn't even a percentage of the real news, but figured it was a good place to start.

"Oh, that's sad." He glanced away again, and Cricket could tell his mind went straight to Vanessa and the father who never forgave her. "Give the family my condolences."

"Well, you see, there's a bit more to the story."

Cricket swallowed, taking a breath before continuing. "Vanessa came back to Rosemary Beach."

His face tightened ever so slightly at the mention of her name, but he brushed it off in seconds. "I imagine she would, for her father's funeral."

"Right, yes, but...she's here to stay. She needed a fresh start, so she came back to Rosemary Beach to try to talk to her dad one last time, but he passed right before she got here. Anyway, she's in a weird spot, trying to figure out—"

"Mom, I'm sorry," Noah interrupted. "I don't mean to be rude, but Vanessa Young's life doesn't concern me. She walked out on me twenty-nine years ago, pregnant with my child, and completely broke my poor teenage heart. She messed me up. Badly."

"I know, honey. I was there."

"So, if it's all right with you, can we not talk about Vanessa Young? It was decades ago, and I don't have any kind of feelings left for her. I hope she figures things out, and I wish her the best. But I can't go back down that road, Mom. I can't. You know...sometimes I feel like I can't trust anyone because of how she treated me."

Cricket felt her eyes shutter, thinking back to those dark days, so many years ago. Vanessa, at the disownment by her nasty father, had fled her pregnant self out to California, where her father had a distant cousin who agreed to take her in.

Before her departure, she had promised Noah that after high school, when they'd both graduated, she'd come back. She'd return to Rosemary Beach and they'd be together. He'd clung to that hope for two long years.

But Vanessa slipped away, and with the help of her aunt, found a private adoption for Emily, stayed in L.A., and followed her dreams.

Despite how mad Cricket was when it first happened, she'd softened toward Vanessa over the years. She didn't entirely agree with her decisions, but she understood them. They made sense for a teenage girl.

But Noah? It was as bad as Cricket had feared. The fact that Nessie was back in Rosemary Beach for the indefinite future was only making Noah want to stay away more.

But then, she had one more little explosive to fire. "Emily is with her," Cricket said softly.

Noah froze, his face blanching. "Em...Emily? Mom, you can't possibly be saying that the—"

"Yes, that's what I'm saying, honey. Vanessa reconnected with the daughter she gave up. Emily has faced some trials of her own, and they ended up deciding to come here together, to start over." Cricket practically held her breath while she watched Noah process this shocking revelation.

"No, that's insane," he replied, shaking his head with a frown. "Vanessa gave up the baby in a private adoption to a single mother named—"

"Joanna. Who passed when Emily was three, leaving her to be raised by her grandmother, called Gigi, who also passed about a year ago. When the grandmother died, she left Emily a note that contained Vanessa's name and information, knowing that Emily would be left with no family in the world. During a turbulent and scary time in Emily's life, she called Vanessa. And now, they're living together in a rental on the beach, starting over."

Noah was silent for a few beats, staring at the camera with his jaw slack and his eyes wide. "This is...wow. That's...yeah. Nuts."

Cricket laughed softly. "I know it is. I could hardly believe it at first, either, but...it's true. They're here."

"I have to get to the office." He shut his eyes, his jaw clenching. "I'm sorry, Mom, I need to go. I can't...I can't deal with this right now. This is way too much."

Just as she had feared.

Cricket felt her eyes sting with threatening tears as she forced a smile and said goodbye to Noah, and the video call clicked off. He hadn't even *asked* about Emily.

She'd had to tell him the truth, right? Maybe she could have done it differently. Or maybe she should have figured out a way to get him up here for a visit, and then he'd have to come face to face with them.

Oh, heavens, no. He'd have never forgiven her for setting him up like that. She'd done what she could. It was clear that the wound Vanessa left on her boy's heart was still sore, even almost thirty years later.

Chapter Nine

Vanessa

As a kid, Vanessa had always thought of Bill's Sporting Goods as a boring, masculine, dingy warehouse full of fishing supplies, surfing equipment, and all manner of snooze-worthy items for a little girl.

But today—as the new owner—she saw the space through an entirely new lens. Standing outside of the corner property on the edge of the town square, she saw nothing but...potential.

The storefront was an old bluish gray color that could definitely use some refreshing, but the big windows and cheerful awnings were inspiring.

Inspiring for what? Vanessa still had no clue. She just knew she felt inspired.

"Here it is," she announced brightly to Emily, who held Ruthie's leash in one hand and a phone in the other, taking a photo of the building. "I mean, I know you've seen it passing by and all, but now...it's mine."

"It's amazing," Emily said, squinting into the afternoon sun. "What are you going to do with it?"

Vanessa let out a breath, truly not knowing the answer. "I don't know, honestly. It's a retail store. I've never even worked in a retail store, let alone owned one, and I'd suppose there's oodles of work involved in deciding what the demographics want and how it would fit into the neighborhood. Truth is, I don't know the first thing about running a retail business."

Emily turned to her, lifting a shoulder. "You wanted a new beginning. I think you're looking at it."

She certainly was.

Vanessa waved them toward the glass front doors. "Come on, let's go inside."

Emily and Ruthie followed as she twisted the lock and swung open the doors, entering the completely emptied-out remains of Bill's Sporting Goods.

"Wow." Vanessa looked around, inhaling the faint scent of dust and leather as she flipped on a light switch—not that the place needed it, with the two walls of windows. Sunlight poured in.

"This is an incredible space," Emily exclaimed as she stepped slowly onto the old vinyl plank floors, which was just about all that was left of the shop.

"It's so weird, seeing it nearly empty like this." Vanessa walked around to the checkout area, running her fingers along the dusty countertop. "I spent so many hours in here as a kid. Bored out of my mind."

"I bet a lot of people had their eyes on this place." Emily turned a full three hundred and sixty degrees, taking in the space and the perfection of the location.

Likewise, Vanessa took a moment to really drink in the full scope of the shop. Some display tables were stacked in the back, along with racks that used to hold surfboards and boogie boards, and behind the cash register area, a hallway led to the back office and spacious storage room.

She stood in the middle of the space, side by side with her daughter, who wasn't new but felt new, and tried to get a grip on this whole "fresh start."

"Maybe I'm in over my head," Vanessa mumbled, letting out a sigh. "I mean, what am I going to do, open a restaurant? That's Glo's department, not mine. And can you imagine the work that would go into trying to transform this place? I don't know the first thing about how to go about any of this."

"Hang on, just...think for a minute." Emily paced around a bit, with little Ruthie trotting along her heels. "It's a blank canvas, just like our lives. It's fitting."

Vanessa brushed some hair off of her face, wondering how it could possibly be that at forty-five years old, she was reevaluating her entire life and staring at a...blank canvas.

"I don't know, Emily. Maybe I should just insist on giving it to Glo." She pressed her lips together, shaking her head.

"She won't let you," Emily said. "And I agree. Your dad left this for you. He put it in your name for a reason, and he wanted you to have it. So does Glo."

Vanessa sighed, glancing at Emily, happy about how seamlessly she was beginning to fit in with the family she never knew she had. "Okay, Miss Optimism. Do you have any ideas?"

"It's hard to be anything but optimistic when you're

no longer living in fear," Emily said, raising a brow. "Trust me. Everything is hopeful."

Vanessa stepped close and put an arm around Emily's narrow shoulders. "I'm so glad you're free of that fear. And I *need* your optimism. What do you think I can do with this place?"

"Well...what do you know the most about?"

"Style," Vanessa answered without hesitation. "Fashion and accessories and how to get a celebrity ready for a photoshoot or plan their red carpet look down to the nail polish color."

Emily looked at her, her eyes wide and starry. "That is still so beyond cool to me that you do that."

"I used to be cool." Vanessa leaned against the checkout counter, shaking her head. "Until I didn't have enough social media skills and TikTok followers. The next generation of stylists came in guns blazing and iPhones out. Now I'm just a Hollywood has-been."

"You are not a has-been," Emily said on a laugh, giving Vanessa a nudge of encouragement. "You have a ton of experience in a fascinating field. You know about celebrities and their looks and trends! There's got to be something you can do with that."

"In a corner store in Rosemary Beach, Florida?" She huffed out a sigh. "I could become a style consultant or something, but this place is way too big for that and there honestly isn't the clientele."

"Hmm." Emily frowned. "What if you turned it into a studio and had photo shoots for aspiring models or actors or something?"

Vanessa chewed her lip, mulling over the idea and appreciating Emily's unwavering enthusiasm. "Well, that's a good thought, but again, right idea, wrong place."

"Fair." Emily paced around, the sunlight casting a glow on her newly highlighted hair. "I mean, I know you said you don't want to run a store or a retail business, but I do think we're kind of dancing around the obvious here."

"And that is?"

"A clothing store. High-end, super fashionable, and a fabulous place to shop. Plus, you can offer your stylist advice, and maybe even do personal shopping for the wealthier clients around here."

Vanessa paused, a ripple of excitement zipping down her spine at the prospect of that particular future. "I could do that, but—"

"Then do it!" Emily exclaimed, her smile wide.

"Emily, I know how to dress people in high-level fashion. I don't know how to run a business. I mean, there's so much involved in that—finances, fashion shows, buyers, and logistics, and inventory. Ugh. I don't know the first thing about any of that. I can style a person with designer clothes and put together a darn good look. But I can't *run* a clothing store for a profit."

"That's where I come in." Emily stepped closer to Vanessa, nodding with certainty. "We'll do it together. I'll handle all the logistics, numbers, spreadsheets, and scary stuff. I used to be an administrator back before...everything, and I'm great with computers. You? You just handle the clothes. Choosing them, buying them, keeping up with trends and seasons, and helping customers pick out the perfect pieces when they shop."

Vanessa's jaw went slack as she, for the first time in her entire life, felt like a proud mother. Unexpected emotion tightened her throat.

"Are you serious?" she whispered. "You really want to do this together?"

"We promised each other a fresh start." Emily lifted a shoulder. "Besides, what better way for some mother-daughter bonding than to open a business together?"

Vanessa laughed, wiping a tear as she pulled away. "This is crazy. I'm gonna need you so much. I don't know how to—"

"I know. I do." Emily nodded, a big, excited grin spreading across her happy, beautiful face. "I worked for a small startup before I married Doug, and I know a lot about getting a business off the ground."

"Only if you agree to be my fifty-fifty partner. I'll handle the initial investments because I have money saved, but when we start getting profitable, we split. Until then, I'll pay you as an employee. Fair?"

Emily dropped her head back and hooted. "More than fair!"

"Holy cow, girl. We're really going to do this." Vanessa looked around at the empty store, her mind already spinning with ideas about clothing displays.

"We have to do this." Emily grabbed her mother's hand and gave it a squeeze. "Together."

"Together." Vanessa agreed, a little shaky with the daunting, but thrilling, decision.

Was this what a true fresh start felt like?

"Now, one question remains..." Emily tapped her temple. "What do we name our fabulous boutique?"

"New Beginnings? Nah, too cliché."

Emily scrunched up her face. "What about just Vanessa's?"

"Snooze, boring. Besides, it's half yours!"

They tossed around some ideas for a while, but nothing really stuck.

"What about something with our last name? Young? I legally changed it back when I got my real ID again." Emily smiled. "Forever Young?"

"Ooh, that's cute." Vanessa wagged a finger. "I like that a lot. But it's awfully close to Forever 21."

"We're close, but not quite there." Emily paced, Ruthie followed.

"Pretty Young Thing?" She cringed a little at her own suggestion.

Emily laughed. "It's a little too Michael Jackson. What about...Young at Heart?"

"That's it!" Vanessa blurted out, gasping with surprise and excitement as she clasped her hands together. "The boutique will be called Young at Heart. I love it."

"Yes! It's awesome." Emily bounced on her toes. "I can't wait to get started. I'll have to tell Glo my stint at the diner won't be terribly long-term, but I'm sure she won't mind."

"Are you kidding? She's going to flip when she finds out what we're doing with this place."

"We should paint the outside," Emily suggested.

"Pink," Vanessa said. "Don't you agree?"

"Oh, absolutely." Emily laughed. "We're about to girl this place up, aren't we?"

"As we should."

"I'm really excited to do this with you." Emily bumped her hip against Vanessa's playfully. "*Mom*."

LATER THAT NIGHT, after the two of them had exhausted every last detail about Young at Heart, making notes and sketches and memories, Emily left to take Ruthie for a long walk on the beach.

As evening fell over Rosemary Beach, Vanessa poured a glass of white wine and sat out on the back deck of their beach house, pondering her new reality. After a few moments, Gloria walked in through the front door of the house, holding a plastic bin full of books and papers propped against her hip.

"Hey, you." Vanessa turned to greet her sister through the open sliding glass door. "Come join me. I just poured a glass."

Glo set the box down in the living room. "Don't mind if I do. I just brought over some stuff from Dad's house that's yours. Hadn't been touched in decades, so go through it whenever you get the chance. Or don't." She picked up the bottle of wine and poured some into a stemless glass, then walked out to the patio to join Vanessa.

"So, I have something to tell you." Vanessa turned to her sister.

Glo perked up with obvious intrigue. "I'm all ears."

"But I don't want to upset you."

Glo frowned and set the glass on the table, as if she didn't want to drop it from whatever shock was coming her way. "Okay..."

"It's about Dad's store. I know it might be a touchy subject, you had such big plans and I still can't believe you're giving them up—"

"Tell me!" her sister gasped, her brows raising high with anticipation. It was more than evident that the hurt, resentment, and shock of Dad leaving the property to Vanessa had been handled and put to rest by Gloria.

"Emily and I are going to open a clothing boutique we're calling Young at Heart."

"Oh, Nessie!" Glo reached down and threw her arms around her sister, squeezing tightly. "What a fantastic idea! And, wait—did you say you're doing it together? Emily's going to work there?"

"Yes." Vanessa nodded proudly. "It was Emily's idea. Everything was, actually. She knows how to run the administrative side and she's a whiz with computers and numbers and all that. I just get to select the clothes we buy, plan the storefront, and help customers. It's kind of..."

"Perfect." Glo leaned back, her eyes misty. "It's beyond perfect, Vanessa. What a beautiful way for you two to start this new chapter as mother and daughter."

"Going from zero contact to opening a store together," Vanessa said on a dry laugh. "Quite the transition."

"You and Emily have a natural connection, anyone can see that." Glo dropped into a seat and picked up her glass, raising it in a toast. "To Young at Heart, which is the cutest name imaginable." She sipped and smiled. "This is going to be wonderful."

"I'm hopeful, I really am. And that's a good feeling." Vanessa sighed and took a sip, watching the orange and pink sky change before her eyes as the sun set over the Gulf. "It feels right, you know?"

"Oh, I know," Glo said. "A perfect fit for a former stylist. That's such a credit for the store. Your client list and knowledge will actually be a big draw for fashion-conscious customers and walk-ins, too."

"I hope you're right," Vanessa said, dropping her head back and closing her eyes. "Because it's scary to start a new business at my age. Especially after walking away from one because I failed."

"You didn't fail!"

"I...fizzled." Vanessa laughed to herself as she sipped the chardonnay, truly amused by how life could take such shockingly unexpected turns, and still work out for the best.

"Hard to believe, because you were obsessed. All the classes you took and conferences you went to, all the networking." Gloria shook her head. "You worked twenty-four/seven."

"You know why?" Vanessa swirled her wine. "Because I gave up Emily to pursue that dream," Vanessa said, turning back to face the water as the bitter truth stung her tongue.

"Nessie," Gloria whispered, reaching out her hand to place it on top of her sister's. "Don't be hard on yourself. You were a kid, and you did try to be a mom for a while."

"I did try." She shuddered at the thought of those first six months with baby Emily. Long, upsetting, sleepless nights with a screaming newborn and no help in the world. She'd tried to make a go of it, she really had. "But I realized early on that my life had ended as a teenager. And I wasn't fit to be a mother. I fizzled at that, too." She winced. "Geez, I don't have a great track record, do I?"

Gloria just gave her a look, and let silence settle between the two sisters. The only sound around was the soft movement of the waves and distant singing of birds.

"Nessie," Gloria finally said. "You've got to let go of this idea that you were some narcissistic, self-absorbed woman who gave up her baby because she was getting in the way of her own dreams."

Vanessa leaned back, listening.

"I was there, too, you know. I mean, I was thousands of miles away at college, but you called me. During those six months when you had Emily, you called me. A lot."

Vanessa gave an apologetic smile. "I bet I did."

"You decided to give her up for adoption because you knew she needed a stable home with a support system and a family. It had nothing to do with your own personal dreams and pursuits." Gloria gave her a stern look. "Don't forget that."

"I just felt like I owed it to her to be at the top of my

field and make something of myself. Because...I sucked at being her mother."

"Vanessa..." Gloria reached for her sister. "You've spent so many years wishing for forgiveness from Dad, I think it's time you forgive yourself."

She sipped the sweet wine and let her sister's brilliant and powerful words wash over her like the waves in front of them. "I've spent so many hours thinking about her, Glo. Thinking about how she must hate the woman who gave her away after six months."

Gloria arched a dubious brow. "It doesn't appear that she's holding a grudge."

Vanessa laughed, thinking about the glimmering excitement on Emily's face when they came up with Young at Heart earlier that day.

Gloria was right, as usual. It was time to let the past wash away. Easier said than done, of course, but Vanessa was ready.

Chapter Ten

Gloria

Gloria had intended to tell Vanessa about the envelope full of Mom's letters tonight, but the time just didn't seem right. Her sister had been through such a roller coaster of emotions this past week and a half, and airing out decades-old grief about their Mom's tragic passing and the parent they never got to have just seemed like too much.

Besides, for the first time since she'd arrived in Rosemary Beach, Vanessa seemed excited and hopeful. She just didn't have the heart to ruin that elevated mood by bringing up their dead mother and her mysterious letters.

Sticking to her plan, though, Gloria left the envelope untouched despite her curiosity, knowing she would find the right time to open it with Vanessa.

Alone in her condo, Glo washed her face, wrapped herself in a soft robe and got ready for bed, since she had to be at the diner early tomorrow.

In the quiet of the living room, she suddenly missed Daisy with a sharp pang. She'd loved when her daughter lived here. Her bedroom was still in her favorite bold colors, decorated with framed inspirational quotes and cheery silk flower arrangements. When she came home after a long shift at the hospital, she'd dance around in her scrubs, still energized despite the hard work, frequently fueled by iced coffee.

The two of them would spend late nights together laughing, talking, and binge-watching soapy TV shows.

Although Gloria knew eventually Daisy was going to move out and move on, she could have stayed like that—the two of them in this condo together—forever.

And that would have been wrong for Daisy, even though she'd always been a Mommy's girl. She and Christian had never been close. Jeremy had a better relationship with Gloria's ex-husband, who had devoted a good portion of his fatherhood time to their son's baseball career.

That had paid off with a scholarship and the two of them in Boston.

Glo, of course, had gone to every tournament and travel game she possibly could, with Daisy frequently being dragged along. Everywhere they went, Christian bragged about how Jeremy was going pro someday.

When Christian would go on like that, fawning over Jeremy and his talent, Daisy would lean close to Gloria and whisper, "I'm not going to the pros of anything." Glo would laugh and tell her that was perfectly fine.

Gloria loved her two kids fiercely and equally, but Jeremy the golden boy and baseball prodigy was always the clear favorite to Christian. That reality just drove Daisy and Gloria to be essentially inseparable, and solidified their relationship—before and after the divorce—as lifelong best friends.

Hopefully, that wouldn't change too much with Daisy's marriage. She should be closer to her husband than anyone, but Gloria's jealousy over the pull the Whittington family had couldn't be denied. It was small and wrong, but real.

So was her fear that she'd lose Daisy completely.

Would she? Had she already?

She poured herself a cup of hot tea and settled into bed to read and get her mind off of things. She was not losing her daughter and best friend to some millionaire family. This was just...a hectic time. Things would settle down. Of course, in a few months, she'd be married and officially part of that family...

The thought made Gloria wince. Daisy was young. She was excited about Kyle and caught up in the fun of it all. She'd figure things out and, while she did that, Gloria would never waver in her love and support.

That's what she'd done with Nessie, after all.

"Okay." Gloria let out a long sigh, sipped her tea, and picked up her Kindle, excited to dive back into the world of fiction and forget about life for a little while.

Once she was about a chapter in to her latest read, Gloria could feel her eyes getting heavy, so she set the reader on her nightstand and clicked off her lamp.

A second later, she was jolted into awareness by a knock on her front door.

Adrenaline zipped through her as she shot up out of bed and slid on her slippers, trying to figure out who would be here this late. She hadn't missed any calls, either.

Gloria hustled to the front door, peeking out the side window to see...*Daisy?*

Whipping the door open, she blinked back in surprise at the sight of her daughter, standing outside in the drizzling rain, her wet hair stuck to her face.

"Mom, can I..." She sniffed. "Can I stay here tonight?"

"Of course. Oh, my heavens!" Gloria hurried her inside, closing and locking the front door behind her. "Daisy, you don't have to knock, you can just come in." Gloria grabbed a towel from the hallway linen closet and handed it to her. "I still think of this as your place, too. I was just missing you, as a matter of fact."

"I lost my key," Daisy said, drying her hair with the towel.

"Sweetie, what happened? Is everything okay? Why aren't you at Kyle's? How about a tea?"

Daisy gave her a sideways glance. "The Gloria Bennett cure-all? Thanks, but I'll just get a glass of water."

Gloria laughed, remembering how frequently Daisy teased her for being a tea addict.

On a long sigh, Daisy wrapped the towel around her hair and sat on the edge of the couch, pulling a throw blanket over her legs. "We had a fight."

She'd suspected it might be something like that. "And he kicked you out into the rain?"

"No," Daisy said quickly, accepting the water Gloria brought over. "I left."

"Well, what was the fight about? Is it something with the wedding?"

Like possibly the fact that it was too rushed and too soon and they were too young to get married?

Hold your tongue, Glo.

"No, no." Daisy sipped her tea. "It's not about the wedding. It was something else. You're going to think it's stupid."

"Daisy, come on. You can tell me anything. I'm not going to judge you or Kyle or anybody else, okay? I just want to be here for you. I know when my girl needs me."

Daisy gave a smile that seemed appreciative. "Okay, well, basically Kyle was out golfing with his dad today, and I didn't have a shift, so I was just hanging out at his— I mean, our, apartment."

Gloria nodded.

"Anyway, my laptop died and I needed to check my work schedule, and it won't pull up on my phone. So I decided to just log into the hospital portal on Kyle's computer, which was sitting on his desk."

"Okay..." Gloria said slowly, unsure about where this was going.

"And on his computer, I stumbled upon some..." Daisy scrunched up her face. "Messages."

Worry and slightly premature anger swept over Gloria, but she kept her cool and narrowed her gaze. "What kind of messages, Dais?"

She swallowed, glancing away, as if ashamed to say the next part. "From his ex-girlfriend. The one he was with at Yale."

Gloria sucked in a small gasp, her protective-mother instincts already kicking in enough to have her ready to hop in the car and go give Kyle Whittington a piece of her mind. "Did you read them?"

Daisy cringed, tears filling her eyes as she squeezed them shut. "I couldn't help myself. I just skimmed through them, and, honestly, it all seemed pretty innocent. I don't think he's cheating on me or anything like that. I just...I didn't know he still talked to her."

Gloria, having a few more decades of life experience under her belt, was not so easily convinced. "What do you mean innocent? Wasn't he pretty serious with this girl? I mean, what could they be texting about that's appropriate when he's engaged to someone else?"

Daisy sniffled, wiping her eyes. "They were just, like, catching up I guess. She texted him first saying she missed him and wanted to know how he was doing. I'm really upset that he didn't tell me, because it feels like he was keeping it a secret and—" She let out a sob, and Gloria's heart wrenched.

"Oh, honey." She reached over and wrapped Daisy in her arms, stroking her hair like she would when she was little and couldn't sleep. "I completely understand why you got upset about that. I think anyone would have. He shouldn't be talking to his ex-girlfriend, and he definitely shouldn't be hiding it from you."

Daisy pulled away from her mother's embrace and took a drink of water. "Well, when he got home I told him that I saw the messages and he got super mad at me. He accused me of snooping around and invading his privacy."

You're about to marry this guy, the voice in Gloria's head screamed. *There should be no such thing as invading privacy!*

But Glo knew her daughter's buttons, and she wasn't about to push them right now. "So, he got defensive about it?"

"Yeah." Daisy nodded. "Because he said it was completely innocent and he did nothing wrong."

Gloria wasn't sure she agreed with that but, again, buttons. And it wasn't actually cheating to catch up with an ex, was it? Still, he should have told Daisy.

"Okay, well, he still owes you an apology for having hidden conversations with this girl, no matter how 'innocent' they may be."

Daisy laughed dryly through her tears. "I don't think I'll be getting an apology anytime soon. He totally blew up on me and is very certain he didn't do anything wrong and that I was being a psycho for looking through his texts."

"He called you that?" Glo gritted her teeth. "A psycho?"

Daisy, sensing her mother's anger, shrugged it off. "It's fine, we'll get past it. I'm just upset because we argued."

But *should* they get past it? Gloria couldn't help but visualize a sea of red, red flags waving in a stiff breeze of discontent.

Gloria swallowed, choosing her words carefully,

knowing how fragile her daughter was. It was enough of a victory that Daisy came running to her, because it meant she still trusted and needed her mother.

Despite the circumstances, Glo couldn't deny that that fact alone was a relief.

"Daisy, when things calm down and emotions are settled, the two of you really should sit down and have a conversation about this. I mean, marriage is serious. We're talking about the rest of your life, here. You don't want to be with someone who treats you—"

"It was my fault, Mom." Daisy looked up at Gloria, her red-rimmed eyes shadowed with darkness. "I shouldn't have read through his texts."

"Daisy!" Gloria felt her voice raise but couldn't help it. "He shouldn't have been texting his old girlfriend from college! That's the real wrong here."

Daisy shook her head, tears falling down her soft pink cheeks. "I don't want to lose him, Mom. I love him so much. I just want this to go away and be happy with him again."

Gloria let out a sigh, softening as she folded her daughter back into her arms once more. "I know, honey. I get that. I'm sure things will be better soon and you guys will talk it out. Want to get some sleep for now?"

"Yeah." Daisy stood up and wiped her eyes again, picking up the water glass. "Maybe I'll just stay here a few days, let things cool off and give him some space."

Gloria nodded, admittedly a bit happy about that plan. "I think that's a really good idea. You've got clothes here, and some scrubs for work. Everything will be fine with a little time and space. You two are together a lot."

"Thanks, Mom. And...I hope this doesn't make you, like, hate Kyle. I was probably overreacting. He's a really great guy."

Glo shook her head. "I don't hate Kyle, I promise."

But as she stood up and turned around to walk back to her bedroom, the words tasted bitter on her tongue. It was true, she didn't hate Kyle—she hardly knew him, actually. But, boy, she hated seeing her daughter like this, that was for sure.

"HE WAS TEXTING HIS EX-GIRLFRIEND?" Cricket's dark brown penciled eyebrow shot up like a rocket. "Some snobby priss from Yale, I assume?"

Gloria sighed as she, Cricket, Vanessa, and Emily walked along the white sand of the beach, the morning sun rising overhead.

Gloria had gone to the diner early to help get everything ready for opening and to check in with her manager, then texted Cricket and Vanessa to see if they were free for a beach walk. She was so happy Emily had come, too, and even through her worries about Daisy, Gloria couldn't deny how joyful it was to have these women here.

"That sounds really fishy to me, I'm not gonna lie." Vanessa shook her head, the soft breeze of the Gulf blowing her hair around her face. "There's never a good reason to text an ex."

Gloria groaned, squishing the cool, damp sand between her toes. "I know. I have such a bad gut feeling about the whole thing."

Cricket turned to her. "The marriage or the fight?"

"The fight," Gloria said, not entirely sure if that was the truth.

She couldn't deny the heavy weight of worry that pressed on her chest anytime she thought about Daisy and Kyle. The weight had only gotten more difficult to ignore after Daisy showed up in tears last night.

"You sure about that?" Cricket challenged, her signature raised brow once again in full force.

Gloria sucked in a breath, then let it out, shaking her head. "I don't know. I don't know, you guys. I'm freaked out. I mean, Daisy is enchanted with this guy. She really seems to see something in him. Shouldn't I trust her judgment and trust that, in time, I will understand their love and relationship? I can't bear the thought of pushing her away even more."

"And..." Vanessa held up a finger. "If you push her away by telling her you're not super supportive of the marriage, you'll just push her right into his arms."

"Yeah." Gloria wrinkled her nose. "And into the toned and Pilates-fit arms of *Linda Whittington*."

"Oh, spare me," Cricket said with an exaggerated eyeroll. "I still can't believe Daisy wants anything to do with that insufferable family."

"How well do you know this Kyle guy?" Vanessa

asked. "Daisy could get her heart seriously broken, and marriage is a big deal."

"No kidding." Gloria lifted a shoulder. "I mean, I know Kyle, I guess. He's...fine. Sort of unremarkable, if you ask me. The Whittingtons are a very wealthy and important family around here, but I certainly don't run in their circles."

"Nor do I," Cricket added. "But I hear things at the salon. No one—and I mean no one—can stand Linda, and not because of her arms. She loves to flaunt her wealth and it's tacky, if you ask me."

"Like mother, like son," Gloria murmured. "From the Rolex to the Porsche, he likes everyone to know he's rolling in the dough, not that I think money inherently makes a person bad," she added. "But I do think he's been spoiled his whole life and has a strong sense of entitlement. He's never made much of an effort to get to know me, and they spend the vast majority of their time with his family. I don't blame Daisy. I mean, it's not like I have a yacht or a seven-million-dollar beach house."

"You shouldn't need a yacht for them to want to spend time with you, Glo." Vanessa placed a hand on Gloria's arm. "This is really hurting, you, isn't it?"

Unexpected emotion burned in Gloria's eyes as she held her breath to try not to cry.

"Well, yes, it is. Daisy and I have been glued together since the day she was born and...and I feel that I've been dumped for another family. One that I simply can't compete with."

"You should not have to compete, Gloria," Cricket asserted, her tone stern.

"Tell us more about this fight," Vanessa said. "What was he talking to the ex about? And he didn't tell Daisy? You said she discovered it on her own?"

"Even fishier," Cricket whispered.

"Yes," Gloria said, splashing some gentle waves around her ankles. "She was using his laptop and I guess a message popped up or...whatever. I guess he dated this girl for almost three years in college. She's from another prominent family."

"I can imagine that made Daisy so insecure," Cricket said. "And she shouldn't be! He should be kissing the ground our girl walks on. Does he not know what a prize he has?"

"I don't know," Gloria shook her head. "I just know that she was wrecked last night. Not as much about the messages, but about the fight. I guess he got really defensive and mad at her."

"Red flag, red flag, red flag." Cricket clicked her tongue. "I know the wedding is coming up and it's all very fun and exciting but I'm so worried for Daisy."

Gloria chuckled. "You and me both. I have to support her, you guys. I have no choice. She's an adult, and she'll make her own decisions and figure things out. Maybe we're wrong about Kyle, maybe he does treat her really well and whatever connection they seem to have is genuine and can be lasting. I have to believe that. I have to cling to that hope." She swallowed. "They're getting married, and I cannot lose my daughter by not being one hundred percent supportive of it."

"We totally understand." Vanessa wrapped her arm around Glo's shoulders and gave her a squeeze as they walked along the sand. "We support her, too."

Emily, who had been quiet, pushed back a strand of her hair and turned her head to meet Gloria's gaze as they all walked side by side. "Is she really into the money? I haven't met Daisy, I'm sure she's wonderful. However, I know from experience that it's easy to get swept up in gifts and trips and lavish things and lose sight of...red flags."

Gloria turned to look at her "new" niece, who she was starting to learn was reflective and insightful and wise.

"It's surprising, honestly, but it does seem to be the case that she's at least a little taken with his luxurious lifestyle. I gave her everything I could, but...I couldn't give her all of that."

"Gloria." Cricket turned and narrowed her fierce gaze. "You are a wonderful mother in every way. Don't you dare say a negative word about yourself."

Glo smiled, grateful for the dear woman.

"It's just, um..." Emily swallowed, frowning as she thought carefully. "My ex-husband, Doug, came from family money. Not Whittington kind of money, but more than I'd ever had. He used it to really captivate me early on with gifts and vacations and a lifestyle that I never could have imagined for myself. I'm not suggesting that Kyle is a bad person like Doug," she added quickly.

"But it can be intoxicating," Vanessa noted.

"Yes," Emily agreed with a voice that sounded very much like an experienced one. "It can also accelerate things like engagement and marriage. And lead a girl into cutting off..." she hesitated, her eyelids shuttering closed. "Important people. People you love."

"Oh, Emily, would you talk to her?" Gloria asked, not caring about the desperation in her voice.

"Oh, I don't know," Emily said. "I've never even met her, and I really don't feel like it's my place to—"

"You must!" Cricket insisted. "Emily, you're young, only a few years older than Daisy. And you've been through a horrendous hell of a marriage and a painful breakup. Such a struggle that she could learn from if you shared it."

"I can tell her my story, if it's appropriate," Emily said quietly. "It might not change her mind."

"Maybe you can get the full story, at the very least," Vanessa said, shrugging her shoulders. "Figure out why she's so crazy about the guy and help us see the good in the relationship."

"Yes, yes." Gloria nodded. "I'm not suggesting you try and talk her out of the marriage or anything like that."

Cricket snorted. "I am," she said, clearly only half joking.

"But maybe she'll open up to you," Gloria said. "You're her age and a new, fresh face. I'm afraid she's holding things back from me."

The reality hurt worse than it should. Of course her

daughter was going to grow up and find a guy and not be attached to Gloria.

But...for whatever reason, her relationship—er, engagement—with Kyle Whittington didn't sit right with Gloria at all. Was she just being selfish, wanting Daisy to stay her little girl forever? Or was her gut instinct trying to tell her that her daughter could potentially get really hurt?

Gloria didn't know, but she liked the idea of Emily getting to know Daisy and maybe helping her navigate some of this stuff.

"You are cousins, after all," Gloria said.

"I mean, I'd love to hang out with her and get to know her," Emily said. "It seems like she could use a friend—we both could. Maybe I'll find out that Kyle isn't so bad, and there's nothing to worry about."

"I do hope that's the case," Gloria said, chewing her lip.

"I'm not even remotely convinced." Cricket crossed her arms and shook her head. "Personally, I think we should find a way to break them up and get this whole thing canceled. I can start plotting something tonight."

"Cricket." Gloria frowned, shooting her a look. "That would break her heart."

"In the short term, yes, but we need to be thinking long term."

"I am not getting involved in sabotaging my daughter's engagement, thank you very much, Crazy Woman." Gloria laughed and looked skyward.

"I'm just saying. Those Whittingtons are no good," Cricket insisted.

"Give me Daisy's phone number," Emily said. "I'll find a time for us to get together. No recon, no ulterior motives, just...get to know each other. I'm busy today, I've got the later shift at the diner and then I'm meeting up with this guy to try and fix his laptop...long story." She waved a dismissive hand. "But I'll get something planned with her."

"Okay," Gloria said. "That sounds great. Thank you, Emily."

Vanessa smiled. "It's a good plan." She draped one arm around Glo and the other around Emily as the four women continued their beach walk.

"I'm so happy you guys are here," Gloria said, meaning it in her heart and soul.

Chapter Eleven

Emily

As soon as Emily finished her shift at the diner, she pulled out her phone to read through the string of texts from Reed Collins, the unfortunate recipient of her clumsiness, hoping she could try to fix his laptop as soon as possible.

If there was one thing Emily hated, it was unpaid debts, and she felt as if she owed this stranger at least her very best effort after dumping a liter of iced tea onto his precious work computer.

She said goodbye to Liz at the hostess stand, brushing crumbs off of her black jeans and heading out the front door of Gloria's Diner as she glanced at the address again.

Too far to walk, since he didn't live in Rosemary Beach, but a nearby town that she'd heard of but hadn't visited, called Panama City Beach. She wondered why he frequented the diner so much when there were probably plenty of places closer, but maybe the food was that good. Not the clumsy service, though, she mused.

Could she Uber there?

Shielding her eyes from the afternoon sun, she squinted at her GPS and zoomed in on his...no, not a house or apartment.

Was that...a marina?

He had said in his message that she could stop by "his place," but this was literally on the water...or a dock. At least that's what it looked like in the satellite image.

Fueled a little by curiosity and a lot by the desire to help restore the computer she'd carelessly ruined, Emily called an Uber and soon, she was heading south along the beach, past shops and homes on her left and the blue water of the Gulf on her right. Traffic was heavy and it took nearly a half-hour to get to the marina, making her wonder again if his business brought him to Rosemary Beach.

The driver brought her to Treasure Island Marina, after giving her a detailed rundown of the geography of the area, which was actually quite helpful.

Looking around to get the lay of the land—er, water—she took her hair out of the ponytail she'd had it in for work and shook it around. Only then did she realize she was in her black Gloria's Diner T-shirt tucked into black skinny jeans and paired with white sneakers, complete with a mayonnaise stain on one thigh. Yikes. So not... yachting clothes.

For half a second, Emily wished she'd have changed into something else before coming here, but...whatever.

"Okay..." She glanced around, taking in the scenery and wondering where she was supposed to meet Reed.

The marina was small, a tad rundown, but it had charm. Rows of docks lined the gently lapping water, each hosting a wide array of boats.

Most of the boats were pretty small, but toward the

far end there were some sizable vessels. Each boat rocked softly as the water moved, with very few people about.

Emily knew one thing for sure—Mr. Collins didn't live in a house, condo, or an apartment. Unless he worked here?

She pulled out her phone and sent him a text message, admitting her confusion.

As soon as the text delivered to him, she heard a somewhat familiar voice from several feet away.

"Emily, hey."

She turned, doing a double-take at the man in the baseball cap, although this one read "Yellowstone National Park." He was taller than she remembered, with broad shoulders and a purposeful gait as he walked toward her.

"Oh, hi," she said. "I guess I am at the right place."

"Yep." He held out his arms and gave that same, tiny, barely noticeable smile that he'd flashed her a couple of times at the diner during the incident.

"You live..." She furrowed her brow, looking around. "On a dock?"

"On a houseboat." Reed notched his head toward the other side of the marina, where some of the larger boats, and, evidently, houseboats were situated.

"That's so cool," she blurted out, genuinely excited to see his "place."

Liz was right about one thing—this Reed dude was definitely mysterious, and already full of surprises.

What other surprises were below the surface of the baseball cap and playful smirk?

It doesn't matter, Emily reminded herself. *Fix the laptop and leave.*

Reed led her down to the far end of the dock, where a row of big, boxy-looking vessels with windows and rooms and even front doors floated gently on the water.

Houseboats. Huh. How charmingly Floridian.

"Welcome to my humble abode." Reed stopped in front of one of the boats, gesturing toward the wooden deck on the front of it.

"Wow." Emily smiled, stepping back to take in the dark green floating house. It was small, likely the size of a one-bedroom apartment, but nicely finished with wood trim and vineyard lights and a very rugged feel.

"Come on in." Reed hopped down onto the deck, making the whole thing sway a bit. He reached out to help her on.

Emily took his hand and stepped on, feeling the deck shift under her feet. "Thanks. This is really cool."

"It's not much, but it does the job for now." He walked into the cabin and down the narrow center of the boat, which had a tiny kitchenette on one side and a two-top table on the other. "This is...well, it. Then there's a small bedroom in the back. Here's the computer."

"Right, yes." Emily nodded, following him to a small, maroon fabric futon next to the dining table.

Emily had no clue what a houseboat cost, but she couldn't imagine it was all that much. Weird, since she couldn't help but notice that he wore a Rolex on his left wrist, and the computer she'd so callously destroyed was a top of the line, stupidly expensive MacBook.

New Beginnings in Rosemary Beach 145

What was this guy's deal?

"Okay, so what's its current status?" She sat down, opening the sleek, silver laptop and tapping the space bar to wake it up.

"It seems to be running fine." Reed sat next to her and shrugged. "Apple products are usually pretty good about handling water damage these days. I'm not too worried about the hardware itself, but when it first got wet it crashed and I hadn't saved the files I was working on."

The knowledge that the computer was running fine gave Emily hope. If this was purely unsaved file recovery and not a hardware issue, she actually had a pretty decent shot at fixing it.

"What software were you using?"

He hesitated for a second, his jaw clenching as he glanced away. "Just, uh, Microsoft Word."

"Oh, okay." For some reason, that surprised Emily. With how important his lost work seemed, she'd assumed he was using a powerful work software or a high-tech program to work on...whatever these mysterious files contained. But Word? That made it even easier. "Can you open up the latest version of the document you lost changes on?"

Reed let out a sigh, pressing his lips together. "Yeah, I guess...yeah."

Okay, seriously? *What* was this guy's deal?

"I just..." She slowly handed him the laptop and forced a smile. "I just need to access the files so I can find the version history. Don't worry, I'm not gonna read through your personal or professional stuff."

He glanced at her, his dark brown eyes softening. "Thanks. I promise it's not anything creepy or weird. Just...private."

"And private it'll stay." She raised her hands.

But curiosity burned in Emily's mind like wildfire. The mystery man who showed up in town, doesn't talk to anyone, works on strange, secret documents and lives on a houseboat. Who also happens to be, yes, definitely good-looking. Even Emily, who had sworn off men forever, couldn't deny that.

No wonder Liz said every young woman in town was enchanted by the enigma of Reed Collins.

"Here." He tapped a key and handed her the computer back. "This is the most up-to-date version I have. Before the, uh, spill happened."

Emily laughed softly and shook her head, meeting his gaze. "I am still so sorry."

"Hey, if you can recover everything I'd done on this file before the spill, you'll be my hero."

She nodded and began to search around through the file settings. "Consider me Superwoman, then."

Fighting curiosity, Emily kept her focus on the top of the screen at the control panel where she was looking for the version history.

Yes, she was aware that the document was full of words, but she forced her eyes not to read them. He'd said it was private, and she was determined to respect that.

"And this is the file you were using when you lost the changes? For sure?"

"One hundred percent."

Her gaze flicked to the top of the screen at the file name.

The River of Blood – Day 43

What the ever-loving heck was this document? River of blood? Was he a serial killer or something?

A sudden chill marched up her spine as Emily realized she was alone with a man—a stranger, no less—and completely vulnerable. She knew all too well what men were capable of.

And...*a river of blood?*

But her fear melted away as soon as she looked over at Reed. Something about him, despite the air of mystery and the scary-sounding Word document, was comfortable and relaxing and not scary at all.

Focus, Emily. Version history.

"Okay, so that would have been April 16th, right?"

"Yeah, that...that sounds right."

Disappointment hit her as she looked through the history of changes on the file in the Microsoft Word Autosave database. There were no changes past this current version. The post-spill version.

"Darn it," she whispered.

"It's not there?"

"It didn't back up in the Office database." She frowned, searching the screen for answers. If whatever words he'd lost had been written down in this file at some point, they could be recovered. Of that she was certain.

"It's okay." He sighed, waving a hand. "I appreciate you trying."

"I'm not done yet," she said.

She started searching every setting and menu option, all while trying her absolute hardest not to read a single word that was on the screen.

Of course, it was impossible not to see a few lines, despite her best efforts.

She saw descriptions of blood and a dead body. Lines of dialogue and emotional words and internal thoughts.

Was this...a novel?

Her eyes fixed on a particularly gruesome description of what sounded like a bloody stab wound, but Emily forced herself to pay attention to the software settings.

Wow, he really could be a serial killer.

"It's, uh, it's a book," Reed blurted out, as if sensing Emily's slight discomfort at the subject matter on the screen, which they both realized was truly impossible to ignore.

"Oh, I...I wasn't reading it." She smiled and turned to him.

"You're a terrible liar," he said with a wry smile. "And you're alone with a stranger. I don't want you to think I'm some psychopath."

She chuckled, jutting her chin toward the document on the screen. "Would a psychopath talk about the 'pools of deep ruby blood glistening in the white of the snow'?"

"It's in the villain's point of view," he explained quickly. "He's a twisted guy, but the reader is in his mind right now. Although they may not know it yet, since I planted a red herring in Chapter Six, and...anyway." Reed shook his head and cleared his throat. "It's not important."

It sounded important, and Emily was fascinated to find out that he was writing fiction, but Reed had already told Emily more than it had seemed like he would, so she didn't pry any more.

"Wait a second..." She glanced at the top bar of the laptop, where she saw a Dropbox logo. "Do you use Dropbox?"

"Yeah, I back up all my files to Dropbox. But I already checked—the stuff I lost isn't in there because I never saved it."

Yes! This was it, Emily was certain. She could find it.

"That makes sense, but Dropbox has a much more comprehensive version history for recovering documents. It saves automatically every thirty seconds or so, which it had to have been doing before I spilled the tea."

Reed perked up, leaning over to watch what Emily was doing on the screen. "Really?"

"Yes." She clicked the icon and turned the keyboard to face him so that he could type his username and password into the login.

"I hope you're right." He let out a breath.

"Let's see..." She clicked on the name of the file—River of Blood Day 43—and right-clicked on the version history. "Look, see here?"

He craned his neck. "What am I looking at?"

"Change the setting to 'auto-saved version.' You didn't save it manually, but Dropbox did." She clicked the button and the computer loaded a long list of documents, each saved and backed up within a minute of one another.

"Holy cow." Reed laughed, and his smile was bright and wide. This was the first real smile Emily had seen on him that wasn't a smirk. "There they are."

"There they are." Emily beamed with relief as she scrolled to the most recent version of the file—time-stamped at 12:38 p.m. "This looks to be just moments before the, uh, river of tea."

Reed laughed again, deep and genuine and infectious. "Click on it. Let's make sure."

Emily hadn't wanted to assume it was okay for her to see the file but then again, she'd seen the older version and had a somewhat loose idea of what he was working on.

"How does this look?" She turned the laptop to face him when the new document loaded onto the screen.

"It's there." He scrolled to the bottom of the page, shaking his head with disbelief. "It's all there. I don't even know how to thank you, this is so important. I could never have recreated this." Reed turned to her, his dark brown eyes glinting with gratitude. "Thank you, Emily."

"I'm just glad I could help. Whew!" She laughed, falling back on the cushion with relief.

"So how do I get this auto-saved version into my regular files?"

"Oh, that's easy." She clicked out of the file and went to transfer it into his documents by moving it to the desktop folder.

Once she clicked Confirm, the screen switched over to his list of document folders.

"Which folder do you want it in?"

"The one titled 'River of Blood.'" He pointed at one of the blue folder icons with that name underneath it. "There."

As she was moving the mouse to click on it, Emily couldn't help but notice the surrounding folders' names.

The Year of Lies
Last One to Die
Secrets Among Us

They were all so strikingly familiar, and in a split second she realized why she knew those titles so well.

They were freaking *bestsellers*.

"Are you...kidding me?" Emily turned to him with a gasp, her brain putting two and two together.

Those titles, which were massive, chart-topping mystery thrillers, were written by R.C. Anderson, who some had hailed as the "next Stephen King." R.C. Anderson was a famous author. He was a big deal. He was...

Reed Collins.

He was sitting right next to her.

"You're R.C. Anderson!"

He shut his eyes, holding his hands up. "Okay, please don't tell—"

"This is insane!" Emily stood, covering her mouth with her hands. "You're a celebrity!"

"I wouldn't quite call it that, but could you please just keep quiet about it?"

"I mean, sure, I guess. But this is so cool! I've never met a famous author before. My Grandma Gigi would be flipping out right now. She was a huge fan. Wow." She shook her head, blinking back as she tried to process the bestselling author who, for some reason, lived on a houseboat and kept his identity a secret. "I have so many questions, I—"

"Okay." Reed stood, too, unable to hide his soft laughter as he put his hands—strong, she had to note—on Emily's shoulders. "I'll answer your questions, just sit down and please don't shout my pen name anymore. Sound carries on the water."

"Okay, okay." Emily gathered herself, sitting back down on the futon and seeing the mysterious diner man in a completely new light.

"Yes, I'm R.C. Anderson." He let out a sigh of resignation. "And, yes, I keep it a secret. My identity is totally anonymous, and that's very much on purpose."

"So... no one knows your face? How is that possible?"

"I was really strategic about my anonymity. My family knows, obviously. I have an agent and an editor and a publisher who, of course, know what I look like, but we signed a contract that if I took their exclusive deals, they'd keep my real identity private. No book signings, no public appearances, no social media. I get to just write, without all the other garbage. And that's what I do. I write."

"Yes, you do. At a local diner in Rosemary Beach, Florida. Why?"

"Simple." He tapped the laptop. "*River of Blood* is set

in Florida's panhandle. It's another reason I keep my identity private. I move around a lot. Basically, I go and live in whatever random town or city I decide to set my current project. I immerse myself in the scenery, the culture, and, of course, the crime history. Then, when I finish the manuscript, I leave and move on to whatever place I feel intrigued by next."

Well, it certainly explained why Reed kept to himself so much, and why no one in Rosemary Beach knew anything about him.

Except Emily. Now, she knew. But she had no idea what to do with this stunning bomb of information.

"Not to sound like a total fangirl, but your books are incredible. I had no idea I was spilling iced tea all over the next greatest thriller novel of the decade."

Reed laughed, shaking his head. "We'll see about that, but thank you, Emily. I appreciate it. And I hate to ask this, but...I've developed a way of living where no one knows who I am. And I really, really prefer it like that."

Emily lifted her fingers to her lips and made a zipping motion across them. "I won't tell a soul."

"Thank you." The smile in his eyes was sincere.

"You picked a good person to know your secret." She lifted a playful shoulder. "I'm new in town and hardly know anybody, and I know a little bit about a secret identity."

He arched an eyebrow. "You're Gloria Bennett's niece, right?"

She frowned, angling her head. "Yeah..."

"You'll know everyone soon enough, then."

"How did you know I'm Glo's niece? I thought you didn't talk to anyone."

"Just because I don't talk doesn't mean I don't listen." He shut the laptop and set it next to him on the couch. "Thanks again for your help. And for your...loyalty. I appreciate you keeping it quiet."

"I got you, Reed. Or should I say..."

"Please don't say it."

"R.C. Anderson, the next Stephen King." She winked jokingly, although he seemed young to carry that mantle. Maybe not even thirty-five. "Okay, I'm done now."

Reed couldn't help but laugh as he walked her to the front deck of the houseboat and helped her back up onto the dock.

"Thanks again, Emily." He waved to her from the boat, his eyes glinting in the sunlight, even in the shadow of his ballcap. "I'll see you around."

"Bye, Reed." She turned to walk away, then glanced over her shoulder. "Good luck with everything."

As Emily headed toward the entrance of the marina to call an Uber back to Rosemary Beach, she found herself smiling.

She'd just met a very talented and famous author, and was the only one who knew about him. She'd successfully helped salvage his files, which were, in fact, super important. He was also seriously cute and clearly brilliant.

In some other universe—one where Emily was not in the process of getting out of a hellacious marriage, permanently bruised and scarred by her ex-husband, and certain she wanted to be alone forever... In that universe?

Emily just might have a tiny little crush.

Clearly, that hypothetical other universe was not this one. And in this one, she was still married to a monster and broken forever.

But she had a fun secret. She had a little bit of knowledge that was all her own, and the thrill of that was enough to have her smiling the whole drive home.

Chapter Twelve

Cricket

Ever since Noah moved away for college and law school, Cricket wanted to be a grandmother more than she wanted to breathe. She always thought she was a good mother, but knew she'd be an even better grandmother. It was all the fun of parenting without any of the stress.

Of course, things hadn't worked out. First, Vanessa left and gave the baby up for adoption. Then Noah married Rebecca ten years ago, and she barely was out of her wedding gown when she announced she didn't want any kids to interfere with her law career, much to Cricket's dismay.

But now...everything had changed. The world had shifted and would never be the same, because her granddaughter—the baby she'd never met—was sitting across from her at an outdoor café, scanning the menu.

Emily was beautiful, especially now that her rat's nest of box-dyed hair was totally fixed. She had Nessie's features, but Cricket was certain she could see glimpses of Noah in the young woman. The way her nose wrinkled when she laughed, or the way she gestured with her hands when talking. Her quiet insight and keen, unassuming wit.

There was plenty of Noah in her, and therefore, plenty of Cricket.

"My darling granddaughter," Cricket said, resting her chin in her hands as she shamelessly admired Emily Young. "How blessed am I?"

Emily looked up from the menu and smiled, a bright and cheerful grin that lit up her eyes.

Cricket swore that the light in Emily's expression had grown brighter and brighter every day, even just in the short time she'd been in Rosemary Beach.

She knew Emily had a sad past, and it broke her heart. She hoped desperately that her dear granddaughter would find healing here.

"I'm blessed, too." Emily set the menu down and sighed. "I never thought I'd have another grandma after Gigi passed."

"And I must make it clear that I am by no means trying to replace the woman who raised you." Cricket nodded seriously. "She sounds like an angel."

"Oh, I know that, Cricket." Emily laughed softly. "I just feel so lucky that I get another grandmother. A whole family, actually. I mean Vanessa, and Glo and Daisy... I've never had a family. It was always just Gigi and me."

"What about the family who helped you out and gave you a job down in Cocoa Beach? Before Nessie found you?"

"They were incredible." Emily glanced off into the

distance. "The Sweeneys saved my life, and they were an amazing family. I miss them, but they weren't *my* family, you know? Even Grandma Gigi wasn't actually biological family, either, but that didn't matter. This is all so new and...different."

"It's a bit much, I imagine." Cricket stirred her icy cold glass of sweet tea and studied the young woman.

"It's definitely an adjustment, especially after having been alone for so long. Like, truly, truly alone."

Cricket felt her heart tug as she shook her head, unable to think too deeply about the horrible things this sweet girl had been through. "Nessie told me a bit about your marriage. I don't know much, but it does sound truly awful. I'm so sorry, my dear."

"Thank you." Emily flipped the white paper napkin off the table and onto her lap and let out a gentle sigh. "I'm doing so much better now. It was scary and really difficult at times, but I seriously do feel like this is a fresh start for me, as cheesy as that sounds. And Vanessa. The timing of it all was really something, how we found each other, both basically at rock bottom. It was almost like..."

"Divine intervention." Cricket finished with a sip of her tea. "Absolutely."

"Everything I've been through..." Emily closed her eyes, the salty breeze sending her soft waves of light brown hair swaying around her face. "Has brought me right here, to this moment and this place and this family. It's where I think I'm meant to be."

Emotion squeezed Cricket's chest tight. She'd pulled a lot of strings in her day in order to get exactly what she wanted. But this? This was no typical feat of Cricket Ellison manipulation and orchestration. Even *she* wouldn't have thought this possible. This was pure fate.

"Now tell me." Cricket met Emily's gaze. "I want to hear all about your and Nessie's plans for the corner store. All I've heard is 'clothing boutique' and 'we'll share more later' and I'm simply withering away with the lack of details." She pushed her pink glasses up the bridge of her nose. "I must know!"

Emily brightened up even more, her blue eyes glimmering as her smile reached them. "So, we're going to call it Young at Heart. You know, like our last name."

"A-stinking-dorable."

"Right? And Vanessa is going to handle all of the purchasing—clothing, accessories, whatever we carry. That's her area of expertise, of course. But I have a good bit of experience with administrative work, so I'll be doing all the behind the scenes. Logistics, finances, bookkeeping...boring business stuff."

"Wow." Cricket shook her head slowly. "It's truly amazing, you know? You and Nessie had never spoken as of a month ago, and now you're mother-daughter business partners! How beautiful!"

Now, if only Cricket could get Noah here and the whole little family could reunite and be together, all would finally be right in the world.

Her mind bounced back to the FaceTime call the other night. He wasn't going to budge.

"It's been so wonderful getting to know my mom. And everyone here." Emily grinned. "I never thought I would get to live somewhere like this or have a family or start a business."

"You're finally free, my dear."

Emily nodded, but glanced away like she wasn't so sure.

Cricket prattled on about the comings and goings of Rosemary Beach locals, and how they'd all adore Young at Heart.

Emily was so easy to talk to, curious and responsive, and lunch flew by without a moment of awkward silence.

"So that's why I opened the salon," Cricket finished her story after they'd eaten their lunches, leaning back in her chair and sipping the last of her iced tea. "Noah was a young boy, and Gene and I wanted a business of our own."

"Did you always know you had a passion for hair and beauty?"

"Oh, heavens, no. I just knew the salon would be a good way to keep up with town gossip, which I *did* have a passion for."

Emily cracked up.

"But once I finished cosmetology school and really got into it, I did find that I absolutely love it, yes."

"That's wonderful. I always—" Emily's phone rang from her purse. "Hang on one second, sorry."

"No worries, my dear. Take your call."

Emily smiled with gratitude and lifted the phone to her ear.

"Hello? Yes, this is Emily. Yes. Oh, my papers were sent over a week ago. I filled everything out..." She frowned, listening. "No, I don't have a lawyer, um, yet, but..."

Cricket tried not to eavesdrop on what seemed to be a serious phone call, but the mention of a lawyer and papers made it clear that the subject matter was likely Emily's divorce.

"Wait, *what*?" Emily gasped into the phone, her eyes suddenly wide and shadowed. "What do you mean? What's taking so long? I mean, he's in jail, isn't he? Doesn't he have to sign the papers as soon as—"

Oh, boy. Cricket's heart dropped a little.

Emily stood up, the phone still pressed to her ear as she turned around and began to pace down the sidewalk, obviously distressed.

After several long moments, Emily returned to the table, her eyes worried.

"What's the matter?" Cricket asked.

"That was Doug's lawyer." She shook her head, squeezing her eyes shut, not even sitting down. "Of course, he hired the best lawyer of all time—big shocker —and he's not going to make this easy. He's out on bail, which already makes me nervous. He wants the assault charges dropped, the restraining order lifted, and..." Emily's eyes filled and she tried to swallow her emotions.

"Oh, honey, no." Cricket got up to give Emily a reassuring hug.

This was unacceptable. This just would not do. No one was going to cloud up Emily's new life here, not if Cricket had anything to say about it.

"How can that evil, evil man continue to try and ruin your life?"

Emily sniffed, wiping a tear. "I don't know. But...I'm going to need one heck of a lawyer."

Cricket clenched her jaw and stroked Emily's back. There was an obvious solution here—Noah was both Cricket's son and Emily's father. And a darn good lawyer.

But he shut the conversation down so hard last time, Cricket would have to tread *very* lightly. She'd sworn she wasn't going to try to manipulate Noah coming home anymore, but these were desperate times. Desperate times indeed.

SHELLY AND PAULA stared at Cricket slack-jawed after she'd told them about Emily's terrifying situation.

"Of course Noah is the answer!" Paula exclaimed, setting down her knitting needles to give this conversation her full, undivided attention. "How can there even be any doubt in your mind, Cricket?"

"I have no doubt that he could help her," Cricket said, tip-tapping her needles around the yarn as she bit her lip and thought. "I have doubts that he wants to get involved at all. And I fear the more I bring up Vanessa and Emily's names, the further away I'll push him."

Shelly clicked her tongue and gave a sassy eyeroll. "That boy. Doesn't he know what's good for him? I mean, what kind of life is it to live in an apartment alone in a big city at forty-five years old? Has he lost his mind?"

"Surely he'd help his own daughter." Paula's eyes widened. "Noah has a good, good heart."

"That he does," Cricket agreed. "But I'm not sure he sees Emily as his daughter. Not yet, at least."

"Well, what does he see her as? She's got half his DNA!" Shelly flicked her needle before returning to her wintry scarf that would get mailed to a northern relative next Christmas.

"As far as he's concerned, Vanessa gave her up for adoption and all parenting rights were relinquished."

"That was a hundred years ago," Paula said, shaking her head. "Emily is a grown adult who is now building a relationship with her birth mother. Shouldn't her birth father want the same thing?"

Cricket huffed out a sigh and shrugged, reaching over to grab her mug of tea and take a sip. "Who knows? I thought I knew what Noah wanted, but here he is—a forty-five-year-old bachelor with no kids who claims he's 'living his dream.'"

Shelly narrowed her gaze. "You do know what's best for him. You just need to make him see it."

"And besides," Paula interjected. "Even if Noah is too stubborn to see that his life is superficial and boring—sorry, but it is—he should at the very least help Emily with this situation. I'm sure he'd realize how serious it is if you explained it to him."

Cricket pondered this while she knitted rapidly with thick, purple yarn. "I know he'd be able to help, but you guys didn't hear him on the phone last week. He shut the whole topic down hard. I can see it in his eyes. They darken at the very mention of Vanessa Young and the 'baby' who isn't a baby anymore."

Shelly let out a soft sigh. "She did hurt the boy, that's for sure."

"But...we need him." Cricket swallowed, nodding her head with certainty. "Emily needs him. And I think if I make it very clear to him what's going on, he'll do what he can. He'd do it for a stranger, my Noah."

"Then he'll certainly do it for his own flesh and blood," Paula said.

Cricket wanted to believe that, she really did, but she wasn't entirely sure her dear friends understood the depth of how badly Noah had been hurt by the way everything transpired with Vanessa all those years ago.

Staying away was his way of protecting himself.

"Oh, gosh." Cricket groaned and shook her head, dropping her whole knitting project into her lap with frustration. "What do I do, you guys? I feel so stuck."

"Well..." Shelly turned to Paula and they shared a look. "I think you might need to make a little road trip down to Miami."

Cricket paused to consider this.

Paula held up a needle. "I know everyone these days uses Zoom-this and FaceTime-that and text messages about all of life's problems, but...call me old-fashioned but I think there are some conversations that have to be done face to face."

Maybe it was her age talking, but Cricket couldn't

help but agree. If she was going to have a serious—and quite possibly emotional—conversation with her son, it couldn't happen on a phone screen. Not about this subject.

"You're right." She sighed. "I'll get down there one day next week. He can help. He'll help. He has to."

But...he didn't *have* to. He could just as easily say no in person as he could over the phone, devasting Cricket and ruining poor Emily's only chance at having a fantastic lawyer handle her case.

Cricket had to try. She was not a quitter, that was for sure. Besides, this was not a selfish goal. Of course she wanted her darling son to move back to Rosemary Beach and stay there forever.

But this short-term goal mattered far more. Maybe she'd get her big family party one day—the gathering she'd always dreamed of. Not yet, though. Right now, the only thing to focus on was helping Emily, and how wonderfully fitting that the best person in the world to help her...was her dad.

Chapter Thirteen

Vanessa

Vanessa and Emily wasted no time diving into the official transformation of Young at Heart. Cricket helped them snag a great contractor who had a hole in his schedule, and since the store was already arranged for retail, they didn't need to do major construction.

Emily had been a godsend, diving into the renovation logistics while Vanessa focused on the job of building their inventory. She called on former contacts at the designer fashion lines, and consulted old friends in retail all over L.A. for advice and guidance.

She spent every waking moment of the past week on the phone, learning a whole new vocabulary and acronyms like SKUs and order cycles and MOQs—minimum order quantity.

Without hesitation, she dipped into her savings, tapped her investments, and started the process of selling her L.A. house, knowing that huge windfall would go right back into her new business. That would still leave her able to buy or rent something small here, thanks to the tidy divorce settlement she got from Aaron. Theirs hadn't been an acrimonious parting, and he'd been more than fair.

And she was deeply grateful for that, now that she wanted to open this boutique.

She slowed her step as she looked around the store, seeing two men installing large, white wooden shelves onto the back wall while another installed clothing racks. A few painters were rolling sample colors onto the walls, because God knows Vanessa was not ready to commit to a color yet.

"Whatcha think?" Emily stepped back, pointing at one of the side walls where several paint samples were spread across the old gray drywall. "I like the peach, but I feel like on the full wall it might be too much."

Vanessa stared at the multicolored wall, her eyes scanning the shades of cream, peach, soft blue, and light green. "I, uh...gosh. I don't know. I have no idea."

She glanced around at the total disarray, alternately overwhelmed and excited.

"Well..." Emily crossed her arms. "What's your vision?"

She willed herself to see the potential in the store, to visualize what it could be, but all she got was...a little freaked out. "I'm not sure," she admitted.

A tap on the glass front door startled her out of her thought spiral, and Vanessa walked toward a woman who was definitely not dressed to be part of the construction crew. Whoever she was, please don't let her be one more person who required her to have a *vision*.

As Vanessa pushed open the door, she met the smiling eyes of a woman who looked to be in her mid-fifties, holding a notebook. She wore a soft green blouse and white jeans—a nice choice, the stylist in Vanessa noted—with blunt-cut dark brown hair framing her face.

"Can I help you?" Vanessa asked.

"Hi, yes, I'm Robyn Riley, I'm with the *Rosemary Beach Reporter*." She gestured at the notebook. "I was wondering if I could have a few minutes of your time. We'd love to do a profile on you and share some early information to get the locals excited about the store."

"An interview..." Vanessa swallowed, glancing behind her at the messy, vision-less store.

"A feature piece, really." Robyn lifted her shoulder. "Some local press would help drive enthusiasm for the grand opening. Plus, I've heard you come from a Hollywood background as a stylist to the stars. That might be my headline, you know."

"Well, not sure I'm ready for a major piece, but..." Vanessa ushered her in, already comfortable with the sweet lady. "Also, it's loud in here. Why don't we go chat in the back office."

Robyn smiled brightly. "Sounds great."

Vanessa shared a look with Emily, who had heard the whole encounter. "Robyn, this is Emily, she's my business partner and my...daughter."

Whoa, that still sounded foreign on her lips.

"Oh, a family business! That's fun." Robyn shook Emily's hand. "Would you like to be a part of the story? We certainly can—"

"No, no, that's okay." Emily held up her hand. "Vanessa is the face of Young at Heart, I'm behind the scenes. Not really one for...publicity."

Vanessa understood and gave Emily a nod.

"Very well, then. Good luck to you, Emily!" Robyn said as she followed Vanessa down the small hallway behind the checkout counters into the back office.

"Sorry it's a mess." Vanessa frantically moved aside some of the stacks of clothing catalogues and papers she'd been looking over that morning.

"Oh, please don't apologize!" The woman waved a hand. "You're starting a brand-new business from the ground up. I'd be concerned if it wasn't at least a little hectic."

She was probably just being polite, but her words somehow actually brought Vanessa a little peace.

"So. An interview." She pulled up two chairs, sliding them over to the corner of the room to face each other.

Robyn sat down in one and pulled out an iPhone. "Nothing serious, I assure you. This is what you call a puff piece, I promise. Over at the *Reporter*, we've been hearing so much buzz about what's going to go in Bill's old sporting goods store, but I must say, no one predicted a boutique. I insisted on doing the story myself because the idea excited me so much."

Robyn's enthusiasm was genuine, but Vanessa still had some nerves fraying.

"It's definitely a surprise, but—"

"Sorry, would you mind if I recorded?" She grinned and held up her cell phone.

"Oh, of course. Go ahead." Vanessa had done her fair share of press, publicity, and interviews back in Hollywood, where she prattled on and on about the fabulous custom-made pieces she dressed her clients in for this red carpet or that gala.

She always knew what to say and how to say it, and she never struggled to share her passion or her vision for a look with anyone who would listen.

That was her comfort zone. This? Was somehow way outside of it.

"Okay, Vanessa Young." Robyn smiled and set the phone down on her lap. "Tell me a little bit about your background before coming here to Rosemary Beach."

"Well, I grew up here, back when it was just Inlet Beach, so it's still home, I suppose. But I left when I was a teenager, and I went out to California, where I pursued a career as a stylist."

"And you were quite successful," Robyn prompted.

Vanessa smiled. "I had some famous clients, and I was incredibly blessed to be able to work with such talented, high-level designers in Hollywood. I styled singers, actors, producers...all kinds of stars for a wide variety of different occasions. It was an exhilarating, fast-paced career, but I never got tired of sharing my passion for clothes and styles with the world."

"That sounds unbelievably cool." Robyn grinned. "Who was the most interesting or fun celebrity that you styled?"

Vanessa leaned back, shuffling through memories of her career, which felt like both yesterday and a lifetime ago. "I actually got to dress Taylor Swift for the Grammys a few years ago. She was a total sweetheart, and her outfit was just divine."

"Taylor Swift!" Robyn gasped, laughing with bewilderment. "My daughter is going to freak out when she hears this."

Vanessa chuckled. "It was a lot of fun."

"And now, you're here. Back in your hometown, the polar opposite of Los Angeles, and you're creating a brand-new dream—opening your own clothing store. What brought you back to Rosemary Beach?"

She swallowed. "Well, actually, my father passed away a couple weeks ago. As I'm sure you know, this used to be his store."

"I heard about Bill. I'm so sorry for your loss."

"Thank you, Robyn. I came back here when he died and was absolutely shocked to find he left his incredibly prime piece of property to me. I tried my hardest to give it to my sister, who runs the diner next door, but she insisted I have it and stay in town and... start a new life."

"Why quit the star-studded L.A. life?"

She thought about it, then smiled, wanting to be honest. "Dressing the stars is a younger woman's game. Professionally, I've decided to use my skills for the 'everyday' woman who wants fashion but not haute couture. And on a personal level?" She sighed. "I like being near my sister. And to start a business with my daughter? That's a dream."

"Well, Hollywood's loss is our gain." Robyn smiled. "And what a beautiful story of not only a new start for you, but the reunion of sisters. Now, tell me more about Young at Heart. What can the locals and tourists of Rosemary Beach expect from this exciting new clothing store run by a famous stylist? What's your vision?"

And...there it was again. If she heard the word *vision* one more time that day, she just might lose it.

She didn't even know what color she wanted on the walls. How in the world was she supposed to express a vision that she didn't even see?

Vanessa folded her hands in her lap, trying to see her whole life and skill set as she might a woman standing in her underwear, waiting to be decked out from top to bottom with a style that captured her essence, complemented her best features, hid some flaws, and made a statement.

Wasn't that all this woefully undressed retail space really was?

"Beauty for all ages," she said, speaking slowly as the concept took shape. "Not just the young...but the young at heart."

"Oh, I see what you did there," Robyn said with a laugh.

"But it's true, and not just my last name. With my background, I experienced firsthand the constant quest for youth that drives women absolutely crazy. The plastic surgeries, the injections, the agony of trying to be in style when that means crop-tops and ripped jeans."

"Oh, the worst," Robyn joked.

"They have their place, but maybe not on all women. But all women should feel beautiful and confident and delighted with their style choices. Every woman's heart has an inner beauty," she added, leaning forward as the vision finally took shape. "I want the styles at Young at Heart to reflect the inner woman that's elegant, fun, and trendy without ever losing the air of classic fashion."

Robyn's eyes danced. "That sounds absolutely wonderful, Vanessa. I must admit, I'm your target market. I can't wait!"

"I would love to help you find some new clothes and feel your absolute best. You and so many other women," Vanessa continued, words and truth pouring out of her as she finally began to see things in color. "You know, I worked with celebrities and actors and singers, but so much of their styling was for the camera, for show. In this new phase of life, I want to help style women for the everyday. Women who are just as amazing as Hollywood stars, and deserve to feel just as beautiful, all the time."

Robyn sighed, a wide smile on her face. "Young at Heart is going to be a massive success, I can feel it. We simply don't have anything quite like that here, you know? Seems like all the boutiques, while lovely, cater more toward twenty-somethings."

"Young at Heart will be for everyone." Vanessa sat up straighter, a sudden glimmer of excitement dancing through her chest. "Elegant and fun, to bring out every woman's inner beauty."

"What kind of clothes will you be carrying primarily? Casual, fancy...?"

Vanessa thought, but she no longer felt overwhelmed. She was starting to be able to see an intimate, high-end but affordable boutique where she could spend personal time with each and every customer. A small, elevated stage outside the dressing rooms with a three-way mirror. Subtle, ambient lighting. Soft Fleetwood Mac music in the background. A dazzling jewelry counter and accessory table in the corner. Dresses hanging on the walls, styled on mannequins with full outfits. The vibe was beachy, but not too laidback. Peach paint on the walls.

She could see it.

Vanessa felt a real smile pull at her face as she turned her attention back to Robyn and the interview. "A wide range, I would say mostly what I'm calling 'coastal chic,' a slightly elevated take on resort beachwear. Ranging from casual shorts and summer tees to beautiful dinner dresses and everything in between."

"How fabulous is that?" Robyn smiled. "Is there anything else you'd like Rosemary Beach residents to know about this exciting new business coming to town?"

"I just want everyone to know that…I'm honored and humbled to be able to do this, and I get to do it with my daughter. That's a long story, and probably not for publication, but it's a very unexpected and incredible surprise."

They finished up the interview with pleasantries and some more chit-chat about the store, and Vanessa knew that Robyn's intentions were pure and good. And she was, in fact, her target market for the store.

As she was walking Robyn out the front door and saying goodbye, Vanessa felt a new swell of confidence and assurance in her chest.

She closed the door and turned around, leaning

against it as she scanned the inside of her soon-to-be boutique and felt her vision materialize.

The images in her mind came to life before her, splashing the whole space with colors and sleek designs and the lovely little world she suddenly knew she wanted to create.

"How'd it go?" Emily walked up to Vanessa, giving her a nudge.

"Let's go with the peach." She turned to her daughter, nodding with certainty.

Emily lit up. "Really? Oh, yay! I love the peach."

Vanessa nudged Emily affectionately as they watched the workers drill shelves and assemble racks all throughout the space.

"You seem a heck of a lot more confident," Emily remarked.

She turned to face Emily, meeting her gaze, which was sometimes like looking into a mirror. "I have a vision and it's a good one."

"Cool. I hope I'm in it."

She wrapped her arm around the young woman who was becoming as much of a friend as her long-lost daughter. "Oh, you are, Em. You absolutely are."

Chapter Fourteen

Gloria

It had been a few days since the infamous ex-girlfriend texting fight, and in any other circumstances, Gloria would have been thrilled to have Daisy back at the condo for three days.

But these were *bad* circumstances. Ever since the fight, Kyle had effectively cut off communication with Daisy, or kept it to a harsh minimum, and the poor girl was just about shattered.

To Gloria's surprise, Daisy had picked up some extra shifts at the hospital since the argument, which was encouraging to see. She'd basically worked as little as possible ever since she'd started dating Kyle.

Plus, it kept Daisy busy and distracted when Gloria was at the diner much of the day, which was a lot better than her sitting all alone at the condo feeling blue.

But this evening was officially Day Three of Daisy being home—well, back at Gloria's—and they were both slumped on the sofa in the living room after long respective days at work.

"How you feeling, honey?" Gloria asked, placing a gentle hand on Daisy's leg.

Daisy stabbed at some ice cream in a bowl with her

spoon, lifting a shoulder. "We still haven't really talked. It's so hard, Mom. I can't believe he's still mad at me. I feel like I should just apologize."

Gloria felt her eyes shutter closed. "You have nothing to apologize for."

"I was snooping." She stirred the ice cream. "I shouldn't have. And I just want this fight to be over, it's been three days and he's only texted me twice."

That fact alone made Gloria's blood boil, but she was determined to keep her cool. Expressing feelings of worry and doubt about Daisy's fiancé would only push her further away.

"I can't believe he hasn't called." Gloria shook her head. "He knows you're hurting. He knows you're upset. He has to."

"Yeah. He does." Daisy looked up and sniffled, her eyes heavy with sadness. "And he doesn't care enough to call. How do you treat someone you love like this? I mean, doesn't he miss me?" Her voice wavered. "Because I really, really miss him."

Gloria swallowed and took a deep breath, scooching closer to her daughter on the couch.

She had been quiet for many months. She had been kind and polite and nothing but respectful and supportive, even when she saw red flags flying when it came to Kyle Whittington.

But Daisy was hurting. Over the past seventy-two hours, she'd watched her daughter ache and cry and shut down and...break.

This was not how a wonderful, brilliant, amazing

young woman should feel four months out from her wedding day, that was for sure.

"Daisy..." Gloria inhaled slowly and leveled her gaze with her daughter. She admired Daisy's brown eyes, remembering how big and bright they were when she was just a baby. She had such a sparkle about her, a wit and dazzling personality.

But her sparkle was gone, replaced with a veil of sadness and a haze of disappointment.

"Are you absolutely, one hundred percent sure that this is the man you want to marry?" Gloria asked softly and gently. "Because a man who loves you and protects your heart would not be making you suffer like this. I can't stand seeing you so hurt, Dais, and it really worries me, I'm not going to lie."

Daisy paused for a long time, her spoon frozen in her nearly empty bowl of chocolate chip cookie dough. She inhaled like she wanted to say something, but stopped herself, shaking her head. "I don't know, Mom. I love him. I really, really love him..." Her voice broke and she started to cry.

"I know you do, honey." Gloria wrapped an arm around her daughter, her heart aching for her girl.

"But this is really weird." She wiped her cheek with the back of her hand and took a shaky breath. "He's never gone cold to me like this. We've had fights, and we always get over them and move on, you know? This is different and...it's scaring me."

Glo swallowed. "It's scaring me, too."

Daisy looked up, her red-rimmed eyes watery. "Mom. What if I'm making a mistake?"

Gloria held her breath for several moments, debating how to answer this massive question. The reality was, Gloria didn't know for sure if Daisy was making a mistake. Yes, she had her gut feelings about Kyle and his high-flying family, but those things didn't necessarily mean he and Daisy were wrong for each other.

Just as she'd always told herself, if Daisy was happy, then so was she.

Right now, Daisy was about the furthest thing from happy. And that made Gloria want to say, "Yes, honey, I think you're making a mistake." But it was too late for that, wasn't it?

They were engaged, Gloria reminded herself as she stroked Daisy's hair. Engaged, but not married. Maybe this was her chance. Maybe this was the only opportunity she'd get to save her daughter from a miserable marriage and, even worse, the pain of divorce, which Gloria Bennett knew all too well.

"Daisy, to be honest with you, I—"

A knock at the front door cut her off.

Daisy shot up off the couch, eyes wide with anticipation. Of course, she hoped that was Kyle knocking at the door.

Before Gloria could respond, her daughter jogged across the living room and into the small entryway of the condo, opening the front door.

Gloria peered over her shoulder to see tall, slender

Kyle Whittington in a polo and khakis, holding a giant bouquet of flowers.

Of *course*.

Disappointment punched her in the stomach, because Gloria knew without a doubt that Daisy would swoon over this romantic gesture and leap back into his arms.

"Oh, my gosh, Kyle..." Daisy gasped, turning over her shoulder. "Mom, look!"

"Hey, Gloria." Kyle waved a hand, the orange glow of the sunset casting light on his youthful face.

Kyle was cute, in a frat-boyish sort of way. He had soft brown curls and a pretty chiseled jawline, with blue eyes and a smile that always seemed the tiniest bit untrustworthy.

"Hi, Kyle." Gloria walked over to the front door and stood next to Daisy, getting the full scope of the colorful bouquet. "It's good to see you again. I assume you're here to apologize." She added a playful smile to the comment, even though she didn't want to.

If this kid was going to be around for the long haul, Glo would make it work. She didn't have a mean streak in her personality, though if she did, he'd be the one to trigger it.

"Kyle, you are so sweet," Daisy cooed, setting the flowers down on the entryway table. "I really appreciate this, and...I missed you."

Gloria could tell Daisy was doing her best to hold off on leaping right into his arms.

"I missed you, too, baby." He kissed her a bit too aggressively for Gloria's taste, and she tried to look away.

"Kyle, you're welcome to come in." Gloria gestured, breaking up the make-out session happening on her front doorstep. "I can fix you guys something to eat."

"Sure, that would be great." They stepped inside and shut the front door behind them. "And, actually, Daisy there's something inside the flowers. For you."

Daisy's eyes widened with surprise and she glanced at her mother, then back at Kyle. "In the flowers? A note?"

Kyle lifted a shoulder smugly, the smirk on his face revealing that, whatever this was, it was more than just your average note.

Gloria grew suspicious.

"Okay..." Daisy said slowly, drawing out the word as she separated the blooms in the bouquet and pulled out a little black box from the center of the florals. "Kyle, what is this? I mean, you already proposed to me," she said on an emotional laugh.

"I just felt really bad for how things went down, and I'm sorry we had an argument."

Gloria swallowed. It wasn't exactly, "I'm sorry for texting a past girlfriend and hiding it from you and yelling at you and not calling for three days..." but she let it go because she had to.

Daisy's hands toyed with the box.

"And I really, really wanted to make it up to you and show you how much I love you, Daisy."

Glo held her breath as Daisy slowly lifted the velvet

lid, waiting for some dazzling diamond necklace or sapphire earrings to blind her.

But when Daisy opened the jewelry box, inside it was...a key.

Daisy held it up, and it only took a few seconds for her to notice the Mercedes-Benz logo glimmering on the black plastic.

You have got to be kidding me.

Daisy gasped, her hand flying to her mouth in shock. "Kyle...what...what is this?"

He nudged his head toward the front door. "Go look in the driveway. I got you a little 'I'm sorry' present. I know your old GMC has been having problems, so..." He shrugged. "Figured it was time for an upgrade."

Daisy, with stars in her eyes, glanced at Gloria and leapt out the front door, squealing when she saw the vehicle parked in front of Gloria's condo.

"Oh, wow," Gloria said, following them around the hedges and looking at the pearly white, glimmering Mercedes convertible. "Kyle that's...quite a gift."

"Oh. My. Gosh!" Daisy bounced with joy and threw her arms around Kyle, kissing him again. "Thank you so much, babe! I can't believe you did this. This is literally the best thing ever!"

"I love you, Daisy. I'm sorry we fought." He patted the open door of the car. "She's all yours."

Daisy screamed again, running around to sit in the driver's seat, covered in smooth, luxurious tan leather with every imaginable bell and whistle.

In a flash of disappointment, Gloria couldn't help but

think that she was watching Kyle buy her daughter's love before her very eyes...but she shook away the thoughts.

"Kyle, this is so unbelievably generous of you," Glo said, smiling at the kid. "I hope it means you won't go three days without talking to her again," she added with a playful wink, simply unable to help herself. He needed to know how unacceptable that was. All of it.

Kyle's eyes flashed. "Sorry, Gloria. Daisy just was acting really crazy. There was a huge misunderstanding, and I knew she needed some time to cool off. And see? Everything worked out."

Gloria clenched her jaw and looked forward, watching Daisy honk the horn and dance around in the new car.

Would it work out? She didn't trust the boy, that was for sure. Now, less than ever.

All it took, though, was one look at the giant, glimmering smile on Daisy's face, and Gloria willed her anger to fade away. Daisy was happy again. That was all that mattered, and she could have peace. For now, anyway.

To THE SURPRISE of no one, Daisy and Kyle rode off into the sunset—back to Kyle's apartment—in her new, flashy, rich-girl-mobile, and Gloria was alone once again.

Plagued by some seriously mixed emotions and concerns about her daughter, she decided to take a drive —in her now sad-looking Toyota Camry—over to the corner store, where Vanessa and Emily had spent all day overseeing renovations and getting set up.

She texted her sister to make sure they were still there, and then took the short drive into town, parking behind her diner.

Gloria sighed, thinking about Daisy and replaying everything in her mind. Was she being overly cautious? Closed minded? Or were her fears valid?

She walked into the soon-to-be boutique and gasped with surprise at how much progress had been made.

"Hey!" Vanessa jogged over, looking bright-eyed and effusively happy in her ponytail and athletic getup, complete with some paint stains. "It's still just getting started, but..."

"Oh, Nessie." Gloria scanned the inside of Dad's old pro shop, which already looked completely different. White wooden shelving was installed on all four walls, rods had been hung by the large windows for curtains, and about half of it was painted a soft, feminine peach color. "It's going to be fabulous."

Gloria waited for a pang of jealousy, a wishful thought about how this was supposed to be her expanded diner, her full-service restaurant...the future she had planned for herself. But those feelings never came, because when she looked at her sister and her niece, she knew that *this* version of the future was so much better.

"You like the peach?" Vanessa asked eagerly. "I was on the fence about it and, well, everything."

"I adore the peach."

"I was just all over the place." She pushed back a

strand of blond hair that had escaped her ponytail. "But then, I don't know, it started to come together. I know exactly what I want it to be now."

Gloria walked over and put her hands on her sister's shoulders. "You're exactly where you belong."

"Hey, Aunt Glo!" Emily said as she strode toward them, wearing a paint-splattered smock, brush in hand.

"Look at you, really on the front lines."

Emily waved the brush. "The sooner we get done, the sooner we open."

"Well, you can't be too far off, right?" Gloria looked around. "I mean, it's not done by any means, but is there that much more to do before you can make it a clothing store?"

"Actually, no." Vanessa lifted a shoulder. "Once interior updates are done, I'm going to start ordering clothes."

"I've filed the permits with the state and town, and locked down our corporation." Emily grinned proudly. "Once Vanessa narrows down her shipment selections, we've just got to set those up, hire some staff, and get rolling. We should be able to open in a month."

"I can't believe how fast this is happening!" Gloria grinned.

"It was just meant to be. All doors are opening." Vanessa sighed, shaking her head as if she, too, couldn't believe the turn of events that had led the two women here. "Glo, I can't thank you enough. Your generosity is..." Her eyes grew misty. "Astonishing."

"Your presence here is a gift, believe me. Got time for

a coffee break?" Gloria asked, jutting her chin toward the door.

"Please, I'm desperate. We've been at it since seven a.m."

"I'm gonna keep painting." Emily held up her peach-dipped brush. "But you guys go! I'll be here."

"Thanks, Em." Vanessa smiled over her shoulder as she and Gloria walked out of the store and down Main Street.

"Are you okay?" Vanessa asked softly, placing her arm on Gloria's.

"Me? Yes, I'm fine!"

"Okay." Her sister chewed her lip. "I just...you know. With the store. Obviously, I'm excited about it, but I know it might be hard for you. It was supposed to be yours and you had planned on it and..."

"Oh, Nessie." Gloria flicked her hand dismissively. "I've basically already forgotten that. It's a decision I have never, and will never, second guess."

Vanessa sighed. "You're such an angel. But you seem a bit blue. Are you sure it's not upsetting you? Even a little bit?"

"It's not." Gloria shook her head as they walked up to the order window of 3rd Cup and placed an order for two decaf cappuccinos, agreeing it was way too late in the day for actual caffeine.

"Then what is it?" Vanessa grabbed the two hot to-go cups and handed one to Gloria as they walked over to a sidewalk bench. "Something's bugging you."

Glo shot her a look. "You know me too well."

"I may have been gone for the better part of thirty years..." Vanessa lifted the cup to her lips and flicked her brows. "But you're still my big sister."

"It's Daisy. Again." Gloria sighed as they sat down together.

The evening air was slightly cool, and the colors of sunset painted the sky. Rosemary Beach's town square bustled with people walking dogs, riding bikes, laughing, talking, *being*.

"What's wrong? Did they have another fight?"

"Not exactly." Gloria sipped her coffee. "The fight was bad, though. Bad enough that she stayed with me for three days."

"Oh, my." Vanessa's eyes widened. "Was she icing him out? Silent treatment?"

"More like the other way around," Glo said softly. "He wouldn't answer her calls."

"For three days?" Vanessa frowned and shook her head. "When *he* was the one texting his ex? He should have been groveling."

"I know, I know." Glo held up her hand. "Please. I'm trying so hard to forgive him and like him and support this relationship."

"I know, I get that. So what happened? Did they finally make up?"

Gloria gave a dramatic eyeroll. "He showed up with a bouquet."

"Classic."

"It gets worse. There was a box in the middle of the flowers with a key in it."

"A key?" Nessie drew back. "To his apartment? Doesn't she already live there?"

"To a brand-new Mercedes convertible."

Vanessa's jaw fell as she gasped loudly. "You are *kidding* me."

"Nope."

"So, I assume he's forgiven."

Gloria laughed dryly. "Yeah, I think that's a safe bet. I don't know, Nessie. I'm just so troubled by it all. And the car? Is Daisy really that shallow?"

"Daisy is a twenty-four-year-old girl who clearly has a teeny-tiny taste for the finer things in life." Vanessa shrugged. "Maybe she'll outgrow it."

"I didn't raise her to be materialistic." Gloria pursed her lips. "I just hate that her love can be bought."

"Her love isn't being bought, Glo. She's obsessed with Kyle, for better or for worse, but that's the truth. It's not like she's only with him for the money." Vanessa rubbed Gloria's arm lovingly. "Relax. It was just a grand gesture."

"An obnoxious one. It's like he's..." Gloria took a deep breath, emotion tightening her chest as the truth slipped out of her mouth. "It's like he's giving her everything that I never could, and now she's ditched me for him and his wealthy family."

The reality of that pressed on Gloria like cinderblocks, and every passing day was one day closer to Daisy legally becoming a part of the Whittington family...only to leave her own, real family in the dust.

"She'll come back, Glo. You two are so close."

"Were," Gloria corrected sadly. "Now it feels like she

only wants me the second things go south with Kyle. When they're good, I hardly hear from her."

Vanessa sighed, shaking her head as they sipped their decaf drinks and watched dusk fall over the town square. "Do you think there's any chance this won't work out?"

"With the wedding in four months?" Gloria blew out a breath. "I doubt it. Linda Whittington has already flown Daisy to New York City twice for her preliminary dress fittings."

"Eesh."

"Yeah. I'm going with them to the final fitting, though, in a couple of months. That'll be nice."

Vanessa offered a sympathetic smile. "That should be nice. But hey, you never know. Maybe things won't work out. They aren't married yet."

"But I don't want to hope for it not to work out." Gloria heard the whine in her voice, but couldn't help it. She was pained over this. "That would mean I'm hoping for Daisy to get her heart broken and be devastated."

"Of course. But if it's the best thing for her in the long run? She really does need to talk to Emily. They made plans, but Daisy kind of blew her off."

"Sounds like Daisy. As of recently, anyway."

"Well, Emily said she's going to keep trying. She really wants to get to know her cousin. As she put it, she's never had a cousin before."

Gloria smiled. "She's too precious for words. How has it been for you? Having a daughter for the first time ever?"

"It's been fascinating, honestly." Nessie shook her

head and laughed. "It's odd, because I didn't raise her, so I didn't see her grow up. And we're so close in age for mother and daughter, it really feels more like friends."

"That's not a bad thing."

"No, it's not." Vanessa set her coffee on the bench next to her and leaned back, the warm breeze blowing her hair around her face. "I don't know. I can't explain it, but it feels like that parental bond just...isn't there. Like we get along great, and we're obviously insanely similar, but I don't feel like she sees me as *Mom*, you know?"

"Well, honey, you only just met!" Gloria laughed. "I'd give it some time."

Nessie took in a slow breath. "I know, I know. I feel like it's partially my fault because I just don't know how to be a mother. I didn't know how to be a mother to her when she was a baby and...I'm not sure I know how now."

"Hey, ease up on yourself. Give it some time. Emily is still healing from trauma and figuring out how to have a family." Gloria draped an arm over her sister's shoulders and pulled her close for a sideways hug.

"Oh, these daughters of ours." Vanessa laughed softly.

"We are blessed to have them. And each other now. We'll figure out life and all the ups and downs together." Gloria turned to Vanessa. "You better not run off again, because now I'm attached."

"I'm not going anywhere, Glo."

They finished their drinks and walked back to the boutique, and Gloria thought back on the great heartbreaks of her life. Mom dying when she was five—top of the list. Nessie leaving was up there, along with her divorce from Christian.

She thought about him, a typical, fleeting curiosity about his life, but pushed it away as quickly as it came.

She'd stopped allowing herself to miss Christian a long time ago, and now would be no exception.

Gloria willed herself to do what she'd always done—focus on the positives, of which there were many, and move forward with hope.

She would leave Christian Bennett in the past, where he belonged, and pray that Daisy never had to go through the agony of divorce.

Chapter Fifteen

Emily

Emily had spent the past few days so deeply immersed in the creation of Young at Heart, she'd almost—*almost*—been able to drown out the words that played like a broken record in the back of her mind.

Doug is out on bail.

Yes, he had a restraining order. And theoretically had no idea where she was. But people broke restraining orders all the time, and he could easily find her. Doug wasn't exactly scared of the law, although Emily sincerely hoped his time behind bars had changed that.

Of course he'd hired some top-notch defense attorney, and of course he was doing everything in his power to make this as difficult as possible for her.

Why did he hate her so much? Why had he dedicated his life to ruining hers?

She clung to some other words that his lawyer had said on the phone the other day, expressing that Doug legally had to stay in Colorado, his state of residence, while he was on bail and probation.

People were monitoring him, and his job was at stake, which gave Emily more certainty that he wouldn't come after her again.

But he wasn't going to let her freedom come easily. It didn't help that she hardly had a penny to her name for a lawyer of her own, and she didn't feel comfortable asking Vanessa for anything, especially money, although she got the feeling her birth mother had no shortage of it.

She was not wracked with the intense and overwhelming fear that had consumed her after she ran away, and that was a relief. She was safe here, as safe as she could be, and she chose not to let the fear of him eat her alive.

The justice system was involved now, and all Emily could do at this point was wait and hope that justice would, in fact, be served.

And she could distract herself. Which was not hard to do when one was getting to know a new family, opening a business, and discovering all the hidden gems in what had to be Florida's most adorable beach town.

Today was sunny and gorgeous, and Emily had finally made plans to meet up with Gloria's daughter, who had been difficult to pin down. Grabbing an old yellow bicycle that Gloria had loaned her to get around town, she headed to the beach where she was meeting Daisy to hang out.

Emily was vaguely aware of Gloria's concerns about Daisy's fiancé, and knew that was what had precipitated this meeting. But she didn't need an ulterior motive—Daisy was her cousin and she'd actually never had one of those.

She parked her bike by the edge of a wooden boardwalk where Daisy had said to meet her, and scanned the area for Gloria's daughter.

Emily had worn a bikini underneath an orange sundress and sandals on her feet. It was probably too chilly to swim in the Gulf just yet, but a beach day was a beach day, after all.

"Emily?" a young woman's voice called.

Emily turned around to see a pretty twenty-something jogging toward her with long brown hair and big sunglasses. Daisy wore a bikini top and jean shorts, looking too cute for words.

"Hey!" Emily held up her hand and waved. "It's so great to finally meet you."

"Yeah, seriously." Daisy pushed some of those thick locks out of her face and slid her sunglasses on top of her head. "It's so crazy that you're here. The whole story is nuts."

"Tell me about it." Emily laughed, gesturing toward the wooden staircase that led down to the blue water and creamy white sand. "Shall we?"

"Let's do it. I'm desperate for a tan."

Emily glanced down at her pasty pale arms and legs. She, evidently, was desperate for a tan, too, although she hadn't thought about it until just now.

Daisy already looked bronzed and sun-kissed.

As they settled down on the sand, making slightly awkward small-talk and first-meet kind of conversation, Daisy spread out a blanket and lay down flat on her back with a long sigh as the sun baked into her skin.

"So." She turned to Emily. "We're cousins."

"*First* cousins." Emily sat, then dropped back like Daisy, folding her hands behind her head. "How about that?"

"I'm not gonna lie, it's pretty weird. I mean, Aunt Vanessa was always this sort of elusive figure that Cricket and my mom would whisper about. I have to admit, though, her life sounded super cool. A Hollywood stylist."

"Right?" Emily turned to face Daisy. "She's worked with so many famous celebrities."

"So what about you? What did you do before you came here with Aunt Vanessa?"

Emily paused, knowing that if she opened up and got real, Daisy would be more inclined to do the same. And all Emily really wanted was a legit friendship.

"I used to be an administrative assistant, after college. I worked for a small startup business in Denver, and I ended up taking on a really big role there, and handled basically all of their logistics and running of the business. I learned a lot, and I loved it."

"So that's what you're going to be doing with the store, right?"

"Yeah, exactly. I haven't done that sort of thing in about four years, though, so I've got some technology to catch up on."

Daisy turned, her interest piqued. "Wait, why? What did you do for four years?"

So Gloria and Vanessa hadn't told Daisy about

Emily's marriage, which she was kind of glad about. She was grateful for the chance to tell her herself, in hopes it could help them bond.

"Well, I got married."

"Oh, so you stopped working." Daisy smiled and turned her head back toward the sky, readjusting her designer sunglasses. "That's the dream."

"More like the nightmare," Emily said quietly, making Daisy turn to face her again, frowning with confusion.

"What do you mean? That's, like, the perfect life. Kyle said that after we get married, he wants me stop working. I get to just be...his wife," Daisy said whimsically.

The words sent icy shivers up Emily's spine, reminding her freakishly and eerily of when she and Doug got engaged.

She could still practically hear his deep voice echoing through her mind.

You don't need to work, baby, I want to provide for us. You should spend your time taking care of yourself and our home so everything is perfect for me when I get back after a long day. Can you do that for me, pumpkin?

The flashback made her nauseous.

"Daisy, are you sure that's what you want? Twenty-four is awfully young to stop working."

"I think so." She toyed with some sand in her palms. "I really do love nursing, but it's exhausting sometimes, and Kyle's mom wants me to get involved in the country club and the DAR."

"The DAR?"

"Daughters of the American Revolution," Daisy explained. "It's a charity. Apparently, you can only volunteer for them if you come from certain ancestral lines, which Kyle's family does."

"How charitable."

Daisy laughed. "I know, it's kind of weird, but they're always throwing these fancy galas and balls to raise money. You wouldn't believe the dresses."

"But what about nursing? You're just going to throw that away for country clubs and...galas?"

Daisy pushed some hair out of her face and turned to Emily, taking her sunglasses off to make direct eye contact. "Honestly? I didn't love the idea at first. I worked really hard in nursing school and I really do enjoy my job."

"Then why quit? Why let him..." *Control you.* No, she couldn't say that. Not yet. "Take that away from you?" she asked instead.

"Kyle lives in a different world. It's hard to explain, but his family has a completely different lifestyle then anything I've ever known. At first I felt like a total fish out of water, but...I don't know. Once I leaned into it and started to see that maybe one day I could fit in with his world, I just sort of let it happen. Linda, his mom, has really taken me under her wing."

"So you're happy?" Emily asked. "That's really what matters."

"I am happy. Kyle makes me happy. The money and the trips and the fancy clothes...it's fun, don't get me wrong, I've really grown to appreciate and enjoy all of that. But I love Kyle, and he loves me, and we're meant to be together. I know it."

It was a tiny bit like looking in the mirror to a younger version of herself, but Emily had to remember that Kyle was not Doug, and even though he was an entitled rich kid, that didn't mean he would ever lay a hand on Daisy.

"So, what happened with your marriage? If you don't mind me asking..."

Not that she loved the topic, by any means, but the fact that Daisy was asking questions was a win to Emily. "Unfortunately, things didn't go well for me. Hence... being divorced. Or trying to be."

Daisy was clearly curious, and her walls were beginning to come down just a bit. Of course, she was skeptical about her random new cousin who had been adopted out of the family thirty years ago and just suddenly showed up. Emily had expected that, but she was glad that she and Daisy were chatting about real things.

"What happened?" Daisy asked softly.

"Doug Rosetti—my husband—is not a good man." Emily swallowed. "Shortly after we got married, he starting getting...abusive."

"Oh." Daisy turned on her side, narrowing her gaze. "Was it bad?"

Emily pressed her lips together. "Very. The worst thing you could imagine."

Daisy stared silently, shaking her head, her initial hesitance and slight coldness dissipating before Emily's eyes. "I'm so sorry."

Emily filled her cousin in on the entire saga of how after Grandma Gigi died, she got a fake ID, ran away, cut and dyed her hair—badly, as Cricket had said—and ended up reconnecting with Vanessa.

Daisy stared at her, her big brown eyes blinking with shock and sympathy. "Is he in jail now? Are you safe?"

"For the time being, yes. At least, I hope. He's out on bail, but legally he can't come anywhere near me."

"Emily that's...that's just so scary what you went through." She sat up now, sunbathing taking a back seat to the story. "And he never showed any signs that he was a total psycho when you were dating?"

"Not in the slightest. He was so romantic and, well, kind of over the top. I guess that maybe could have been perceived as a red flag, but hindsight and all that. I got swept off my feet and...I paid the price."

"I'm sorry." Daisy shook her head. "And I'm sorry for blowing you off at first when you tried to make plans with me, and being kind of rude."

Emily's heart lightened. "You weren't rude, Daisy. It's totally okay."

"I guess I just..." Daisy took a fistful of sand and let it slowly drain out between her fingers. "I was a little salty that your mom got the corner property. I felt like my mom deserved it, putting up with grumpy old Grandpa all those years."

"I completely get it," Emily said, smiling. "I would have been salty, too."

"Really?"

"Of course! But your mom is a selfless saint, and

insisted Vanessa keep it, so that she and I can stay here and make a new life. Gloria is an angel."

Something flashed in Daisy's eyes as she glanced out at the water. "Yeah. She is."

Emily paused, knowing Daisy wanted to say more, and hoping she would.

"We're just, I don't know. We're not as close as we used to be, my mom and me."

"Why do you think that is?"

Daisy exhaled noisily, turning to Emily with an arched brow. "She hates Kyle."

"What?" Emily blinked back with shock, although her surprise was exaggerated, considering she already knew that Gloria wasn't exactly in the Kyle Whittington Fan Club. "I doubt she *hates* him."

"Please." Daisy waved a hand. "She acts like she likes him and like she's so supportive of everything, but I can read her like a book. She's my best friend—or she was. I can tell she has her feelings about him, and they're...less than stellar. I hate that it's driven a wedge between us, but what are you gonna do, right?"

Not marry a guy your mom hates, Emily thought to herself, but she pushed away her judgment. She wouldn't have listened to a soul who tried to tell her that the sun didn't rise and set on Douglas Rosetti and that maybe he wasn't the perfect dreamboat she had thought he was.

Emily knew what it was like to be blinded by love. She just prayed Daisy didn't face consequences a tenth as bad as her own.

"Have you talked to your mom about it?" Emily asked.

"She dances around it." Daisy turned, leaning on one elbow to face Emily. "But there are plenty of subtle hints in the things she says and how she reacts to stuff about him that I can just tell. She would never outwardly say she doesn't like him but yeah. I mean, it's obvious."

"That has to be kinda tough, to have your mom not crazy about your fiancé."

"It doesn't make me love Kyle any less, but honestly? It's made me question the relationship before."

"It has?"

Daisy shrugged. "I value my mom's opinion more than anyone. Or I used to. But she just doesn't know Kyle the way I do. She doesn't get it. What he and I have is... special. Yeah, we have our arguments, we're not always perfect, but what couple is?"

"Well, that's fair." Emily lifted a shoulder, brushing some hair out of her face as she tasted the salt of the breeze on her lips. "So, tell me about the wedding."

Daisy lit up, and all walls and reservations about this cousin relationship came all the way down. She launched into a long description about the venue, the bouquets, the string quartet, the dress, the whole over-the-top shebang.

Emily listened and laughed, watching the soft blue waves of the Gulf of Mexico lap up onto the shore, imagining a wedding of that caliber, happy for her cousin and her dream day.

Thoughts of her impossible divorce and lack of a

lawyer—or help of any kind, really— briefly crossed her mind, but didn't disturb Emily's peace.

She would figure it out. She didn't have much, but she did have something she'd never had before....a family.

Chapter Sixteen

Cricket

If there was one thing on this planet that Cricket Ellison truly and deeply despised—besides an overdone blond balayage—it was the city of Miami.

The traffic, the noise, the tall buildings...it was enough to give a poor old woman a panic attack.

But Cricket was not a poor old woman. She was a determined mother and grandmother who knew what needed to be done and would stop at nothing to accomplish it.

"Come on! Go! What the heck is the hold-up?" She scooched forward in the driver's seat of the candy apple red Mustang she'd bought right after Gene died. Paula had dubbed it a "grief gift," and Cricket enjoyed every second she spent whipping around in her fun little car.

Except this particular second, because all she could see was brake lights and highly congested traffic. She glanced at her GPS; she was only a mile from Noah's apartment building.

So close and yet...so far. At this point, it'd be faster to walk.

Cricket took the opportunity to look around and try

to understand what Noah liked so much about this massive, crowded, blazing hot metropolis.

As she crawled her way down Brickell, she gazed up at the glitzy glass skyscrapers and the tall palm trees that lined the street. Noah had only moved back to this exclusive neighborhood when he and Rebecca separated. When they were married, they lived in a cute house in Coral Gables, which was also wealthy and crowded, but not so skyscraper-y.

Once he left his ex-wife, Noah wanted to be close to the office and back in the hottest spot of Miami, and that's exactly where he was.

This city? For the birds, as far as Cricket was concerned. But she knew she couldn't bring a nasty attitude into her time with Noah, especially since her visit was a surprise.

She'd casually asked him about his work schedule, so she knew he'd be working from home today and she could surprise him at his apartment. Then, she'd tell him all about Emily's divorce struggles and he'd simply *have* to come back to Rosemary Beach.

He'd plan to be there temporarily, of course, but Cricket would make certain that being home would prove to Noah why he needed to leave this cesspool and live where he belonged.

Okay, fine. It wasn't a cesspool. But it took her son away from her, so who could blame Cricket for being a bit bitter toward the city?

Finally, she pulled up to Noah's building, a high-rise with glass balconies overlooking the snaking waters surrounded by other tall buildings. She stopped in front, where a valet was working, and handed him the keys to her car.

"I'm just visiting," she explained, getting out of the car and thanking him.

She walked into the lobby of the condo building, which was as glamorous as anyone would expect it to be. Water flowed gently off of a big fountain in the center of the shiny marble flooring, surrounded by potted trees.

Cricket spotted the elevator in the back corner and beelined for it, but was stopped by a doorman.

"Excuse me, ma'am? Are you visiting?"

"Yes, I'm visiting my son, Noah Ellison. He lives on the twenty-sixth floor."

"Does he have you on his guest list?"

She narrowed her gaze. "He better."

The man moved to a small desk in the corner and typed onto a laptop. "Ellison... And your name, ma'am?"

"I'm his mother. Cricket."

"Okay..." He typed some more. "I'm not seeing you on his permanent list. Do you have a guest pass?"

Irritation skittered up her spine. "He is my son. Can I please go up and see him?"

"I can give him a call, just to make sure—"

She held up a hand. "No, it's a surprise."

The man pressed his lips together. "I'm sorry, ma'am, I can't let anyone up without proper authorization from a resident. It's our security policy."

Cricket took a deep breath and clenched her jaw. "Listen..." She glanced at the gold-plated nametag on the man's chest. "*Brett.* I just drove seven and a half hours and sat in the absolute nightmarish traffic of this horrendous city to surprise my darling son, who I never get to see and...and..." She shook her head and glanced away, shutting her eyes dramatically. "I don't know how much time I have left..."

"O-okay." The man backed away, reluctantly gesturing at the elevator as he glanced around to make sure no one was watching. "Go on up."

Cricket pressed a hand to her chest, smiling gratefully. "Thank you, Brett. You have a wonderful day."

In a few minutes, she was marching down the hallway of the twenty-sixth floor, past rows of white wooden doors with gold knockers. She knew his unit number, of course, and stopped to gather herself when she was finally standing in front of his door.

After a deep breath, she knocked a few times.

The door swung open, and Noah's handsome face brightened with shock. "Mom? Holy heck, what are you—"

"Noah." Cricket wrapped her arms around her one and only child, who was even taller and more built than she'd remembered. "Good heavens, have you been hitting the gym?"

"A bit more, yeah." He laughed. "Mom, what are you doing here? This is such a surprise."

"A pleasant one, I hope."

He smiled at her, his dark eyes warm and kind, just like Eugene's.

Noah was as good-looking as ever, although Cricket

couldn't help but notice a small smattering of gray hairs in the dark brown right around his temples. The work stress was too much, obviously.

"Of course. Come on in. I'll make you a hot lavender tea with honey, your favorite."

"Oh, you know me too well, honey." Cricket walked into the high-rise condo she'd only seen once since he moved in.

It was mostly glass, with an admittedly breathtaking view of Miami. Noah had decorated it with sleek gray and black furniture, with modern finishings and no clutter and barely a thing on the walls. It was a bachelor pad, that was for sure, and certainly not what Cricket had envisioned for her son at age forty-five.

She'd pictured a life with the two women who had spontaneously returned to Rosemary Beach, but she'd get to that in due time.

"So." Noah handed Cricket a hot mug of tea and sat down next to her on his dark gray L-shaped sectional, with the city view behind them. "To what do I owe this surprise?

"What?" Cricket arched a playful brow. "An old lady can't decide on a whim to come visit her only son?"

"First of all..." Noah leveled his gaze. "You are the opposite of an old lady. And second of all, you don't get out of bed in the morning without an agenda."

Cricket laughed and waved a hand. "Okay, okay. There is something I'd like to discuss with you, but I also just...miss you."

Noah's eyes widened with warmth and he laughed softly. "I miss you, too, Mom."

"Before we get into my stuff..." She lifted the mug to her lips. "Catch me up. How is everything? Nice that you get to work from home."

"It's great, and you actually caught me at a perfect time." He jutted his chin in the direction of his office. "I don't have another meeting until after two, and I'm pretty caught up on everything at the moment."

"Wonderful!" Cricket looked around. "Your place looks great."

"Yeah, it's a good condo. Work is...you know, work. It's tough, but being a partner has some major perks."

"Like a major paycheck," she remarked. "And the ability to work from anywhere."

"I still do have to go to the office most days, but yes. The money is nice." He chuckled. "I spend all my time working and any shred of free time I have I go to the gym or catch a game with some of my work buddies." He shrugged. "That's about all there is to say. Nothing new here."

Cricket sighed as she sipped the tea, thinking about how Noah should be raising a family, living in a beautiful house with a backyard, not an ice-cold glass high-rise box. He should be in his hometown, where people knew him and loved him.

"Do you still love Miami?" Cricket asked in her best attempt at nonchalance.

Noah scratched the back of his neck and raised a shoulder. "Yeah, you know. It's Miami. It's a bit exhausting at times, but I'm so used to it now. It's home. I'd like to get out of the heart of the city eventually, but for now, this is my spot."

A glimmer of hope twinkled in Cricket's heart. "Well, the traffic getting in was simply heinous, I'll say that much."

He laughed. "A bit more populated than Rosemary Beach, huh?"

"Oh, it's far too much for me, but worth it to see my boy." She reached out and squeezed Noah's arm.

"All right, Mom." He leaned back, shaking his head. "Go ahead. Skip over the rest of the small talk and tell me why you're really here, because I know you didn't drive almost eight hours to ask me about work and diss Miami, which you could—and happily would—do over the phone."

"Well, I would, but...no. I didn't." She cleared her throat and straightened her back, leveling her gaze with her son's. "You may recall that I told you a couple of weeks ago how Vanessa Young is back in town. With your daughter, Emily."

He winced, averting his gaze as his jaw visibly tightened. "Mom, she is not my daughter, and Vanessa Young's life does not concern me. Did you seriously drive all the way down here to try to convince me to come back and reconnect with my high school girlfriend?"

"Well, she is your biological daughter, and Vanessa is more than just a high school girlfriend. We both know that."

He didn't argue, but his expression was frustrated

and troubled.

"And this is actually more about Emily than Vanessa."

Noah glanced at her, his eyes clouded with the familiar heavy sadness that came whenever this particular part of his past was brought up. "Mom, I know that, biologically, yes, I got Vanessa pregnant and she had a baby. But...I never even met the kid! Vanessa ran off to L.A. and tried to make it on her own, despite all my best efforts to help her."

"I know." Cricket nodded, flashbacks echoing through her mind of seventeen-year-old Noah in tears, asking a thousand times why Vanessa hadn't come back. Why she hadn't called. Why, why, why.

And she'd never had answers.

Cricket chose to forgive Vanessa a long time ago, but these memories brought up some buried frustration and hurt, and she knew it had to be a thousand times worse for her son.

"You remember what happened." He swallowed, letting out a soft breath. "When Vanessa got pregnant, I wanted to figure it out, and you were going to help us. And Gloria."

"Yes, I was. We were." Cricket sighed. "It was a shocker, but we would have handled it."

"And next thing I know..." He leaned back onto the couch cushions. "She left. She took off to live with some bizarre distant cousin I'd never even heard of. She swore it was just while she had the baby, because her dad was so mad."

"Bill practically disowned her, you have to remember that."

"But you would have taken her in!" His voice rose with emotion and frustration. "She knew that, and she left anyway."

Cricket felt even more residual pain and anger toward Vanessa rising in her chest again. "Yes...she did. But she—"

"She promised she'd come back." He ground out the words, clearly still bruised from the memory. "She said she just needed to give her dad time to cool off and she needed to figure everything out and her dad's cousin was going to help her. She promised to come back and then she decided to give Emily up for adoption and...never did."

Cricket just swallowed, watching the decades-old pain in her boy's eyes as fresh as if it had happened yesterday.

He took a deep breath and gathered himself. "Look, Mom. This is ancient history, and it's in the past, where it needs to stay. I get that Vanessa is back, and I know that you've always loved her like a daughter. And the fact that she's reconnected with Emily is...really weird for me, honestly. It's uncomfortable, all of it. I got pushed out of their lives thirty years ago, and out of their lives is where I need to stay."

"I understand."

"No one ever hurt me like Vanessa Young." He took in a deep breath. "I never let anyone else get that close."

"Oh, Noah." Cricket wet her lips and tried to sort

out the medley of emotions coursing through her heart and mind. "I'm so sorry for the way everything played out."

"It's not your fault, Mom." He placed his hand on hers. "You did everything you could. She's the one who left."

Vanessa did hurt Noah, badly. She broke her promise to him, and it shattered him. Cricket had been quick to forgive—she was just a girl, after all—but oftentimes she let herself forget how hard it was on Noah. How he was so young, and so broken, and was never the same because of it.

But Cricket hadn't come here to get upset at Vanessa all over again. "Look, honey, Emily needs help. Real, serious help."

Noah stayed quiet, listening reluctantly.

"She's in the process of getting out of a seriously ugly and abusive marriage."

He grimaced. "Is she okay?"

"Yes, she is now. But it was scary for a while. She had to run away during the night with a fake ID and travel from town to town hiding. It was bad."

His eyes darkened and he ran a hand through his hair. "That happened to her?"

Cricket paused, taking his hand, knowing that it would be difficult to hear this horror story that happened to his daughter, even if he swore up and down he wanted nothing to do with her and never would. Noah had a soft heart, underneath everything else. And nobody knew that better than Cricket.

"Yes, but like I told you, she's safe now. The trouble is...the divorce."

Noah didn't say anything, but he also didn't stop Cricket from talking, so she took it as a clear invitation to continue.

"This Doug character is evil, and he's not making a divorce easy. He was arrested for assault and battery and all of that, and spent some time in the slammer. Not enough, as far as I'm concerned, but he's out on bail now."

"Restraining order, I presume," Noah said.

"Of course. And there are contingencies with his probation that mean he can't leave the state of Colorado, so Emily is okay."

"Colorado?" he asked. "Is that where Emily grew up?"

"Yes, her adoptive grandmother raised her in Colorado Springs." Cricket was pleased to see Noah showing some level of interest, but she tried not to overwhelm him. "Anyway, Doug has money, and he has hired the best divorce attorney in Denver, who is threatening Emily with all sorts of strings and hurdles and hoops to jump through. Starting with the fact that he won't sign the papers she filed."

"What a jerk." Noah huffed a sigh and rolled his eyes.

"No kidding. Worst of the worst. So, she's in a bind. What she needs more than anything is...a lawyer." She wanted to say "a father," but...

Too soon, Cricket. Too soon.

Noah let out a long breath and ran his hand through his hair again, thinking this through and digesting the troubling information about the daughter he never knew. "Well, Mom, I'm really sorry but I can't help her."

"But why not? You're a lawyer. You—"

"I'm a corporate antitrust attorney working in mergers and acquisitions for big tech companies. I don't know the first thing about family law." He lifted a shoulder. "I'm not even really authorized to practice it, since I have zero experience in the field."

"But you're the best there is!" Cricket insisted, pleading with him. "Noah, there's got to be something you can do to help her. She's stuck in this awful marriage and she needs legal protection, and—"

"It's not even remotely close to what I do, Mom." He squeezed his eyes shut, clearly upset by the whole thing. "I'm sure you can find her a decent lawyer up in Rosemary Beach or Panama City. Maybe go to Pensacola. There are good attorneys up there who do this in their sleep."

"But a good, sleeping attorney isn't what she needs. We want an amazing lawyer. We need a lawyer who is going to rake this Doug guy over the coals and get Emily the safety and justice that she deserves!"

Noah pinched the bridge of his nose, stress and conflict written all over his face. It was the opposite of what a mother wanted to see on her grown son. "I'm really sorry, Mom. There's nothing I can do for this type of case."

"Could you at least give her advice? I don't know... some sort of legal guidance?"

Noah shook his head. "It's awful that she went through that type of situation. No one should ever have to face trauma like that. But I'm not a part of her life, I don't practice family law, and there really is nothing I can do."

Disappointment settled in Cricket's gut like the clouds in her now-cold tea. She understood that Noah was hurt by his past with Vanessa but...really? He couldn't do anything at all in the world?

Maybe he was right, it was so far off from the type of law he did that there was really no overlap. Or maybe he was just so bruised and stubborn that he couldn't bear to get any closer to the life he'd never had.

Or the *family* he'd never had.

Cricket decided to drop the subject and enjoy the rest of the afternoon with her son, who insisted she spend the night and drive home in the morning, which she agreed to.

She adored her boy more than life itself, and every second they spent together was just another reminder of how much she missed him and wished he was around.

But the way his eyes darkened when Vanessa's name was brought up, and the way he shut down conversations about Emily and insisted he didn't want to know about her? It all made Cricket less and less hopeful for a future with Noah in Rosemary Beach.

She wasn't ready to give up, of course, but it was beginning to look tragically bleak.

Chapter Seventeen

Vanessa

"Is that box the last of it?" Vanessa leaned against the side of Dad's old wooden desk, watching as Glo hauled out yet another massive box of stuff.

"Not sure." She glanced up with a dreadful eyeroll. "I haven't started on the attic yet."

"I forgot he had an attic," Vanessa said in a mock whine.

"Nessie, please. You don't have to spend your day going through Dad's stuff with me. You have a boutique to get ready to open and probably a million things to do for it." Gloria stood up, fixing the messy bun that she'd covered with a patterned scarf wrapped around her head. "I can handle this."

"Absolutely not." Vanessa folded her arms across her chest. "I promised you I'd help you with this monstrous task, and I'm not just going to abandon you with it. I mean, good heavens, Glo, you've done more than enough for Dad." She snorted softly. "I should really be doing this by myself."

"I would never put that on you." Gloria shot her a look. "Besides, I was with him so much in his last few months, I have a pretty good sense of what's where and what to do with...most of this."

The two sisters leaned against the oversized desk side by side, looking around Dad's office at the semi-organized piles and stacks they'd made of much of his stuff. The office was the biggest undertaking by far, as he didn't have too much anywhere else in the house.

Except, possibly, the attic, and the very thought of that made Vanessa cringe. She'd promised Glo she'd pull her weight on this project, and it was the absolute least she could do after all her sister had sacrificed for Dad.

"Any word from Daisy?" Vanessa asked as she wiped a layer of dust off the top of the alleged last office box.

"She texted me and said she had a lot of fun with Emily." Gloria smiled, crouching down to open the box. "Said she was 'really, really cool' and she's excited to have a cousin in town."

"Emily said the same thing," Vanessa said. "I haven't had much time to talk to her. She's over at the boutique today getting the computer system up and running, and there are a few shelving and furniture deliveries coming in as well."

"That's amazing, Ness." Gloria shook her head, looking up at her sister. "She's so capable, and really putting her heart into this store. You both are."

"She's shockingly capable. I think it's going to be a huge blessing." Vanessa smiled.

"And everything is still good between you two? The long-lost mother and daughter?"

"Oh, we get along great." Vanessa lifted a shoulder

and sighed. "She's incredibly smart, insightful, interesting in every way. I'm loving getting to know her. I'm just still waiting for that...motherly feeling. Maybe it'll never come, because I met her as an adult."

Glo put a hand on Vanessa's knee and gave it a squeeze. "Give it time. That's what I'm doing with Daisy, and I've known her since birth. I'm just letting this new personality run its course and...giving it time, hoping she'll come back to her normal, sweet, not completely shallow self, even if she is married to Kyle."

"She will. What's the latest with the wedding planning?"

"Well, I had the absolute honor and privilege of receiving a text message from the one and only Linda Whittington, inviting me to come to their catering tasting tomorrow. Which, of course, she's organized."

Vanessa made a face. "Linda texted you? Why didn't Daisy just tell you to come?"

"Daisy's scared of stepping on Linda's toes, I think. But, it's my daughter's wedding, and I'm going to go and make the best of it. Linda hired some big deal chef from New York and her personal team."

"At least you know the food will be good." Vanessa patted the plastic lid of the bin. "So, what have we got here?"

"Looks like..." Glo popped off the lid and opened the bin to find old binders full of expense reports and tax returns from the sporting goods store. "More exciting stuff."

"Wow." Vanessa laughed, picking up a binder and

flipping through it to see Dad's signature all-caps handwriting. "I don't think we'll have anything like this for Young at Heart. Emily says it's all digital now."

"Of course it is. The diner is certainly run completely digitally. This is just, you know, Dad. The world moved to computers but he stayed on pen and paper. Remember how he used to keep track of orders with rows and rows of sticky notes? The definition of Old School."

Vanessa swallowed, a wave of sadness hitting her as she thought of him, and the closure, forgiveness, and peace neither one of them ever had a chance to give or get.

Yes, he'd left the property to her, and that had to mean something. But the wound of her father basically not loving her stung like it was fresh.

"Most of this is getting trashed," Gloria said, flipping through the binders and notebooks. "But I'll sort through it just to make sure there's nothing important hidden away. Why don't you go scope out the attic and see how much more there is up there? Just pull the rope to the hatch in the garage and some steps will clunk you in the head, er, come down."

Vanessa snorted a laugh, brushing some dust off her jeans. "The fun never stops," she teased.

"Hey, you owe me, remember." Gloria winked. "I'll be up in a few."

"Take your time. I'll handle whatever I can."

Vanessa walked through the house and out into the empty two-car garage, where there was a small hatch on the ceiling.

Peering up at the rectangular cut-out door in the ceiling, she carefully tugged the rope to open it, which did, indeed, reveal a ladder that snapped into place. Really fast. Startled by the creaking noise and fast-moving ladder, Vanessa jumped back. But it came down in sections, stopping in place on the cement floor.

"Stuff of nightmares, is what this is," she muttered to herself, clamping down on the lower rungs of the ladder, thankful she'd opted for a comfy pair of sneakers today.

Vanessa stared upward into the dark hole at the top of the ladder, and debated for half a second, then forced herself onward and upward. Had to be done.

One step at a time, she headed up the ladder. At the opening, she stuck her arm in to feel around for a light switch.

Her fingertips finally landed on a pull chain, and she yanked it, illuminating the wooden storage hole.

"Okay." Vanessa huffed out a breath as she hoisted herself into the ceiling and crouched down, looking around. "This isn't so bad, is it?"

The attic smelled musty, like wood and dust, and it actually wasn't as packed as she'd feared.

There were some boxes, likely Christmas decorations or extra merchandise from the store, a couple of bags of golf clubs and some fishing rods. Nothing she couldn't handle.

Vanessa wiped her brow as she looked around. It was too small of a space to stand all the way up, but she could hunch over and move around well enough to assess everything.

She poked around at the golf bags, fishing supplies, and a couple stacks of bins. She lifted one of the bins off of another to see what was inside them.

"Not too heavy, thank goodness," she whispered, grunting softly as she moved the top bin to the side.

Underneath it was an old wooden box, covered in a thick layer of dust.

Vanessa sat down on the wooden planks, wiping the dust off the top of the box, and opening it up. Inside was a black plastic...photo album? Scrapbook, maybe?

Her eyes moved to the corner of the dusty book, noticing a small piece of blue tape, with the word "Vanessa" written on it...in Dad's signature all-caps.

"Oh," she whispered at the sight of her name. This must be an old photo album, from before she ran away. Her childhood stuff.

She slowly opened the hardback front and found it to be, in fact, a scrapbook. The old-fashioned kind, with plastic coverings that kept the contents stuck on each page.

The first thing she saw, on the very first space, was a cutout from *Vogue* magazine. It was a 2018 issue, and the actress on the cover had been styled by Vanessa.

"Holy cow." She raised her slightly shaking hand to her mouth as she picked up the magazine, slowly taking it in.

She flipped to the next page to find the spread of the actress's photoshoot, where in the corner the words "styled by Vanessa Young" were circled and highlighted.

This was certainly not a book full of childhood memories that Dad had stowed away when Vanessa left.

With a slightly racing heart, she began flipping through every plastic page of the book. Newspaper articles, magazines, printouts from websites—every single time Vanessa's name had been mentioned in the media, Dad had saved it and stuck it in here.

He had saved every one, and marked them with highlights, circles, and dog-eared pages.

Tears sprang from Vanessa's eyes as she thumbed through the papers. Printouts from *E! News* when she styled her first Grammys outfit in 2011, and the report referred to her as "Hollywood's Newest Fashion Guru." Her first magazine spread in *Cosmopolitan,* where she had dressed a movie star for her photo shoot.

Pages and piles of Vanessa's career, big moments and small ones, saved and marked and tucked away.

As she skimmed over an article praising Vanessa for her "blend of elegant and edgy" styles, her tears spilled onto the plastic cover over the black-and-white print.

It wasn't forgiveness, it wasn't closure, but it was *something*. It was evidence that he cared. He thought about Vanessa, followed her career and saved every piece of it in a scrapbook. In his own weird, messy Bill Young way...he still loved her.

Vanessa wiped her tears and laughed through them as she closed the binder.

"How's it going up there?" Glo's voice echoed from down in the garage.

Vanessa craned her neck to lean over and wave at her sister. "Glo, come up here! You've got to see this!"

In a few moments, Gloria was up the ladder and in the attic, and Vanessa showed her the scrapbook.

"Oh, my word..." Gloria shook her head in disbelief as she ran her fingers over highlighted words of a newspaper article about one of Vanessa's looks.

"Did you know he saved all this stuff?"

"I had no idea."

"Everything in this book...it's my career. Even articles about my wedding to Aaron, and the divorce. He followed it all and held onto it. And highlighted it. Then he packed it away and hid it, but...still. I'm touched."

Gloria lifted her eyes from the papers, and they grew misty as she reached her arms out to hug her sister. "Oh, Nessie. He did love you."

"It's not an apology or making up, but it means he cared." Vanessa wiped a tear. "And I'll take it."

A weight seemed to lift from her shoulders as she set the book aside and pictured her dad cutting out those articles and buying issues of *Vogue* when Vanessa had done work for it.

She might never get to speak to him again in this lifetime, but in a way, in this scrapbook, he spoke to her. And it meant more than she ever could have realized.

"Oh, I keep forgetting to tell you," Glo said, leaning back against the wooden beams on the low walls of the attic. "Speaking of surprising finds in Dad's stuff, I found an envelope in his desk a couple weeks ago."

Vanessa frowned. "What is it?"

"It says, 'Letters from Violet.'" Gloria sighed softly, her eyes sad and hesitant. "It was stuffed to the brim and sealed shut. I haven't opened it."

"Oh, wow." Vanessa blinked back, the impact of that hitting her with yet another emotional wave. "Letters that Mom wrote Dad. When they were dating?"

Glo shrugged. "I guess so. Or in early years of their marriage, or both. Possibly even right up until the day she died. I had no idea she wrote him letters."

Vanessa swallowed. "Let's save that for another day. I think this is enough emotion for now."

"Totally agree." Glo patted the tops of her thighs. "One step at a time, sister."

Vanessa smiled and leaned her head against her sister's shoulder. "I can't believe I spent all those years away from you. I missed you so much."

Glo smiled. "It's a good thing we've both got a lot of years left, God willing."

Vanessa nodded, clutching the scrapbook close to her, letting the powerful meaning of the contents bring her a new sense of peace. "There's nowhere I'd rather be."

Chapter Eighteen

Gloria

Gloria wished that she could be excited instead of feeling nervous and dreading going into the catering tasting for her only daughter's wedding.

But as soon as she looked up at the Whittingtons' monstrosity of a beach house with Linda's Tiffany Blue Bentley parked in the driveway, the dread exploded into...whatever was worse. Fear, she supposed.

Also, insecurity, uncertainty, awkwardness, and a whole bunch of sad. She should not feel this way about her daughter's wedding or marriage or future in-laws.

Trying to shake it off, she focused on the house, a cream-colored, three-story mansion—palace?—with massive windows everywhere and a six-car garage. It backed up to the Gulf for a breathtaking one-hundred-and-eighty-degree water view and a private beach walkout.

Lord knew what *a private tasting* cost, but Gloria shook off the thought as she reluctantly turned her car off and let out a deep breath.

"I am not intimidated by Linda Whittington," she whispered. "I will not be pushed out of my daughter's life."

Gloria closed her eyes for a long few seconds to center herself and visualize the type of graceful and confident woman she wanted to be. It hurt that she felt she needed to compete with this kind of wealth for her daughter's attention, but she had to remember that Daisy loved her, and she would come around, and—

"Gloria?"

A sudden tapping on her driver's-side window and the muffled voice of Linda Whittington startled her.

"Oh! Linda!" She fumbled around to roll down the window, laughing awkwardly as her cheeks burned with embarrassment. "I was just about to come inside."

"Please do!"

Linda, whose face was beautiful—pulled, but pretty—wore a knit skirt with a matching jacket that looked like it could be St. Johns or even Chanel.

Gloria got out of her car and glanced down at her white jeans and blue tank top, suddenly horribly worried she was underdressed. Was Linda wearing heels? For a tasting?

"We are so delighted you could join us today, Gloria." She smiled, her teeth white and perfect and her lips plump and glossed.

"I'm happy to be here," Gloria said as they walked up the driveway toward the massive house. "Thank you for including me."

"Oh, of course. I'm so thrilled it worked out that you could come today. I know how busy your schedule must be running the café and all."

"It's a...diner, actually," Gloria corrected with an

awkward laugh. "And, yes, it can definitely involve some crazy hours."

"Which is why you must be so relieved that we've been able to take the brunt of planning this royal ball of a wedding, yes?"

Frustration burned in Glo's chest, but she pushed it far, far away. *For Daisy.* This was all for Daisy.

"Yes, Linda, you have been so helpful."

Linda waved a hand. "I try, I try." She clasped the enormous metal handle of the front door and pushed it open. "Please, come in. We're all situated in the formal dining room. You're in for a treat. Angelie Auclair is truly the best in the business."

Gloria pressed a smile onto her face as she walked into the house, which was even more gargantuan and over-the-top on the inside than it looked on the outside.

The floors were entirely cream-colored marble, and two curved staircases looped around each side of the entryway, connecting on a second-floor balcony.

Through tall French doors, Gloria could see a resort-like infinity pool in the backyard that looked right out at the Gulf.

"Hello, ma'am. May I take your bag?" Startled by the question, Gloria saw it came from a woman who stood next to her, clothed in a simple black dress, her blond hair in a tight bun.

A housekeeper, of course.

"Uh, yes, sure, thank you." *Take it and save me the misery of someone at that table noticing it's from the sale rack at Ross.*

"Thank you, Melanie," Linda said to the housekeeper, who nodded and hurried off. "The dining room is around this hallway."

"Great."

Gloria followed Linda into the formal dining room, which was exactly what it sounded like. The table could have accommodated sixteen, maybe more, but it was just Daisy, Kyle, and another woman in her thirties or so who Glo didn't recognize.

"Hey, Mom." Daisy smiled, waving one hand, the other interlocked with Kyle's on the table.

The stranger stood up and held out her hand. "Gloria, it's wonderful to finally meet you. I'm Elise, the wedding planner."

Gloria felt a sudden burn of shame for the fact that the wedding was four months away and she hadn't even *met* the planner. But how could she have? Linda was fully and completely in charge. This was basically the first thing she'd been invited to attend, and probably only because Daisy made a stink about it.

She shook it off and stayed cool. "Nice to meet you, Elise. I know this is going to be such a beautiful event."

She sat down across from Daisy, where Linda indicated, and noticed full place settings with a glossy printed menu sitting on top of a cloth napkin.

"Okay." Linda clasped her hands together, standing at the head of the table. "I'll go notify Angelie and her staff that we are ready to start." She clicked off to the kitchen in her red-bottomed stilettos.

"This is very exciting." Gloria grinned at Daisy and

Kyle, holding up the customized menu. "Duck confit, Wagyu beef crostini, smoked trout blinis with crème fraiche... My goodness!"

"And those are just the appetizers," Daisy said, her eyes dancing with excitement.

"Hors d'oeuvres," Kyle corrected. "Appetizers are served as part of a sit-down meal, while hors devours are passed around at a mingling event, such as a cocktail hour."

Gloria watched the bright smile fade from her daughter's face.

"Right," Daisy said quickly. "Hors d'oeuvres. For the cocktail hour. That's what I meant."

"Well, I certainly wouldn't know the difference," Gloria said with a soft laugh and a playful wink at Daisy.

Kyle lifted a shoulder. "I can't imagine you'd need to, working at a diner."

Anger gripped Gloria. "I don't work at a diner, Kyle, I own it. But you're right. We don't serve hors d'oeuvres or appetizers. Just good, old-fashioned meals."

Daisy swallowed and stayed quiet.

"Okay, everyone." Linda click-clacked back into the room with a distinguished-looking woman in a full-on *toque blanc*.

Gloria almost snorted at the head-to-toe chef getup, but quickly realized that this was completely unironic.

"This"—Linda gestured at the chef—"is Chef Angelie Auclair, one of the most highly esteemed private chefs in New York City, originating from Paris. She will be cooking and leading all catering for our big day."

"Wonderful to meet you all," Angelie said with a detectable French accent. "Of course, I will not be doing all the cooking myself, due to the high guest count of the event. But not to worry, I have a magnificent team with me."

Gloria held the glass of iced water that was at her place setting to her lips. "What, uh, what is the final guest count?"

"We're estimating around four hundred and twenty," Linda said.

Gloria actually choked on the sip of water. "Four...hundred?"

Linda frowned. "Arthur and I have a great deal of friends and colleagues who it would be rude not to invite. We've certainly been included in their children's weddings. It's only common courtesy to return the favor."

Gloria snuck a glance at Daisy, wondering how much she really wanted to walk down the aisle through a sea of people she'd never met.

Daisy shot her a powerful look back, her eyes conveying an obvious message of "Leave it alone, Mom."

So, as with everything else for this wedding, Gloria let it be and stepped out of the way. In fact, she'd never felt more in the way in her entire life.

"Here are the hors d'oeuvres." Angelie stood at the head of the table as her team passed out plates containing bite-sized samples of the luxurious gourmet food to be offered at the cocktail hour.

"Wow." Gloria gasped and eyed Daisy. "This all looks amazing, doesn't it?"

Daisy began to smile, but it quickly turned to a frown when she saw Kyle looking less than pleased with the plate.

"What's wrong?" she asked him.

"Mom," Kyle said, ignoring Daisy and looking straight at his mother. "What is the Wagyu served on?"

Linda lifted her head to defer to Angelie for an answer.

Angelie nodded. "It is a crostini with a parsnip and fig puree."

"Toasted bread?" Kyle wrinkled his nose. "I think we can do a little better than that."

Daisy stayed quiet, Gloria clenched her jaw, and Linda nodded in agreement.

"Of course, my dear." Linda clasped her hands together. "You are the groom-to-be. Angelie, could we try something a bit more, hmm, exotic?"

Angelie folded her arms. "It is pan-seared in melted garlic and herb butter and sprinkled with sea salt. It is simple and wonderful, but..." She tipped her head in concession. "I can consider other options."

"Well..." Glo dabbed the corner of her mouth with the cloth napkin. "I personally think everything is absolutely delicious."

"It sure is," Daisy agreed. "I love the duck confit. I wasn't sure about it at first, since I've never had duck, but—"

"You've never had duck?" Linda gasped.

Kyle laughed and shook his head in a way that was so condescending, Gloria visualized what it would feel like to smack him. "Of course she hasn't, Mom. She didn't grow up, you know...eating stuff like this."

Okay, now Gloria had really had it. Fury and offense ricocheted through her as she looked at Daisy for some sort of support or defense, but her daughter kept her gaze fixed downward, right on the food she didn't grow up eating.

Gloria stood up, holding up a finger. "Excuse me for just one moment, please. I'm going to use the ladies room."

"Down that hall to the left," Linda said, gesturing toward a long hallway.

Tears of hurt and disappointment stung Gloria's eyes as she walked down the long hallway and found a powder room.

Shutting the door behind her, she took a deep breath and looked in the mirror.

How had this happened? How had she become such an outcast in her own daughter's circle? Kyle had officially solidified his reputation with Gloria as a complete and total jerk, and it was like Daisy didn't even see it.

She was blinded. But by what? Love? Money? A life that Gloria could have never given her? She refused to believe her daughter was truly that shallow. She'd had a wonderful childhood and always seemed content and happy with everything.

How did she get so wrapped up in this? And how did Gloria, her own mother, get so blatantly left out?

She pulled her phone out of her back pocket and saw a new text from Nessie.

"Hope it's going well, keep me posted!"

Glo closed her eyes and slid her phone back into her white jeans and pulled it together. She had to. For Daisy.

When she got back out to the dining room, entrees were being served.

Gloria cleared her throat and sat back down at her seat, forcing a smile and knowing she had to get through this and try her hardest to accept the situation.

Angelie talked with her French accent about the different entrees—short rib, sea bass, mushroom risotto, and some sort of fancy chicken.

Once they'd served everyone, Gloria lifted her hand. "Um, Angelie?"

"Yes?"

"Will you and your team be making the desserts, too?"

Before the chef could open her mouth to answer, Linda let out a chuckle, waving her hand.

"Oh, good heavens, no! Angelie isn't a pastry chef, Gloria. We've hired a patissière, and a baker for the cake."

"Right, of course." Embarrassed once again, she shook her head. "Duh. Thank you, Angelie."

The chef nodded and headed back to the kitchen with her team.

"Oh, I am so glad everything has turned out so delicious," Linda said, delicately sipping her water. "The food at weddings is so important. I mean, it can really make or break the entire event. Kyle, do you remember when we attended the wedding of Henry Hampton's son, and the prime rib was completely dry?" She groaned and rolled her eyes. "Totally ruined my night."

"Dry prime rib will do that," Daisy said with a chuckle, clearly trying to join in on the conversation.

"Oh, please, Daisy." Kyle glanced at her with an arrogant smile. "Have you ever even had good prime rib?"

Daisy tapped her fork. "Am I not eating it right now?"

"No, that's *short* rib, dear," Linda said gently.

"Oh, right." Daisy shrugged. "I'm not too much of a foodie. But whatever it is, it's amazing."

"It'll pair beautifully with the Stags' Leap cabernet," Linda remarked.

Glo looked at her daughter, remembering how she used to eat a double cheeseburger with caramelized onions and a chocolate shake every time she came to the diner after school, grinning the entire time.

"What kind of food did you have at your wedding, Gloria?" Linda asked with a fake smile.

Glo cleared her throat and set her napkin back down on her lap. "We, uh, we had a taco bar when Christian and I got married."

Linda and Kyle laughed as if that was just the cutest thing they'd ever heard.

"You're kidding," Kyle said.

"That is precious." Linda shook her head. "Charming, truly."

Gloria glanced at Daisy, who was, again, quiet. "Well, we didn't have a lot of money. Christian hadn't risen to the major leagues yet, and I was still in the red from the small business loans I took to open up the diner. But the taco bar was a big hit, I thought."

"I love tacos," Daisy said, glancing at Gloria with a smile, and sending a small ripple of relief through her.

Thanks, Dais.

Linda nodded, still smiling. "Yes, I imagine it was quite...rustic. Oh, Daisy. Don't forget, dear, we have our second-to-final consultation with the florist next Tuesday. I'll pick you up around eleven."

"Okay." Daisy turned to Gloria. "I would have let you know about that, we just...you know, figured you'd be busy with work and it's just easier if we go."

There were those pesky tears again, burning and stinging and threatening to dump out. "Of course." Gloria took in a shaky breath as her throat tightened. "I get it."

"We'll be ordering you a corsage, of course." Linda plastered that fake smile on her face once again.

Gloria had lost her mom, lost her sister—for thirty years, anyway—lost her husband, who she still missed on occasion, lost her father so recently it still stung, and now...she was losing her daughter. To this family, of all people.

She'd never be cool enough, rich enough, or hip enough to stay in Daisy's life if her life looked like...this.

Somehow, the event ended and Gloria escaped. But all the way home and for the rest of the day, she ached for the little girl who ate cheeseburgers in the diner.

Chapter Nineteen

Emily

Distraction was the name of the game for Emily, at least while this divorce was going on and Doug was still lurking in the shadows of her life. Thankfully, distractions were in abundance as she typed up a template for monthly expense reports and went over her finalized paperwork for Young at Heart, LLC.

She and Vanessa had completely cleared out the back office and had new furniture delivered, making it a comfortable and beautiful workspace for Emily to run the logistics and administration of the business.

She tried to focus, but her brain kept sliding back to Doug. Why couldn't he just sign the papers? Why did it have to be such a battle?

Because it was Douglas Rosetti. He'd had a grip on her since she was twenty-four, and the more she ticked him off, the harder he gripped, even from sixteen hundred miles away.

And, boy, she'd *really* ticked him off now.

A knock on the office door caught her attention, and Emily spun around in the brand-new white leather desk chair they'd picked out. "Come on in."

"Hey, you." Vanessa walked in, looking totally put together and fabulous, as always. "How's it all going?"

"Really well." Emily swiveled the computer monitor to show Vanessa. "Our LLC is officially active, so I'm just working on setting up our monthly and quarterly business reports, like P and L statements, expenses, all that fun stuff."

"Wow." Vanessa shook her head in amazement as she leaned close to the screen, admiring Emily's detailed and organized spreadsheet template. "Gosh, I don't know how I would do any of this without you. I wouldn't be able to."

"You'd figure it out. It's not that hard." Emily waved a hand. "Or, you know, hire someone."

"No one is as awesome at this stuff as you are. I'm really grateful." Vanessa smiled, sitting down in a plush accent chair they'd put in the corner of the office.

"I'm so excited to get started." Emily grinned. "I can't believe we've already put in some orders for shipments."

"We will have clothing in this place in two weeks." Vanessa shook her head. "I can't believe it, either. It's all happening so fast."

Emily clapped as she remembered more news. "I've hired those two women we interviewed, who both want limited hours part-time. I think we might need one more sales person. I've got a few more interviews lined up for this week. I'll throw 'em on your Google Cal so you can join."

"Perfect." Vanessa took a deep breath and studied Emily.

"What?" Emily asked.

"Nothing, it's just...you're my daughter. And sometimes I really notice that."

The observation warmed Emily's heart. She liked feeling like Vanessa's daughter. The dynamic of their relationship was still being worked out, but so far everything had been relatively seamless.

"I notice it, too." Emily smiled. "Did you talk to Gloria? How was the tasting thing?"

Vanessa groaned, shaking her head with sympathy. "Not great, apparently. I've only gotten a couple texts since she left the Whittington mansion, but she seemed pretty broken up about the whole thing."

"Oh." Emily pressed her hand to her mouth. "I don't understand. Daisy seems so sweet. We had a really fun time together the other day. She was a bit guarded at first, which is understandable, but she opened up and we connected pretty quick. It's hard to imagine her pushing Glo away like that."

Vanessa lifted a shoulder. "I'm glad you guys got along well. You're young and cool and I think it was probably easy for Daisy to relate to you."

"Yeah," Emily said with a soft snort. "I'm super cool, getting all excited about expense reports."

Vanessa laughed. "You are cool, Emily. And I don't know how to help Glo. I just feel for her. She's getting so undermined by Kyle's mother with the wedding planning and everything."

"I don't know how to help, either." She pursed her lips. "Don't you think once they're married, maybe the excitement will wear off and she'll want to be close with

Gloria again?"

"We all hope so, but it's not looking good."

"I just don't get it." Emily swiveled in the desk chair and clicked her tongue. "How can you push your own *mother* out of planning your wedding? Maybe I'm biased because I don't have a mom, but—" She caught herself quickly. "I mean, that's not what I meant—"

"It's okay." Vanessa forced a smile, but Emily could see a slight shadow of disappointment in her eyes. "I know what you mean."

"No, really, I'm sorry. I do have a mother now, I'm just still getting used to it."

"I know. It's okay, Emily. We're both learning." She stood up and walked over to the desk chair, giving Emily's hand a squeeze. "I'm going to go back on the floor. They're installing clothing racks and setting up the jewelry and accessories table."

"Exciting! I'll keep working in here."

Vanessa headed out of the office and Emily sat thinking about her misspoken comment. She wasn't used to having a mother, and she didn't really think of Vanessa as a true "mom" in the traditional sense.

Should she? Would it come with time, or was the nature of their relationship just different because of the strange circumstances?

Her phone buzzed with a message, and Emily picked it up to read it.

"Huh?" She squinted at the phone screen, the sender of the text message labeled, *Unknown Number*.

An eerie chill crawled up her spine as she clicked on the text and read it.

Abby, it's me. Miss me? I know I'm not supposed to contact you, and don't freak out, it's a one-time thing. You won't hear from me again. I just wanted to let you know that if you don't drop all the charges and the restraining order, I will never sign divorce papers. Is that clear? Don't worry, I'm not going to find you, in fact, I want nothing to do with you. You've humiliated me and threatened my career, so you're going to pay the price. I gave you everything and you stabbed me in the back, so now you have to live with the consequences. If you ruin my reputation any further, you're never getting out of this.

With a shaking hand, Emily dropped the phone back down on her desk and felt the room begin to shift and spin around her.

He was not supposed to talk to her. It was in the terms of the restraining order. He was out on bail, but on probation, and how was this happening? And why was he making it so hard?

With a racing heart and sweaty palms, she stood up and paced around the small office, closing her eyes and trying to focus on breathing in and breathing out to steady herself. It wasn't working.

She ran her hands through her hair, gripping it tightly as stress and fear and anxiety worked their way down her spine and all the way to her fingertips.

"It's okay," she whispered to herself breathlessly. "He's not coming after you. He's just trying to punish you, but he doesn't want you anymore."

And that, she was fairly certain, was true. Running away and getting him arrested was Doug's final straw with Emily, and quite possibly the smartest thing she ever did. It made him so mad that he no longer had a desire to have her and control her, but he did have a desire to make her pay for it.

And his way of doing that? Not giving her a divorce. Why wouldn't he want one?

This could take years. This could take ages to get resolved, and Emily didn't have even the tiniest clue about how to fight him on it—or a dollar to pay a lawyer who could help her.

As she paced around the office, the grueling reality of the situation hit hard. She could be fighting Doug Rosetti for freedom for a long, long time.

Tears began to fall down her face and turned into full-on sobs, and she curled up on the plush accent chair and cried.

Suddenly, the door swung open again.

"Hey, did you check on the— Oh!" Vanessa gasped as she rushed to the corner, crouching down to meet Emily's gaze. "Oh, my gosh, what happened? Are you okay?"

Emily nodded and sniffed, wiping her eyes. "I'm fine, I promise."

"What's the matter?" Vanessa asked, her whole face softening with empathy and concern. That alone made Emily feel the tiniest bit better.

This woman—whatever she called her—deeply cared, and that really meant a lot.

"I got a text." Emily swallowed, willing herself to calm down. "From Doug."

"What?" Vanessa gasped, her brows knitting in a worried frown. "I thought he wasn't legally allowed to contact you. How can he—"

"It came in from some unknown number that I'm sure would be disconnected if I tried to call or text back. He basically just said that unless I drop all charges against him and the restraining order, he's not going to sign the papers. He doesn't want me to be free."

"Oh, Emily. That's unbelievable. I'm so sorry."

"It's ruining his career and reputation, I guess."

"As it should!" She curled her lip. "He doesn't deserve a career or a reputation. Can you fight it somehow?"

Emily moaned softly. "I don't think so. Not right now, anyway. I'll just have to put it on hold until I can get myself a really good lawyer. But even then, I'm not sure what they can do. He isn't exactly willing to come to any kind of agreement."

Vanessa bit her lip, shaking her head as she visibly tried to wrap her mind around the unfathomable evil that resided in the ice-cold heart of Doug Rosetti.

"I'm just so scared," Emily said, her voice wavering. "He's never going to leave me alone. He's never going to let me get away from him and the marriage. My whole life, I'll be tied to him and weighed down by this awful baggage and..."

"Hey, whoa." Vanessa placed a hand on her hand. "No. You will not, okay? You are literally the most resilient, courageous, and strong person I have ever met in my life."

Emily looked up, blinking through her tears. "I am?"

"You're incredible. And I know I haven't known you that long, but... Gosh, I am so, so proud of the woman that you are."

Emily swallowed and pushed a strand of hair out of her face, her mother's words like a soothing balm on her broken, anxious heart.

"Really?" she whispered.

"Are you kidding me?" Vanessa's eyes grew misty, and she kept her hand interlocked with Emily's. "Meeting you has changed my life, Emily. You've inspired me with your grace and your brilliance and your fearlessness. And you'll get through this, just like you've gotten through every challenge so far. You're so much stronger than you give yourself credit for."

Emily felt more tears burn in her eyes, but these were no longer tears of sadness and fear.

She didn't feel alone anymore, because...she had a...

"Mom," she whispered. "I have a mom."

Vanessa lost it a bit, too, and they held each other and happy-cried for a few moments that Emily knew she would never forget.

"I can't believe I was so dumb to think that this problem was behind me when I saw him escorted into a cop car in handcuffs," Emily finally said, swiping at her tears.

Vanessa nudged her. "That had to feel pretty good though, huh?"

Emily managed a laugh. "It was awesome."

Vanessa laughed, too, and wrapped an arm around Emily, which felt seriously comforting and nice. "Look, I don't know any lawyers around here, but Gloria and Cricket know everyone in town. We'll find you some way to handle this."

Emily had no earthly idea how that would happen, but she trusted Vanessa, her mother, deeply and wholly.

Chapter Twenty

Cricket

Troubled and unsettled by her visit with Noah, Cricket found herself preoccupied all day at work. She had three appointments and she just didn't quite feel like herself. Of course, doing hair was a calming and peaceful outlet for her, but she found herself oddly quiet when it came to the conversation portion of her work.

Normally, Cricket Ellison could talk to anyone about anything, especially her clients, who she considered all dear friends at this point, with no shortage of local gossip and drama.

But today she was quiet, with a heavy heart that any mother would feel after seeing her grown son express the depth of his decades-old pain and heartbreak.

He'd never fully healed from Vanessa Young. He couldn't forgive her, and who could blame him, really? Cricket forgave, of course, but maybe she should have considered Noah's pain more.

Maybe she had been too quick to forgive Vanessa and that made Noah feel even more pushed away and alone.

Sure, this was all ancient history and deep in the past, but somehow it was as relevant today as it was twenty-nine and a half years ago.

Because of her troubled heart, Cricket asked Vanessa if they could meet for a glass of wine after her last appointment of the evening, because she knew darn well that bottling up emotions and thoughts would never do anyone a lick of good, and she had to just be straightforward and talk to Vanessa about all of this.

Just because it happened a long time ago didn't mean it wasn't a massively big deal. A deal big enough to change the course of her son's life forever and, worst of all, keep him far away.

She didn't want to harbor bad feelings toward Vanessa, especially since she'd returned to Rosemary Beach and brought Cricket a granddaughter! But it was growing increasingly difficult as the pain of the past reared its quite ugly head.

There were so many questions left unanswered and their implications had become everlasting.

Cricket gathered her thoughts as she swung the door open to the Gulf Coast Wine Bar, a cute two-story spot on Main Street, where they served wine and charcuterie and nearly the entire customer base was women.

When she walked in, Vanessa had gotten a spot in the back corner, with two plush-looking lounge chairs separated by a round wooden table.

"Hey, Cricket." Vanessa stood up and gave her a hug.

Cricket held her breath, trying to figure out how not to be mad at Vanessa. Of course, she'd always known how much Noah had been hurt by everything that happened. But they'd hardly talked about it in the last twenty years!

"Hello, my dear."

"I ordered us each the house sparkling rosé." Vanessa smiled.

Cricket sat down in the champagne-colored velvet chair across from her. "That sounds lovely."

"So, what's going on?"

"Oh, you know. This and that." Cricket crossed her legs underneath her long pink dress and folded her hands.

"Is something wrong?" Vanessa asked, her brow furrowed with a half-smile as she studied Cricket's expression. "You seem...blue."

Cricket paused as the server came over and brought them their glasses of light pink bubbly drinks, took a sip, and leveled her gaze. "I went down to see Noah in Miami on Tuesday."

Vanessa's eyes widened and her smile quickly faded. "Oh." She cleared her throat. "How, um, how is he?"

Cricket took a deep breath and set her delicate champagne flute down. "Well, according to him, he's great. Living the big-shot lawyer dream."

Vanessa's gaze flickered with disappointment, but she forced a smile. "Good for him. I always knew he would be successful."

"Career-wise, he is. Of course." She let out a sigh. "But he's my son and I know him better than anybody, and I don't believe he's truly happy."

Vanessa chewed her lip, pausing and thinking, as if she didn't really know what to say.

It seemed she was every bit as uncomfortable talking about Noah as he was talking about her.

Well, that was just too darn bad. Because these were two adults in their forties and they both needed to grow up, face their pasts, and consider their futures, instead of just avoiding the topic and hiding from reality.

"Why do you think he isn't happy?" Vanessa asked hesitantly.

"He has no love in his life," Cricket replied. "He has his work, and his fancy apartment, and that's it. He and Rebecca are long divorced, not that there was much love in that marriage even when it still existed. Noah had put up every imaginable wall around his heart because of... well..." Cricket cleared her throat. "Because of you."

Vanessa blinked back, her blue eyes darkening. "Because of *me*? Cricket, I haven't talked to him in decades. Noah and I were just kids, we—"

"It doesn't matter, Vanessa." Cricket clenched her jaw and took another sip of the rosé. "I went to speak to him in person to talk to him about Emily."

Her jaw fell. "He knows about Emily? He knows she's here and we're together and—"

"Of course he knows—he's my son. I wasn't going to *not* tell him that his only daughter is living here, in Rosemary Beach, with the only woman he ever loved, who also happens to be the girl's mother." Cricket raised a brow, adjusting her glasses.

Vanessa winced and toyed with the stem of her champagne flute. "How did he react?"

"Shock, at first. And then...nothing. He doesn't want any part of it, because he is still very hurt and broken, and that's why I needed to talk to you."

New Beginnings in Rosemary Beach

Vanessa swallowed, waiting for Cricket to continue.

"Nessie, why didn't you come back?" Cricket couldn't help the emotion that rose in her voice, but she didn't try to hide it. "Why did you promise him you'd come back here after he graduated high school, and you never did?"

Vanessa just swallowed hard and cast her gaze down.

"When you gave Emily up, you hardly discussed it with him, and then you just...dropped him," Cricket continued. "It wrecked him. Destroyed him. And now, even though it's been thirty years and it's all long over, he doesn't ever want to come back here or be in Emily's life or anything." She sniffled and shook her head. "It's very sad."

"Oh, Cricket." Vanessa's brows drew together with sadness. "I was so young, I didn't know what to do. My dad kicked me out, and—"

"You knew I would have taken you in. You knew that."

"I didn't want that. I couldn't put that on you, and on him and..." She shook her head, her eyes misty. "And on myself. If I'm being completely honest, Cricket, I didn't want to give up my life and my dreams. I wasn't ready to be a mother. I tried, for six months, and I couldn't do it. I knew that Emily would be better off with a different family."

Cricket pinched the bridge of her nose. "I understand the adoption, Nessie, I really do. And as much as it pained me to find out that my only grandchild was going to be raised by another family, I respected your decision."

"I know you did."

"But why didn't you come back? Why did you never make another go of it with Noah? Was your career really that much more important?"

"It was important, but..." Nessie plucked at a thread on her dark blue jeans. "I couldn't do it with Noah. It hurt to even hear his voice on the phone. He was my best friend from the time we were four. He was my first crush, my first kiss, my first and possibly only real love."

Her words made Cricket's heart jump.

So the feeling was mutual between them, just as she'd thought.

"I'm not saying I handled it right." Vanessa took a sip of wine. "I regret a lot of what I did and how I did it, but I realized pretty early that I couldn't let the path not taken bog me down. I gave Emily up to pursue a career and a dream, and for that reason, I knew I had to give it my absolute all."

"And my Noah was just...collateral damage."

"No, Cricket. God, no." Vanessa shook her head, pressing her lips together. "But he needed to move on and be free. He needed the freedom to go and pursue his own career and life and let high school stay where high school belongs."

"But you made that decision for him, Vanessa. By not coming back. What if that isn't what Noah wanted or needed?"

Vanessa sucked in a breath, then paused. "But it worked out, didn't it? I mean, he's at the top of his field, he's—"

"Alone, and broken, and refusing to come home." Cricket sighed, her anger fading into sadness. "I know I can't put all the blame on you, Nessie. I'm sorry if it seems I am."

Vanessa's eyes softened. "I understand, Cricket. Frankly, I was shocked that you forgave me at all, let alone continued to embrace me the way you have."

"I'm not like your father. I don't believe in grudges, and I don't want you to think I'm holding one now. I'm just worried about my son, and where his life is at age forty-five. I mean, he's living like a twenty-five-year-old!"

Vanessa smiled. "There aren't a ton of twenty-five-year-olds who are partners at a massive law firm."

"Law, shmaw." Cricket rolled her eyes. "He's all alone."

"And it's my fault."

"No, honey. Well, partially." She offered a gentle laugh.

"Cricket, I am so, so sorry for how I hurt your son. I know this apology is thirty years too late, and I know I can't do anything to change how I acted when I was young. But everything is different now, and I realize how shortsighted I truly was. I hope you can forgive me."

Vanessa had been just a girl, and Cricket had always known that. But Noah had also been just a boy, and he didn't deserve the pain and heartbreak he went through. Cricket decided that forgiving Vanessa had been the right decision by far, even if Noah wasn't crazy about them having a relationship.

"Holding on to past pain does nobody any good."

Cricket reached across the table and took Vanessa's hand. "But sometimes, I really, really wish you had come back."

Vanessa took in a shaky breath, closing her eyes as she admitted a quiet whisper of truth. "Sometimes I do, too."

AFTER A LATE-NIGHT KNITTING SESSION, Paula and Shelly left Cricket's loft. So she turned on *Gilmore Girls* reruns—why couldn't Vanessa and Emily have lived like those fictional females, who were also sixteen years apart?—and finished the last of her evening tea.

A nearly completed cardigan lay spread on the couch for her to admire, and she decided she wanted to give it to Emily. It had turned out pretty small, so it would fit her perfectly. Probably not the most useful item of clothing going into the girl's first Florida summer, but alas. Cricket didn't know how to knit a bikini just yet.

She'd spent the evening mulling over all the things with her two best friends, who know how to shoot straight and be real, just like Cricket. Paula and Shelly were in total agreement that while Noah's hurt was completely understandable, he was being a bit closed-minded and, frankly, stubborn.

There was no use in dwelling on the past, but there was also no use in trying to change Noah Ellison's mind, heart, or life.

Cricket sighed as she placed her mug in the dishwasher and closed it, leaning against the countertop in her tiny corner kitchen with light blue cabinets and floral wallpaper.

Now that Vanessa and Emily were here to stay, and Noah had made his feelings pretty clear, she might have to come to terms with the fact that he wasn't coming back, at least not anytime soon.

It was wrong on every level and totally unfair, but as Cricket glanced at the sweater on the sofa, she remembered that God had blessed her with a new and totally unexpected gift—her granddaughter.

She felt like this evening had truly cleared the air with Vanessa and made it so that they could all move forward and be a family.

Maybe one day, in the faraway future, Cricket would get the big family party she'd always dreamed of. It just... might not include Noah.

On a sigh, she started the dishwasher and turned off the kitchen lights, closing up for the night as she shuffled along the carpet in her slippers to retire to her bedroom.

She loved this little one-bedroom loft above her hair salon. It had been a tiny and wonderful home for her ever since Gene died. Of course, they'd lived in a house a few miles from downtown, but she couldn't bear to be there all alone after his passing, so she'd moved in here after the renter moved out.

Cricket had sold nearly all the things she and Gene had accumulated together, bought herself a pink and purple lacey bedspread, and moved into her own little space.

With precious few accent pieces and delicate,

eclectic décor, Cricket adored her home. Contentment settled over her as she pulled back that bedspread and climbed in for the night.

"Let's see what the girls are up to," she whispered to herself as she picked up the old, worn copy of *Little Women* from her nightstand to continue on what had to be her fifth time reading it.

Just as she'd sunk into the lives of the March girls, her phone rang loudly from where it was sitting on the charger.

"Who the heck could that be?" she mumbled, getting up to retrieve the phone from its place on top of her white dresser.

Incoming Call: Noah Ellison

Noah? Calling this late?

Cricket slid her finger over the Answer button and held the phone to her ear. "Noah, honey, is everything okay?"

"Hey, Mom. Yes, everything's fine, sorry to bug you so late."

She sighed with a small wave of relief. Those motherly worries never really did go away, did they?

"That's okay, I was just settling in to read for the night. What's going on?"

"Look, I just..." He sighed noisily. "I'm not saying I can help at all, and I don't want you to get your hopes up or think there is anything I can do, because there really is not. But...can you just send me over all of Emily's documents? Her filed charges, the divorce papers, case data.

Anything she has, just..." He grunted softly. "Just send it to me."

Cricket nearly squeaked with joy, but she tamped down her excitement in an attempt to heed Noah's warning that he actually couldn't help her. "Yes, of...of course. I'll ask her for copies of it all tomorrow and mail it to you."

Noah laughed softly. "You, uh, you don't have to mail it, you can just forward it in an email. I'm sure they're all digitally filed PDFs."

"Right. Well, I will email it, then."

"Thanks," Noah said after a long pause. "And, Mom, this doesn't mean I'm going to get involved in any way, okay? You know that, right?"

"I know, honey. I understand."

"I've just been thinking about it, and...figured I could take a glance at it and...pass it along."

Cricket couldn't help but smile. "Well, anything at all that you can do is really appreciated."

"No promises that I can help even a little bit. I don't know the first thing about family law and certainly not domestic violence cases like this. I can't... Anyway." He stopped himself. "Just send it over when you can. And please don't tell Emily that you've talked to me about this or that I asked for the papers. I don't want her to get her hopes up that I can wave a magic wand and make this disappear."

How would she get the files without telling Emily? She'd cross that bridge tomorrow. Tonight, she was simply grateful.

"Don't worry, Noah. I'll keep this just between us. I understand there may be nothing you can do, but...I appreciate you looking at it."

"Of course. Get some sleep, Mama. I love you."

She smiled at the childhood endearment. "I love you, too, hon."

Cricket set the phone back down and climbed into bed.

She'd raised a man who cared deeply, even when he didn't want to. A man who had thought about this, struggled with it, and knew the right thing to do was at least look it over and consider it, to whatever degree he could.

She picked her book back up and snuggled into her silky sheets, smiling to herself.

Perhaps there was still hope yet.

Chapter Twenty-one

Vanessa

The moment had finally arrived—Young at Heart's first official shipment of clothing. And, wow, they were beautiful.

Vanessa beamed with pride and shook her head in utter disbelief as she and Emily and their two new employees—Gayle and Lynn—helped unload the truck and began sorting out boxes and garment bags of clothes.

She stood in the warm sun, holding a hand up to shield her eyes as she watched them roll the last rack of clothes through the back entrance of the store.

The driver walked up to her with an electronic machine. "That's the last of it, ma'am. Just need your signature right here. If anything is wrong or missing, contact the supplier directly." He smiled. "I just drive the truck."

"Understood." Vanessa nodded and scribbled a signature onto the pad and thanked him again.

The truck drove away and she headed inside into the back storage room, which they'd cleared out and organized for inventory.

"Holy cow, these are beautiful!" Emily pulled the

protective plastic off of a long chiffon maxi dress with off-the-shoulder sleeves and a flouncy hem.

"Ooh! This jacket! To die for." Gayle, a woman in her mid-forties with the energy of someone half her age, grinned with joy as she uncovered a stack of white denim jackets. "These are perfect for Florida and those chilly air-conditioned restaurants. Everyone thinks it's so hot here, but the truth is, I can't go out to dinner without something on my arms."

As they unpacked the boxes and began organizing the garments by size and style, Emily stood next to Vanessa. "How does it feel to be a boutique owner?"

"Absolutely incredible. I feel like a kid in a candy store. I am so excited to sell these clothes!"

"You're an artist..." Emily gestured at the garments. "And these are your paints."

"And you are one heck of a manager. I can't believe we came this far so fast."

Emily shrugged. "None of this was that hard. All the stars are aligning, for both of us. For Young at Heart. It really feels like it was...meant to be."

"I know it was." Vanessa crossed her arms and watched it all unfold—the vision she didn't know she needed, the future she never could have dreamed, and, best of all, the daughter she never thought she'd have the chance to know.

"I'm going to finalize the plans for the main floor while you guys sort through the shipment," Vanessa said to Emily with a joyful grin.

"You got it, boss."

"Business partner," Vanessa corrected, holding up a finger.

"How about 'Mom'?"

Her heart tugged. "I like that one the best."

She walked through the hallway, past the back office where Emily had been working tirelessly to set everything up in the computer systems, and into the main store.

It was empty, but it was ready. Right down to the decorations on the walls and the soft turquoise and cream curtains that covered the dressing rooms in the back. Two cash registers were set up at the check-out area, on a gorgeous counter they'd had installed that also had shelves to display jewelry and trinkets.

It was real, it was happening.

And it was set to be celebrated tomorrow at Vanessa's beach house, where Cricket had announced she'd be throwing a big party, just like she'd always dreamed of. Vanessa got the feeling she was using the opening of the boutique as an excuse for a get-together, but the thought made her smile.

Vanessa's life had taken a lot of unexpected turns, but this one might have turned out to be the best yet.

As she was walking around admiring everything and making sure there were no missing pieces or final touches that needed addressing, the front door swung open.

She turned around, surprised to see Barry Martinez, the lawyer who had handled Dad's will, standing in Young at Heart.

"Barry!" Vanessa walked over with a bounce in her

step to shake his hand. "How perfectly fitting that you stopped by. You're the one who gave me the news that this place is mine, and now you're seeing it right before it truly comes to life."

"Hey, Vanessa." Barry cleared his throat, glancing past Vanessa with a strange anxiety in his eyes. "Place looks awesome."

She grinned. "We're excited."

"Listen...can I, uh, talk to you for a second?"

She inched back. "Sure. Is everything okay?"

Barry gestured toward the back hallway to the office. "Let's chat."

Vanessa swallowed, her mind racing. What could be wrong? Was there something else with Dad's will?

"Come on in," she said, opening the door to the office, inviting him to sit in the chair across from the desk.

Vanessa sat down in what had basically become Emily's seat, in front of the computer where she'd worked weeks of magic to make this place a reality.

"What's going on?" she asked, tapping her fingers on the desk.

Barry crossed he legs, letting out a sigh. "Vanessa, this is extremely unprecedented. In my thirty-one years as an estate planning attorney, I've never run into anything like this."

Okay, now her palms were starting to sweat. "Barry, you're freaking me out," Vanessa said on a nervous laugh. "What happened?"

He folded his hands and leveled his gaze. "I received something in the mail this morning, and I went through the process of verifying its legitimacy before I talked to you, and, as it turns out, it's totally legitimate."

"Received *what* in the mail?"

"An updated will. From you father."

Vanessa's throat constricted as she sucked in a gasp. "An updated..." Her voice trailed off, just knowing this was bad, bad news.

"Like I said, Vanessa, this is completely unprecedented. It appears that your father filed an updated will with a *different* attorney—not me, and I knew nothing about it—in Pensacola, only six weeks before he died."

She blinked back, her jaw slack. "Six weeks?"

Barry nodded. "And I only just now received it because of the legal process it went through in a different city, with a different lawyer. Vanessa, I had no idea he did this."

"I...but...why..." she stammered, barely able to gather any thoughts. "Okay, well...what does it say?"

As if she even had to ask. Obviously, six weeks before he died, Dad changed his mind; realized that Vanessa was going to be forever unforgivable.

That didn't explain why he'd filed it with some random lawyer two hours from here, but...whatever. He was weird.

Barry pressed his lips together, thinking hard before he answered her question. "He changed the inheritance of this property."

Even though she knew he was going to say that, her heart still sank and her eyes began to sting. "He gave it to Gloria," she whispered.

Already, Vanessa's mind was spinning with how they were going to handle this. She knew that Glo would insist she kept the store and refuse to take it back, even though it was rightfully hers.

But the whole thing was tainted. He didn't forgive her. He hated her so much that on his deathbed he changed his mind about giving her anything at all.

"Actually, no." Barry's words caught Vanessa's attention and she blinked at him.

"Excuse me?" She shook her head. "He didn't leave it to Glo?"

Who the heck else did he have?

Barry reached down into a briefcase and pulled out a folder, sliding a packet of paper out of it and flipping to a marked page.

Vanessa stood up and walked around the desk, wobbly on her legs from the impact of this terrifying news.

"Here." He tapped the top of the page, showing her the name that had been inserted where hers was in the original will.

Right next to the address of what was now supposed to be Young at Heart, a name was written in that Vanessa had never heard in her entire life.

"*Clarinda Smith?*" She breathed the name, her voice shaky, frowning with complete confusion as she looked at Barry. "Who is that? I've never heard of a Clarinda Smith. It sounds made up."

He sighed, sliding the papers back into the file folder. "I was hoping you'd have some idea."

"I don't," Vanessa said, her heart aching. "But, Barry, what does this mean? We don't even know who this person is. I mean, was my dad just losing it or something?"

He lifted a shoulder. "Whatever lawyer he worked with in Pensacola deemed him mentally sound enough to adjust his will, so I can't say that."

"Can you talk to that lawyer?" she pleaded, nerves and anxiety fraying more and more each second. "Figure out what my dad was thinking or talking about when he requested a new will? And why didn't he file it with you?"

He shook his head. "It seems he didn't want this to be...local."

Was he hiding something? Having an affair? Who the heck was Clarinda and why would Dad leave his biggest asset to her?

Disappointment and frustration nearly knocked Vanessa off her feet as she started pacing around the office, running her fingers through her hair.

What was *wrong* with that man? It was one thing to leave the store to Glo, which everyone assumed he'd do. But then he pulled a big shocker by giving it to Vanessa, giving her the closure and peace and the slightest, tiniest feeling that he maybe possibly loved her.

But...he didn't. At all. And maybe he didn't even love Gloria or anyone, because who the heck was Clarinda Smith and why would Dad go out of his way to ruin *everything*?

Did he just want to make a mess? Was the whole

thing just a trick to try and screw up Vanessa's life even more? Was Clarinda even real?

He couldn't possibly have been that evil…right?

"Vanessa, I am so, so sorry." Barry stood up, picking up his briefcase. "I wish there was something I could do."

"Can you find something out? Who she is and what my dad had to do with her?"

"We will be investigating starting tomorrow. My firm has good connections with a PI who will get on it, but, nothing is going to happen overnight."

Sadness weighed on her as she pulled in a breath, her heart pounding in her chest. "What does this mean for me?"

He paused, giving her a look of sympathy. "It means that you have no right to this property. You can't run a business here. Even if we don't know yet who this person is, legally, this building isn't yours."

Vanessa blinked as her vision swam, her eyes filling with tears. She had a million questions, but not one of them would solve this problem.

"What do I do now?" she asked Barry in a quivering, broken voice.

"Everything has to go on hold until we find the rightful owner of the property. Depending on who she is, you could try to buy it from her, but—"

"I don't have that much money," Vanessa moaned, knowing this property was worth far more than she had on hand. Could she get a loan? Could she…

All she could do right that minute was fight bitter, stinging tears.

"I'm really sorry, Vanessa." He let out a breath before turning toward the door. "I'm as baffled by this as you."

"I'm not just baffled..." She squeezed her eyes shut. "I'm heartbroken."

"Clarinda Smith?" Gloria's expression froze with utter confusion and shock. "You can't be serious, Nessie."

"Does it look like I'm kidding?" Vanessa groaned audibly, flopping back onto the bed in her room.

After Barry came and dropped the horrifying bombshell, she had told Emily and her new staff to put the unpacking on hold and head home for the day, due to an unforeseen emergency.

After locking the store, Vanessa and Emily returned to the beach house. When Emily left to take Ruthie on a walk, Vanessa texted her sister, who showed up as quickly as she could.

Glo had no answers, but plenty of sympathy.

She sat on the edge of the bed and placed a loving hand on Vanessa's leg. "I'm at a loss. I'm completely and totally at a loss."

Vanessa sat up, feeling like her shoulders were carrying a thousand pounds of weight. "Did he mention anything to you about adjusting the will or filing a new one?"

Gloria shook her head with certainty. "No, never. I knew that he'd filed one with Barry, and that was that. You said this was another lawyer?"

"Yeah." Vanessa slumped against the pillows. "In Pensacola. He kept Barry totally in the dark. He got it in the mail today, since he's listed as Dad's legal estate representative or whatever."

"Nessie, this is insane. Absolutely insane." Gloria ran a hand through her hair.

"You're telling me." Vanessa covered her face with her hands and sighed, wishing for the thousandth time since that afternoon that this nightmare would end. "I was so excited, Glo. I really felt like I had found a new purpose, a new direction. Young at Heart was—"

"Don't you dare talk about Young at Heart in the past tense." She pointed a stern finger. "We're not just going to give up. We don't even know who Clarinda is yet."

"She isn't me, and that's all we need to know." Vanessa swallowed. "I can't legally run a business on that property."

"Yet," Glo corrected.

"Unless Dad comes back from the dead and changes the will back, it's pretty set in stone." She stood up, resuming her pacing, around the bedroom this time. "I mean, did he really hate me that much? If he did, why wouldn't he have just left the property to you, like we all assumed he would? It would have been a lot less of a stab in the back."

"Nessie, he didn't hate you..."

"Please." Vanessa shot her sister a "get real" look. "He went out of his way to file two separate wills, with two separate lawyers, in order to remind me that he will never, ever forgive me. Even from the grave."

The truth of that hurt almost as much as losing the property.

Who was Vanessa kidding, thinking that her dying father had decided he loved her after all and wanted to show her that with a surprising inheritance?

"He hated me," she whispered tearfully. "He always did."

"Oh, Vanessa." Glo stood up and held her arms out, giving her younger sister a hug. "Honey, you don't need his approval or forgiveness to let you forgive yourself. That's what truly matters."

Vanessa nodded slowly, her heart feeling like it could actually break. "Oh, man, Cricket's party tomorrow. She was so excited."

Glo gave her a deeply empathetic look, squeezing her hands. "I'll worry about Cricket."

"I just don't get it." She sat down on the floor and pulled out the scrapbook she'd stored under her bed.

"See? That's evidence that he loved you," Gloria insisted, sitting down on the floor next to her.

Vanessa sighed and flipped through the book again, trying to imagine Dad cutting out these articles and magazine pages, highlighting her name and carefully tucking them under the plastic covering of each scrapbook page.

"If he cared about me enough to save all this..." She ran her hands over the yellowed edges of a *People* magazine spread. "Why would he do this with the property? He cared, I mean, he had to...but he didn't. He unforgave me at the very end. Decided I wasn't worth it."

"But then why wouldn't he have just left the property to me, like you said?" Glo asked. "We always assumed he was going to."

"Because he knew how golden your heart is, and he knew there was a chance you'd give it to me. If I came back to town or whatever."

Gloria made a dubious face. "I think you're overestimating Dad's foresight and empathy. He didn't think like that."

Vanessa slowly flipped through the pages, stopping at a newspaper profile that the *L.A. Times* had done on her when she was first building a reputation in the fashion world.

Her headshot was in the corner, in black and white. "I remember this day," she said softly, looking at the picture of her thirty-year-old self. "So, so clearly."

"You're so beautiful, Nessie. I'm so sorry this happened."

Vanessa leaned her head on Glo's shoulder. "Thanks."

As she wiped her finger across the layer of plastic to get a better look at her old headshot in the feature article, she noticed how loose it was.

"Gosh, this thing's falling apart."

Vanessa pulled back the plastic covering, which was easy to do, and took out the old newspaper article.

As soon as she lifted it, something fell from behind it.

A small, cardstock square fluttered out of the scrapbook and onto the carpet floor.

"What's that?" Glo asked.

"Don't know. It was stuck behind this article." Vanessa picked up the piece of cardstock, which was old and yellowed and frayed at the edges.

The glint of gold embossed lettering caught her eye as she held it up to read it.

You are cordially invited to the wedding of Clarinda "Violet" Smith and William Patrick Young

"Oh my gosh." Vanessa could hardly breathe as she stared at the words on the fifty-five-year-old wedding invitation. "Clarinda Smith is...*Mom*."

"It can't be." Gloria grabbed the card, staring at it with a gaping jaw and wide eyes. "Mom's name was—"

"Violet." Vanessa pointed at the name on the card. "Evidently, her name was Clarinda, and she just went by Violet." She gave a dry laugh as relief washed over her. "Wouldn't you?"

Of course, it was sad how little she and her sister knew about their late mother. Dad never, ever spoke of her, and they learned quickly not to ever pry.

They just knew she was named Violet, she died in a car accident when they were little, and Dad was so overcome with grief that he moved the girls from Alabama down to Rosemary Beach to start over. That was all they knew...including, evidently, her name.

"Oh, my goodness, Nessie!" Gloria held her hands to her mouth.

"He left the property to Mom..." Vanessa stood up and began to pace once again, her heart thumping and her thoughts circling. "But Mom is *dead*."

"Has been for forty-five years." Glo tapped the

wedding invite against her hand. "Why would he go to an attorney and change his will to leave it to a dead woman?"

"Maybe he was really losing it," Vanessa said hopefully. "Which would mean the original will was valid."

"And the property is yours." Gloria stood up, joining Vanessa eye to eye. "Now do you feel better?"

Had he been that out of it? He drove to Pensacola, hired an attorney, and...

She had to stop questioning it, she decided, flopping on the bed again with a rush of relief and confusion washing over her. "So, this is good, right? I can keep Young at Heart?"

"Yes!" Gloria smiled and nudged her playfully. "This is wonderful! The store is yours, just as it should be."

"But...why would Dad do that?" She sat up, troubled. "You have to admit it's bizarre, even for Dad."

"Yeah, it's more than bizarre." Gloria shrugged. "I wouldn't use the word 'dementia,' but he certainly had his moments. He was really tough to handle toward the end, and honestly? I'd say, yeah, he was losing it a little."

"Enough to drive to Pensacola and change his will with some random attorney? And leave his property to a dead woman?"

"I guess so." Gloria stared at Vanessa, her eyes wide. "There's no other explanation, is there?"

Vanessa thought for a moment, racking her brain for any other imaginable possibility of why Dad would pull this staggering move six weeks before passing away. "No, I suppose there isn't."

"Hey." Glo turned to her, wrapping an arm around her shoulders. "Doesn't matter what crazy old Dad was thinking. Whatever grudges or motives he had, maybe he had just completely lost his mind. The only thing that matters is you get to keep the store."

Vanessa nodded, trying to feel true joy and relief of that. But still, it was all...tainted.

"You're right," she said. "Dad was weird, no need to dwell on him anymore."

"He's taken enough of our time, Nessie. He's siphoned enough of our energy. Let's just be grateful you still have your new dream, yeah? I'll call Barry when I get home and let him know that we figured out who Clarinda is, and the whole thing is just a crazy misunderstanding."

"Are you sure?" Vanessa asked. "I can call him."

Glo waved a hand. "Let me handle it. You run a hot bath, make some tea, and put this emotional day behind you. I'm sure Emily will be home soon and you'll have much to fill her in on."

Beyond grateful, Vanessa gave her sister a big hug, knowing that she was right. It didn't matter what was going through Dad's head. All that mattered was here and now, and she had her store, her future, and her new life.

Chapter Twenty-two

Gloria

As Gloria drove home in the waning evening light, she tried to sort through the complicated storm of emotions swirling through her. She was deeply happy and relieved for Vanessa, who'd finally found a direction —and a home here in Rosemary Beach.

But as Glo turned the steering wheel and pulled into the driveway of her condo, she couldn't help but ask herself the same burning question over and over.

What was Dad thinking?

Yes, he had been aging. He'd certainly become more forgetful and scatterbrained in his advancing years— though he wasn't by any definition old and senile. It was no secret that his mental state spiraled considerably in the last several months of his life, but he wasn't delusional.

He didn't have Alzheimer's. He knew darn well that his wife had died forty-five years ago. If he was ever unstable enough to think otherwise, he'd certainly never made that obvious to Gloria.

She sighed as she went up the walkway to her front door, sliding the key in and walking inside, relieved to be home for the night.

Maybe Dad was more out of it than he'd let on. Maybe he'd just wanted to make a statement about how much he still loved his wife, even decades after she'd passed.

He'd never remarried, after all. Never even dated. He always said Violet was the only woman for him, but that was *all* he said about her.

"Weird," Glo whispered to herself, kicking her sandals off by the front door. She hung up her purse, and walked into the kitchen to warm up her tea kettle. "Weird, weird, weird."

She shook her head as her chamomile and vanilla tea steeped, gathering her thoughts and questions before she picked up her phone to call Barry Martinez.

Barry certainly knew Gloria better than he knew Vanessa, simply because she'd stayed local in Rosemary Beach. So maybe he'd share something else with her. Like whether he had any clue why Dad would do this.

She dialed the phone and held it to her ear, gently swirling the teabag around in the mug of hot water.

"Hey, Gloria." Barry answered the phone with an obvious tone of sympathy and understanding, as if he knew exactly why she was calling, and had definitely expected it.

"Barry, hi."

"I'm guessing you've talked to Vanessa." He sighed audibly. "I know she's seriously broken up about not being able to keep the corner property. That was a shocker."

"Actually, Barry, we found out who Clarinda Smith is, and...it's not going to be an issue."

"What? What do you mean? Who is she? Gosh, I've been racking my brain all day trying to remember if Bill ever mentioned a Clarinda, but came up blank."

"That's because we all know her as Violet," Gloria said softly.

"Your mother? Bill's wife who died before you three moved here?" Barry stammered, his confusion and astonishment palpable even over the phone. "Gloria, that's impossible, she—"

"Died when I was five." Gloria took a sip of tea and set the mug down. "I know. I have no idea why Dad would do this, but problem solved. Vanessa keeps the store. The old will stands?"

"Not exactly. The new will takes precedence, but if the heir to an asset or estate is deceased, then it would be released to next of kin. Which would be you or Vanessa. But..."

"I know," she said quickly, laughing dryly. "It's beyond weird that he did that. Maybe he was just trying to have some dying closure with his wife or...something. I don't know. It doesn't make sense."

"And why would he file the will with a different lawyer and in a different city?" Barry mused.

"Probably because you would have refused to make that change to his will, knowing that my mom is long dead."

"Well, I don't know. He might have just given the

name Clarinda Smith. I'd have never known that was your mother."

"Anyway, he's dead, so we may never know his motive or if he was just out of his mind, but...at least the problem is resolved." Gloria sighed and shook her head.

"Yes, that it is. I'm glad, too," he said. "Vanessa looked like she was just bursting with joy about her shop when I stopped by today. Delivering that news was miserable."

"I can imagine," Glo replied. "Well, no more misery here. Just blue skies ahead."

"Whew. I'm glad we cleared that up." He cleared his throat. "All right, thanks, Gloria. I'll sleep a lot better tonight knowing the mystery is solved."

She chuckled. "You and me both. Bye, Barry."

After hanging up the phone, Gloria took her tea out to the back deck to catch the tail end of the sunset and some fresh air.

She thought long and hard back on her last few months with Dad. He did seem to talk about Mom more. Not a lot, but the occasional comment. Gloria had figured he was just facing his mortality, and thinking about the only woman he'd ever loved.

He never did seem to fully get over his grief. It lingered on and on, making him bitter and sad and deeply lonely. It made sense that she was heavy on his mind in what he might have known, deep in his heart, were his final days.

As Gloria watched the sky turn to night and the moon begin to shine over the Gulf, she remembered the envelope full of "letters from Violet" that was shoved in her nightstand.

She hadn't looked at the letters Mom wrote to Dad, knowing that it would be emotional and that she and Nessie should take that journey together.

But now, she was more curious than ever. What if Viole— Clarinda mentioned something that gave insight into why Dad left his biggest asset to a dead woman? What if there was more to their love story and Mom's life than Glo and Nessie knew?

They hardly knew anything about their mom, and those letters might contain more than they'd ever learned about what she was like.

Maybe she could just take a peek.

ONCE GLORIA finally talked herself into opening the letters, she sat down on the edge of her bed and slid open the drawer of her nightstand.

There it was, an envelope stuffed full with handwritten words from their enigma of a mother—a woman Gloria had never gotten the chance to know, not even her real name, apparently.

She toyed with the envelope, tugged at the seal, and—

The front door opened. "Mom!"

"Daisy! Hi!" Glo shoved the letters away, slammed the drawer, and walked out into the hallway to see a bright and beaming Daisy coming through the front door. "What's going on, girl? You look happy."

And thank God she did, Glo thought to herself. She didn't know if she could physically handle another Kyle-induced breakdown.

"I am happy, because..." Daisy sang the word. "My wedding dress is done! And I wanted to show you a picture, here." She reached in her pocket and pulled out her phone. "They'll still need to make final alterations a month out, but this is—"

"Wait a second." Gloria's heart dropped hard and her stomach suddenly felt sick. "Daisy...your wedding dress is *done*? I haven't even..." Her voice wavered as sadness pressed on her. "I haven't even seen it."

Daisy had been up to New York with Linda three times for custom wedding dress consultations and fittings, but Gloria had been assured that when it came time to do the final fitting, she'd be joining the trip.

Daisy pulled the phone away and frowned. "Yes, you have. You saw the pictures and I FaceTimed you at the most recent fitting in New York."

"But you said that there would be one more trip to New York. You told me you were flying back up there next month and I would be coming with you. I planned for it, Daisy, I...I..." Her chest tightened as hurt hit her like a gut punch. "I was supposed to be a part of this. It's your *wedding dress*."

"Mom, I know, but the designer determined that she didn't need to do another fitting. Everything came together perfectly, and they're shipping us the dress." She frowned, a look of frustration in her eyes. "Why are you freaking out about this? I thought you'd be excited..."

"Freaking out?" Gloria took in a shaky breath and turned around, pacing through her living room, fighting tears. "My daughter has a wedding dress and I haven't even seen it!"

"You've seen pictures," she shot back, her tone rising.

"Daisy, I'm your mother! I should have been there. I should have been in the bridal shop with you, watching you try on dresses and laughing together and sharing those moments. I feel like..." She swallowed hard. "I feel like so much of this has been stolen from me."

"Oh, my gosh, Mom, you can't be serious." Daisy rolled her eyes. "Stolen? Linda had a designer she'd already planned to have make my dress ever since Kyle and I got engaged. I hardly tried anything on, it's all custom."

"Oh, believe me, I know."

Daisy furrowed her brow. "What's that supposed to mean?"

"Nothing, Daisy." She threw her hands up, surrendering to this devastating disappointment and the harsh reality of what had happened between her and her daughter. "The dress is custom, the chef is world-renowned, the florist is probably some sort of magical flower guru who Linda is flying in from Switzerland or something."

Daisy made a face. "What?"

"My point is, it's all just too *good* for me. It's been made very obvious to me, by everyone involved, that I have no place in the planning of an event of this caliber, and I don't fit in enough with Linda and her millions to even see my daughter's wedding dress."

"You're mad because I'm having a nice wedding." She clicked her tongue and nodded. "Seriously?"

"No, Daisy, I'm mad because you're having a nice wedding that I'm not a part of!"

"Of course you're a part of it! I came over her as fast as I could to show you the final dress! You came to the chef tasting!"

"Where I was made to feel like some sort of loser outcast."

Daisy closed her eyes. "Mom, I'm sorry. I know I'm being nasty and...I don't mean to be. I just feel like you're being so unsupportive, and it hurts."

Gloria gritted her teeth. "I've been completely pushed out of this whole thing. And you know what? I've tried to keep my mouth shut. I really have."

"Really? Because all I've gotten from you since the day I got engaged was doubts and negativity."

Gloria's breath hitched in her throat. "I do have doubts," she said softly, her voice wavering. "I have doubts about a boy who makes my daughter cry for three straight days and thinks he can fix it with a shiny car and a half-hearted apology."

"He was sorry, Mom!" She crossed her arms. "Sometimes it feels like you're, I don't know, jealous or something."

"Daisy, no." She groaned, shaking her head with frustration. "I'm *hurt* by you. And Linda. And Kyle. And this whole thing. None of it is what I pictured."

"Well, I didn't picture you and Dad getting a divorce when I was ten but I dealt with it, and you can deal with this, too."

Wow. That one cut deep.

Gloria winced, drawing back from the impact of what her daughter had just said to her. "This isn't about your father and me. Don't bring him into this. This is about how I've been treated and how you're ditching me for that entitled kid and his obnoxious family."

Her jaw dropped as she stared at Gloria, silent for a full thirty seconds. Then she turned and picked up her purse.

"You know what, Mom? If you're going to hate my fiancé and my soon-to-be in-laws, despite how much they've done for me and the fact that they're giving us this beautiful wedding, then...maybe it's better if you don't come at all."

Gloria stood frozen in the middle of the living room, feeling like the ground was going to open up and swallow her whole. "You don't..." Her voice cracked. "You don't mean that."

"It's just that..." She pressed her hands against her lips, composing herself. Then she looked at Gloria with tears in her eyes. "I feel like you're not even happy for me."

"Of course I'm happy—"

"It's my *wedding* day, and I'm seriously afraid that your true feelings toward Kyle's family will ruin it. I don't want that to happen." On a deep sigh, Daisy swung the front door open. "I'm gonna go."

New Beginnings in Rosemary Beach 281

Gloria stood still while a sob choked out of her throat when Daisy walked out the door.

What just happened? Had she lost her daughter forever?

She began to weep as she walked into her bedroom and sat down on the edge of her bed, wondering how she could have possibly gone so wrong.

What had gotten into Daisy? And why was it getting worse and worse every day?

Gloria had just kept telling herself that Daisy was going to come around and be herself again and they could go back to how they always were.

But this wasn't just a rich, entitled fiancé and a controlling mother-in-law-to-be. This was Daisy's doing. She was choosing them over her own mother, and Gloria was left helpless, alone, and broken.

Chapter Twenty-three

Emily

Emily was, once again, caught in a spiral of thoughts and worries, but with some slow-breathing techniques and quiet prayers, she was able to stay calm and relatively hopeful, despite the circumstances.

Still no luck finding any kind of somewhat affordable legal help, and Doug's lawyer was an aggressive shark who wouldn't leave her alone.

He was in rare form today, having already called her five times. She hadn't answered. She couldn't bear to deal with the stress and panic that it induced. Her only hope was a thin one—Cricket had told her she might have an attorney who would at least look at her case as a favor. She'd emailed all the legal documentation to her grandmother, but tried not to put too much hope into it.

Today, her phone was on silent, because Cricket and Vanessa were hosting a gathering of family and friends here at the beach house to celebrate the upcoming opening of Young at Heart.

It was the big party that Cricket had been talking about since Emily stepped foot in Rosemary Beach, and she wasn't going to let anything ruin it.

Emily took a long look in the mirror, smiling at her

reflection. Her hair was pretty again, her face had color and she'd come back to a healthy weight.

She felt confident in some makeup and enjoyed picking out her clothes. After spending so long living in basically fight-or-flight mode, it was fun to just enjoy life again.

Not that she could enjoy it for long, she reminded herself, as the phone in her pocket taunted her. She knew if she pulled it out and checked her email, she'd have another pushy note from Doug's lawyer, threatening to make everything worse for her if she didn't just agree and let the charges and restraining order go.

"Hey, you." Vanessa knocked softly on the open bathroom door, peeking in.

"Hi." Emily smiled.

Vanessa looked down at her daughter's outfit—white jeans, a cropped floral tank, and strappy wedges. "Oh, my gosh. Cute!"

"Really?" Emily lifted a playful shoulder. "Means a lot coming from you."

"Oh, please." Vanessa flicked a hand.

"When's everyone supposed to get here?"

"Within the next half hour or so." Vanessa, who also looked fabulous in a light wash denim skirt, purple halter top, and sparkly sandals, leaned against the doorway of Emily's en suite bathroom. "Any updates with, you know, stuff?"

Emily wrinkled her nose. "If by updates you mean Doug's sociopathic lawyer calling me incessantly, saying that if I don't drop all charges and agree to his terms there will be 'severe consequences.'" She held up air quotes and groaned with anxiety.

"That's so threatening!" Vanessa's eyes widened. "Does it scare you at all?"

Emily thought about the question. "I don't think 'scared' is the right word to describe how I feel. I'm frustrated, stuck, trapped...and many other things. But he doesn't scare me anymore."

"I hate that you're all the other things, though."

Emily shrugged, trying not to let the heaviness of her messy divorce weigh down the happy day. "No sadness today. This is a special celebration, and Cricket is so jazzed. I can't bear to bring any negativity into her life."

"It's a little too late for that." Vanessa pressed her lips together, stepping into the bathroom.

"What do you mean?" Emily shook her head, confused. "I mean, I know she's worried about me and the divorce situation, but that shouldn't bring down the whole—"

"No, no, no. Not you. Or Cricket."

Emily angled her head and frowned, having absolutely no idea what Vanessa was referring to.

"It's Glo and Daisy. Glo called me this morning in tears. I haven't seen her because she had to go to the diner, but apparently they had a massive fight."

Emily gave a sympathetic whimper, her heart hurting for poor Gloria, who had been bottling up all of her pain and disappointment about Daisy's wedding for quite some time.

"About the wedding or Kyle or both?" she asked.

"The wedding, mostly, but Kyle is at the root of it." Vanessa ran a hand through her hair, her brows knitting together as she thought about her sister. "Apparently, it got pretty ugly. Daisy told her not to come."

"To this party?" she asked, confused.

"To the wedding."

"*What*?" Emily suddenly forgot entirely about her own life, and realized how deeply she'd grown to care about her aunt and the cousin she'd only met a few weeks ago. "I'm sure it was just in the heat of the moment. She'll take it back."

"Hopefully. But Glo is wrecked."

"I can imagine. Is she still coming today?"

Vanessa sucked in a breath. "They're supposed to both be coming, so we'll see. Oh! I hear the door opening."

"Cricket's here, I'm guessing."

Vanessa laughed softly. "You've learned fast."

Emily followed her mother out into the living room of their beach house, which felt bright and airy with the sliders open to the back deck and beach. She closed her eyes for a moment and willed herself to enjoy this afternoon, this celebration, this new life and family she'd been so deeply blessed to find.

Even though stress weighed on her and anxiety bubbled below the surface, Emily already had more than she ever thought she would, and she really did mean it when she'd told Vanessa that she wasn't afraid.

She might not be free just yet, but she would be, even

though she knew the phone in her pocket was silently lighting up with threats.

An hour or so into the party, Emily was sufficiently distracted from her problems, and she hadn't even looked at her phone once. She'd been occupied every second meeting tons of Cricket and Glo's friends, people who'd known Vanessa when she got pregnant and were stunned to see the product of such a scandal standing in front of them, twenty-nine years old.

It was kind of bizarre and also completely fun, and Emily felt like she had, yet again, stepped into a whole new corner of the world, and was loving every second of it.

She was vaguely aware of both Daisy and Gloria's presence at the party, but she hadn't seen them talk.

She'd been fairly preoccupied by the two hilarious and wonderful women who proudly wore the title of "Cricket's best friends."

"And, darling, you just tell us if there is anything you need." Paula placed her hand on Emily's arm and gave her a sincere smile.

"Anything at all," Shelly added with a nod of certainty. "In case it isn't obvious, we kind of own this town."

Paula nodded. "We run it."

"So if anyone bothers you—"

"Or interests you," Paula teased with a playful wink. "Let us know."

Emily laughed, debating for half a second about asking these all-knowing locals what they knew about Reed Collins, a.k.a. R.C. Anderson...but she'd kept his secret this long. And being someone who knew what it's like to need trustworthy secret keepers, she didn't intend to break it, even if she was fairly certain she might never see the guy again.

"Will do, thank you." Emily smiled at Shelly and Paula. "It was so great to meet you both."

"Likewise, honey." Paula glanced over her shoulder. "Now, if you'll excuse us, Beatrice Snyder just walked in, and we need to be a buffer before she beelines for Cricket."

"They've been feuding for years," Shelly explained.

Emily lifted her hand to her forehead and gave a mock salute. "Godspeed."

After her lovely and entertainingly hilarious conversation with Cricket's knitting pals, Emily noticed Daisy alone in the kitchen, pouring a glass of iced tea, and she walked over to talk to her.

"Hey, how's it going?" Emily grabbed a plastic cup and got some tea of her own.

"It's...going." Daisy sipped her drink and glanced around. "Honestly, I'm just waiting for an acceptable time to leave."

Emily frowned. "I heard you had a fight with your mom," she said, lowering her voice and hoping for the nice openness that she'd gotten from Daisy last week at the beach. "Is everything okay?"

Daisy sighed, trying to play off a sassy eyeroll that told the world she didn't care, but the sadness in her brown eyes gave away her real feelings. "Let me guess—she told you and Aunt Vanessa that I'm horrible and mean and nasty and that I'm ditching her for Kyle's family or whatever. Something along those lines?"

"Actually, I haven't even talked to Gloria much today. I only got a super brief story from my mom, and I don't think it included any of those awful things about you." She sipped the tea. "Except maybe the whole 'ditching her for Kyle's family' part."

Daisy bit her lip, glancing off into the distance, looking almost as if she was fighting tears. "It's not like that. It's really not. I just..." She turned her gaze back to meet Emily's, and her eyes grew misty. "I never meant to hurt her, but I have to live my own life, too, you know? It's like she doesn't even want me to get married and have my own future. She wants me to just stay her little girl forever. I sound so mean, I know. I've *been* so mean."

Emily sighed, looking across the living room at Gloria, who was in the corner chatting with some friends, looking as if every smile and laugh was completely forced. She was hurting, but so was Daisy.

"Now I don't know what to do," Daisy continued. "I feel like it's all just screwed up beyond repair."

"Believe me, it's not screwed up beyond repair. Nothing ever is. I mean, my mom gave me up for adoption when I was a baby, and now we're both adults, getting to know each other and starting a business together."

Daisy laughed softly. "It is pretty amazing how much you and Aunt Vanessa have just, like, gotten over everything."

"I don't hold anything against her." Emily shrugged. "But honestly? I wish I'd had a mother guiding me through all those years of my life. I had my grandmother, but it wasn't the same. She didn't warn me about Doug—or if she did, I didn't listen. It really wasn't the same as having your very own mother."

Daisy chewed her lip and looked at Gloria, her eyes darkening with guilt and shame. "I said some awful things. I don't know how to take them back. I just got so mad and hurt and... I don't know."

Emily gave her cousin an encouraging smile. "You'll figure it out. She's your mom."

"And how do I balance everything once I'm married to Kyle? She hates him and his family. And, like, I get it, it's tough for her. But I'm going to be a part of this family, and, yeah it's different, but it's what I want."

Emily wasn't too convinced of that, but now was not the time. "Look, there are still a few months before the wedding. I think you ought to just try to make sure Gloria gets totally included in everything, so she really feels involved and like she's a part of it. I think it's hard that she's been so sidelined."

Daisy swallowed, nodding. "Linda just...she takes over everything, you know? She's a human bulldozer, and loaded. The money gives her all the power."

"Oh, I'm sure," Emily said with a laugh. "I know the type."

"She just has so many connections, and—"

The doorbell rang, catching their attention.

"Come on in!" Cricket shouted. "It's open!"

Assuming it was just another one of Cricket's million friends who had arrived a bit late, Emily turned back around to keep her focus on her cousin.

But the look on Daisy's face instantly made it clear that the person who'd rung the bell was not someone she —or anyone—expected to see.

Emily turned around to see a man walking into the beach house. In his mid-forties, he had dark hair, wore a button-down, slacks, and a serious look on his face.

A hushed silence came over the entire lively party, and everyone turned with obvious astonishment at the new arrival.

"Oh, my heavens!" Cricket's cry of joy and surprise broke the silence as she dashed forward and threw her arms around him. "Noah!"

Noah, Emily thought to herself, her heart pounding. *That's...my father.*

Emily staggered back, gasping with shock as she watched him greet the large group and hug his mom.

She slowly scanned the room and found Vanessa, who looked like she'd seen a ghost, with her jaw gaping and her face pale with shock.

This was about to get really, really complicated. But that didn't stop a zing of excitement at the thought of meeting her biological father.

"Oh, my gosh," Daisy whispered, grabbing Emily's arm. "I just realized he's your dad."

Emily laughed nervously, jitters and adrenaline making her heady. "Yeah, he is. I've never met him, but—"

"I think you're about to." Daisy picked up her cup and gave Emily a "good luck" nod before turning and walking away.

"Emily, my dear." Cricket walked over, holding Noah's arm like he was a trophy. "There is someone very, very important that I would like you to meet."

Emily lifted her gaze, making eye contact with the man who was responsible for half of her genetics. His eyes were blue and his hair was dark, and she definitely didn't see any of herself in his features, the way she did with Vanessa.

But it didn't matter, this was him. This was her dad.

"Hi, Emily." Noah studied her, blinking back with obviously the same feeling that she had.

She felt a little of the same dizziness that wobbled her when she'd met Vanessa, but even more intensely.

"Hi." Emily smiled nervously. "It's nice to meet you."

"You...wow." He stared at her, silent for a moment, then a shaky smile pulled. "Vanessa Young 2.0." Noah shook his head, going back to that very serious expression he'd been wearing when he walked in. "I need to talk to you."

Surprised, confused, and a bit disappointed, Emily swallowed. "Oh, um, okay. Sure."

For some reason, it didn't seem like he was saying he

wanted to get to know her or learn about his long-lost daughter. It seemed serious. Everything about him seemed serious.

"Let's go outside." Noah gestured back toward the front door, and Emily and Cricket followed him out.

What was this about? Her mind raced with possibilities and curiosity as they stepped onto the front porch of the beach house, and the three of them stood together.

"What's going on, honey?" Cricket asked Noah. "I mean, your visit is such a surprise! If you had wanted to come and meet Emily, you should have told me." She nudged his arm. "I would have arranged—"

"I just came here to tell her something," he said, his gaze flicking away, almost as if he didn't want to look at Emily.

Was he not excited to meet her?

She tried not to feel hurt.

"Here." Noah reached into a backpack that he'd left on the front porch and pulled out a packet of papers. "If you sign and initial on all the marked spots, you'll be divorced in thirty days."

Emily's breath caught in her throat and she nearly choked on shock. "I'm sorry...*what?*"

Cricket gasped, her hands rising to cover her mouth in slow motion. "Noah...did you..."

He looked at Emily, a bit reluctantly. "I pushed your case to the front of the line at one of our partner firms that deals with family law. I was able to have the divorce expedited by way of finalizing it in Santo Domingo. It takes a month to finalize, but it will be done."

Emily shook her head, blinking back. "The Dominican Republic?"

"Yes. Due to their policies, there's a loophole in the waiting period for a divorce and my guys were able to get this done in a matter of a few days. All you have to do is sign."

Emily felt like she couldn't see straight. "And...the charges?"

"The defendant—Douglas—is fully facing them and likely some jail time, and that's where the justice system comes in. Your restraining order is up after five years, but can be renewed if you think necessary. I'll give you the number of an attorney who will handle that for you."

"And Doug's lawyer...he agreed to all of this?"

Noah almost laughed. "Not exactly. But he's a pretty small fish compared to the guys I had on your case. With the expedited divorce in the DR, he didn't have much of a choice, or else things would have gotten a lot worse for his client."

Emily looked down at the papers, where small highlighter marks indicated where she had to sign. Nearly blinded by shock and swaying on her feet, she looked back up at Noah and over to Cricket. "This...this is real?"

Finally, for the first time, Noah smiled, and she saw a hint of herself in his face. "Yes, this is real. My mom told me about what you were dealing with and, you know, I figured I could help out."

"Oh, you were the lawyer who agreed to look at the paperwork," she said as the truth dawned on her.

Cricket gave a sly smile.

"Thank you, Noah," Emily said on a soft sigh. "I don't even know what to say. I'm so..." her voice cracked as she looked back down at the divorce papers. In her hands, she held freedom. "I'm so grateful."

Noah nodded, conflict and dissonance evident in his eyes. It didn't take much for Emily to realize that he was not ready to dive into a relationship with her the way that Vanessa had been.

But he cared enough to do this massive, monumental favor for her, so maybe part of him was curious. He was fighting it, though, Emily could tell. Maybe Noah never had wanted to be a father. Maybe he had. Maybe it was about Vanessa.

Vanessa...who was ten feet away in the house.

Super weird, but Emily didn't care. Right now, she didn't have a worry in the world. How could she? She was holding her ticket to true freedom, and it had been delivered by the most unlikely source—her very own father.

"Well." Cricket took Noah's arm with one hand and Emily's with the other. "It's a darn good thing we're already having a party, isn't it?"

"Yes," Emily said with a soft laugh, still completely bewildered as she tried to wrap her head around the events of the past ten minutes. "I suppose it is."

Cricket sighed as she looked back and forth between the two of them. "I have never been so happy, I tell you. I'm finally having the party I've been dying for, my granddaughter is free from her troubles, and my son has returned!"

Noah chuckled softly. "Mom, I, uh, I can't stay in town for very long. In fact, I should probably get going..."

Emily felt her heart sink an inch or two from cloud nine.

Did her own birth father really want that little to do with her? If that was the case, why do all of this pro bono work to save her?

"Nonsense, Noah. You can come in, enjoy yourself, and spend the night at my place. You know I have a sleeper sofa for this very reason."

"Mom, I..." He looked at Cricket, then glanced at Emily, something shifting in his gaze. "All right. I'll stay."

Hope bubbled up in Emily's chest as they walked back inside. She felt like she was floating, the image of those signed papers bringing her tears of joy. In the corner, she saw Daisy and Gloria talking, which was a good sign. Maybe they'd make up.

Then her gaze landed on Vanessa, and Emily watched as she and Noah—*her parents*—looked at each other for the first time in thirty years.

Chapter Twenty-four

Vanessa

Vanessa had thought many, many times about how she would feel if the day ever came that she laid eyes on Noah Ellison again. She'd pondered it during sleepless nights in L.A., sitting by the window of her crappy studio apartment, watching the city lights and wondering where he was.

She'd thought about him when things with Aaron went sour, and Vanessa would lay far away from him in their king-size bed, surrounded by emptiness in a ten-thousand-square-foot box in Malibu.

She'd especially thought about him when she returned to Rosemary Beach, haunted by the echoes of their teenaged laughter and memories of their stolen moments that seemed to haunt the beaches and boardwalks.

But somehow, when the moment finally came, it hit her like a high-speed train with more power and force than she could have ever imagined.

Noah walked into that party and Vanessa's world stopped turning. She didn't even really know why. It wasn't that much of a shock that he would be here.

Cricket was his mother, after all. But for some reason, it threw Vanessa for a loop.

Maybe it was how serious he looked—with that faraway gaze in his eyes that masked an obvious level of discomfort. Why had he come? Did Cricket know he was coming? It was pretty in character to assume that she would have orchestrated the entire thing, but the older woman had seemed so shocked by his arrival that Vanessa didn't think that was the case.

He'd aged well, she thought as she watched Cricket introduce Noah to Emily and wondered what they had said to each other, how he felt. But he *had* aged, with threads of silver hair and crow's feet and a slightly softer face than he'd had as a teenager.

After the three of them had gone outside, she turned to Glo, no words necessary. She'd assured her sister she was fine, but this didn't feel...fine.

Gloria stepped away and after what felt like an eternity, Noah, Cricket, and Emily walked back in through the front door, and it was impossible to miss the fact that Emily was beaming.

What had he said to her? Did he want to be an all-involved father all of a sudden? How would Vanessa handle that? Oh, God, was he staying in Rosemary Beach for good now that his long-lost daughter was here?

"Look! Look!" Emily rushed over to Vanessa, her face flushed pink with joy.

"What is it?" Vanessa tried to focus her attention on Emily, and not keep glancing back up at Noah in the entryway.

"These are my divorce papers." Emily was breathless as she waved a stack of pages around in front of them. "Noah got some very, very powerful lawyers to handle my divorce in the Dominican Republic and expedited it and all I have to do is sign! Can you believe it?"

Vanessa took the papers with shaking hands as she processed what she'd just heard, her eyes slowly lifting to see him—the only man she'd ever truly loved—looking right back at her. "Emily. This is…"

"Incredible? I know!" Emily took the papers back. "Cricket did this, you know. She reached out to him, and he fixed it and— Oh! Vanessa! I've never had a family like this. Where's Gloria?" she glanced around. "I've got to tell Gloria!"

Vanessa smiled at Emily, trying to keep her eyes fixed on her daughter and not on Noah, who was walking toward her as they spoke. "Yes, go tell her! She's going to be so happy for you."

Emily gave Vanessa a big hug. "Cheers to new beginnings, right?" she gushed.

Vanessa's gaze flicked up at Noah and she felt her heart skip a beat, just like it always did.

"Cheers to that," Vanessa said softly, finally looking Noah straight in the eyes as he stood in front of her.

"Hey, Ness."

His voice washed over her like a wave of familiarity—the chill of nostalgia and memories of the life she'd walked away from flashing in front of her.

"Hey, Noah." She studied him, not surprised that he'd aged like fine wine. Fit and tall and as handsome as ever, he was the grown-up, successful, mature version of the boy who stole her heart and never truly gave it back. "It's good to see you. You look...great."

"So do you," he said with no hesitation. "I'm really sorry to hear about your father. I know the relationship you two had was...complicated."

And there he was, diving into the personal and real. No small talk about jobs and weather. Not with Nessie and Noah.

"It was nonexistent, really." Vanessa pushed some hair away from her face. "But it's okay. I'm doing well. Coming back here has been really, really good for me."

He angled his head. "So the rumors are true, huh? You're here for good?"

Vanessa nodded. "I'm opening a store. A clothing boutique, in my dad's old spot. That's sort of what this party was supposed to be for." She gestured around.

"Until I crashed it. Whoops." He smiled, that crooked, sly, Noah smile that was familiar and...adorable. Time certainly hadn't changed that.

"You didn't crash it." Vanessa glanced over at Emily, who was hugging Glo. "You turned it into a divorce party for my daughter, which is way better, anyway."

His eyes darkened. "*Our* daughter, technically."

"Right," Vanessa said quickly, shaking her head. "She's amazing, Noah. She's brave and smart and as resilient as can be. She's running the entire business for me. We're doing it together."

"So I've heard. Vanessa, when you gave her up for adoption, didn't you sign papers? Wasn't it sealed?"

Worry and disappointment crept over her. "It was private, not sealed. And she came to me as an adult. Which is allowed."

On a sigh, he gestured her into the hallway, ostensibly for privacy.

Uncertain where this was going, she followed, her throat tight.

"So, uh, look," he started. "I get that you two have reconnected. Or, I guess, connected for the first time ever. But just because you're able to erase the past and forget about it doesn't mean I am. This is really awkward for me, Ness. It's really hard. *You're* the one who wanted to give her up."

Suddenly, Vanessa's knees went weak. "I was sixteen, Noah. So young and—"

"And you never came back." His eyes looked smoky with emotion and memories. "You never came back *like you promised*."

"I couldn't! My dad—"

"You could have, and you know it."

Vanessa couldn't believe they were having this conversation here or, frankly, at all. "Noah, I have a lot of regrets in my life, but I've started a new chapter and dwelling on the past isn't helping anybody."

"The past?" Noah notched his head in Emily's direction. "The past isn't gone. She's standing in the living room."

"Emily is a person, Noah. She's more than just a reminder of our mistakes and immaturity." Vanessa swallowed. "Getting to know her has been one of my greatest joys. And...I did come back. Look." She offered a smile and a soft laugh in a weak attempt to lighten this interaction. "I'm here. And I brought Emily."

"Thirty years too late." He pressed his lips together. "I'm glad I could help her out, but...this is too tough for me. Seeing her, and...and you..." He pinched the bridge of his nose, frowning with distress. "I thought I could deal with this, but I don't know."

"I know, it's different for me, too, but..." She shrugged, giving him a playful nudge. "It's just history, right?"

He leveled his gaze with hers. "Yeah. Just history."

As she leaned back and felt her mind race with thoughts, Vanessa realized that her dad was most definitely not the only man who'd held a grudge against her for all these years.

Noah Ellison had not forgiven her. And that just might be the most painful reality yet.

"It was that awkward, huh?" Glo made a face as she handed Vanessa a wine—sometimes tea just wasn't enough—and they sat down together to debrief once the party had finished.

Emily and Ruthie were off on a beach walk with Daisy, Cricket had gone back to her loft with Noah, and all the guests had said their goodbyes and congratulations. That left Vanessa, Gloria, and the need to talk it all out.

"I don't even know if awkward is the right word." Vanessa curled her legs up on the sofa, sipping the wine and thinking. "Nothing with Noah is ever *awkward*, you know? Even with all the time that's passed, we know each other deeply. It was more than awkward. He seemed...strained."

"Well, that eighty-hour-a-week job in Miami will do that to a person." She sipped from her glass, joining Vanessa on the couch. "I'm surprised his hair wasn't more gray."

"He looked good, didn't he?" Vanessa made a face, laughing as she and her sister looked at each other. "It was nice to see him, and after what he did for Emily? It's hard to have anything but positive feelings about him, even if our long-awaited reunion left me with more questions than answers."

"Who knows? Maybe he'll come around." Gloria lifted a shoulder. "If he's the golden-hearted Noah we all know him to be, he won't be able to resist getting to know his only daughter. He'll want a relationship with her."

Vanessa shook her head. "Doesn't seem like it. I don't know, Glo, it's weird. I'd just always assumed Noah would be fine. But he never forgave me." She leaned back in the couch as the reality of her takeaway from the day began to crystallize.

Glo listened intently, waiting for her to continue.

"All this time I was so obsessed with getting forgiveness from Dad, it never occurred to me that Noah would still be broken about it, after all these years." She blew out a soft sigh. "I never really thought that his forgiveness was what I should have been chasing all along. And I didn't, and it's way too late. Wow, I really made a mess of it, didn't I."

"A little bit of a mess, but it's getting cleaned up more and more every day," Glo said

with a loving laugh.

Vanessa wasn't so convinced things would ever be clean between her and Noah, but that was a worry for another day. "Anyway, enough about me. Speaking of cleaning up messes, did you and Daisy work things out?"

"Well, she apologized, and I could tell she felt bad." Gloria lifted a shoulder. "Not that I want her to feel bad. Ever. But it was nice that she cared. We both cried a bit and hugged each other and I think we're on the right track."

Vanessa placed a hand on her sister's arm. "Good."

"But I don't know. As long as she's marrying Kyle, I fear there's more turmoil ahead."

She nodded. "There's always going to be turmoil ahead. What matters is that we have each other to get through it all with. And that's more than I've had in a really, really long time."

"Aw, my Messy Nessie." Glo smiled, wrapping her arm around Vanessa and pulling her in for a hug. "Speaking of going through things together. How about we finally read those letters from Violet to Dad? I brought them."

"Oh, gosh." Vanessa laughed dryly. "I'm not sure how much more I can handle."

"I know that, but I can't wait any longer."

Vanessa took a deep breath, already curious and slightly anxious about where Glo was going with this. "Okay. Let's do it. I can't believe you've waited this long!"

"I wanted to do it with you," Glo explained. "And I knew we had to wait until things had settled down emotionally. We hardly know anything about Mom"—she made a face—"er, Clarinda. Thank goodness she didn't give either of us *that* name."

Vanessa shook her head. "He never wanted us to know about her. Always shut down questions and conversations when you or I would bring her up."

"That he did. And eventually, of course, we just stopped asking." Gloria sighed. "But these letters could tell us things about her. Her favorite color, her favorite food, the type of music she and Dad used to dance to."

"Plus," Vanessa added, "maybe they'll give us a clue as to why she went by Violet instead of Clarinda."

"Or why Dad left the property to her when she's been dead forty-five years." Gloria stood up. "They're in my bag. I'll be right back."

"Okay."

Vanessa smiled wistfully, thinking about the mythical enigma that was her late mother. Having been an infant when she died, and Dad displaying little to no evidence of Violet, she was kind of thrilled to get a chance to see her handwriting and know more about her.

Glo returned with what was, indeed, a fully stuffed manila envelope, and showed Vanessa the writing in the corner that said, "Letters from Violet."

"All right, Clarinda," Vanessa joked. "Let's see who

you really are."

Together, the two sisters gently tore open the seal and pulled out a stack of folded letters—dozens and dozens of them smashed together in the envelope.

The papers were all different stationery, yellowed and frayed around the edges.

Vanessa felt her heart rate pick up as she and Glo began to slowly pull them apart, revealing line after line of an elegant cursive penmanship.

Mom.

She didn't even know where to begin as her eyes grew a bit misty looking at some of the only evidence they'd ever seen of their mother's unfairly short life.

"Wow," Gloria whispered, clearly feeling as mystified as Vanessa. "Do you think they're in any kind of order?"

"When are they from?"

"They're dated, or at least some of them are." Gloria held up the letter that was at the top of the stack, pointing to the date in the corner. "January 12th, 1980."

"Oh, wow." Vanessa took it slowly, staring at the words, "Dearest William" at the top. "I wonder what—wait a second." She squinted at the date in the corner. "Did you say the date on this was 1980?"

"Yeah..."

"Gloria." Vanessa dropped the letter and stared at her sister. "Didn't Mom die in 1979? In December, right? The year I was born, because I was a baby. That was '79."

"Hold on." Glo grabbed the letter and looked again at the clear 1980 in the corner.

In a second, the women began sifting through the

pile, reading the year at the top of each letter out loud.

"1981. 1982."

"1984...'85...1990!"

"Vanessa." Gloria's voice quivered as she looked at her sister, her eyes wide with fear and astonishment. "What does this mean?"

Vanessa swallowed hard, an eerie uneasiness settling over her as she prepared herself to say something she'd never, ever thought she'd utter.

"I think it means that..." She drew in a shuddering breath, taking Gloria's hand. "Mom didn't die in a car accident when we were little."

Glo blinked at her, cheeks pale and eyes wide.

"Based on how recent the dates on these letters are..." Vanessa gulped, chills swirling across her skin. "She might even still be alive."

For a long moment, neither of them could speak as they tried—and failed—to process this news.

"Nessie," Glo whispered.

"I know, I know. We have to...find her."

"Or find out what really happened to her."

They grasped hands and looked at each other, no words necessary. Alive or dead, they had to find out the truth about their mother. No matter what it meant or how much it hurt. They had to know.

"We can do it," Glo said softly.

"Together," Vanessa agreed.

Because they knew they could do anything together, even face the fact that they might have been lied to for their entire lives.

Don't miss **Old Friends in Rosemary Beach: Book 2 in the Young at Heart series!**

The sun-washed saga continues as Vanessa reconnects with Noah Ellison, the only man she's ever truly loved, and the two of them wade through a rocky reunion. With Noah back in town, Emily is now getting to know her biological father, bringing on a fresh set of challenges and excitement as her new life with her birth parents unfolds.

Gloria and Daisy's once-tight bond as mother and daughter reaches a breaking point with Daisy's wedding looming, and Gloria struggles to save the fragile relationship and protect her daughter from making a tragic mistake.

All the while, Vanessa and Gloria dig deep into the truth about their mother's death, uncovering shocking revelations and secrets that could change their lives forever.

Through everything, the women of Rosemary Beach stick together and lean on each other, proving that all wounds can be healed with sisterhood, motherhood, friendship, and a little help from the beach.

The Young at Heart Series

New Beginnings in Rosemary Beach (Book 1)
Old Friends in Rosemary Beach (Book 2)
Golden Sunsets in Rosemary Beach (Book 3)
And stay tuned...there will be more. Sign up for my newsletter or watch my social media for updates, new covers, release dates, and more!

Looking for more Cecelia Scott books? Don't miss the Sweeney House series, now complete at seven books, and available in digital, paperback, and audio.

Introduction To The Sweeney House

The Sweeney House is a landmark inn on the shores of Cocoa Beach, built and owned by the same family for decades. After the unexpected passing of their beloved patriarch, Jay, this family must come together like never before. They may have lost their leader, but the Sweeneys are made of strong stuff. Together on the island paradise where they grew up, this family meets every challenge with hope, humor, and heart, bathed in sunshine and the unconditional love they learned from their father.

Cocoa Beach Cottage - book 1
Cocoa Beach Boardwalk – book 2
Cocoa Beach Reunion – book 3
Cocoa Beach Sunrise – book 4
Cocoa Beach Bakery – book 5
Cocoa Beach Cabana – book 6
Cocoa Beach Bride – book 7

For release dates, preorder alerts, updates and more, sign up for my newsletter! Or go to www.ceceliascott.com and follow me on Facebook!

About the Author

Cecelia Scott is an author of light, bright women's fiction that explores family dynamics, heartfelt romance, and the emotional challenges that women face at all ages and stages of life. Her debut series, Sweeney House, is set on the shores of Cocoa Beach, where she lived for more than twenty years. Her books capture the salt, sand, and spectacular skies of the area and reflect her firm belief that life deserves a happy ending, with enough drama and surprises to keep it interesting. Cece currently resides in north Florida with her husband and beloved kitty. When she's not writing, you'll find her at the beach, usually with a good book.

Made in the USA
Columbia, SC
06 September 2024